THE TENANTS OF MOONBLOOM

Other books by Edward Lewis Wallant

THE HUMAN SEASON
THE PAWNBROKER
THE CHILDREN AT THE GATE

THE
TENANTS OF
MOONBLOOM

EDWARD LEWIS WALLANT

A HARVEST/HBJ BOOK
HARCOURT BRACE JOVANOVICH, PUBLISHERS
SAN DIEGO   NEW YORK   LONDON

ISBN 0-15-688535-2
Library of Congress Catalog Card Number: 63-13501

Printed in the United States of America
E F G H I J

THE TENANTS OF MOONBLOOM

ONE

LASHED IN THE twisted phone wire, Norman was a victim of his own tendency to fool around, but, finally anchored, he became quiet. His brother's voice was a record played at the wrong speed, reminding him unnecessarily who he was. It could have been the voice on one of those primitive recording ribbons used as a novelty in greeting cards or children's cheap toys, which emit a shallow resemblance to human speech when you run your nail over their ridges. Yet there was no real loss of fidelity; even in Irwin's presence Norman felt his brother to be something that was played over and over again. For a number of years he had been away from the powerful incoherence of that voice, but, pathetically, now that he was back, he admitted there was a perverse comfort in its demands.

"We don't rannana rannana, Norman. You can't keep rannana rannana. You've got to rannana rannana rannana and rannana. Responsibility rannana rannana. I am rannana rannana constantly. Rannana rannana rannana . . ."

The wire held him to the phone and thus to the swivel chair and thus to the warped floor, connected him to the dented file cabinets and the desk with its veneer shrunken away like dead skin. There was a cat smell and dust between his teeth.

"I rannana rannana rannana all rannana rannana. *Rannana* rannana rannana! Rannana rannana rannana . . ."

Norman risked putting the phone on his shoulder; he would

know his own cue to speak by the suffocated pitch. He sat between daydream and nothing, looking at what was to be seen. The sunlight had to bend to get down there. Bounced from the sidewalk above, it had almost the look of artificial light. People's headless bodies were a tantalizing parade, and only the children were whole. Idle as he was at that moment, it was some effort for him to resist complete abstraction. He was a hall of mirrors; within him his dream was an infinite series of reflections and all he could be sure of was that it existed and made him sure that *he* existed.

"Rannana?"

He became alert.

"Norman, are you listening?"

"Of course," he said without alarm. He knew that his lines didn't depend upon what his brother had been saying.

"The thing is, Irwin, in spite of all that . . . On Thirteenth Street," he said, hearing his brother's powerful breathlessness, "the roof leaks so badly that the rats are leaving the building. Then there are the toilets on the second and third floor—they're backing up, and the whole house smells. That's a real emergency, of course. But the stair banister between the first and second floor finally fell off altogether. The furnace hasn't been fixed yet and here it is October. Old Karloff on the first floor leaves food around, and the place is filled with *la cucaracha*. Del Rio threatens to call the Department of Sanitation. Oh, and there are now *no* lights in the hallways—that was the last fixture. Then there's a hole in the third-floor hallway floor, six inches wide. I can't imagine how it got there, but it's there. Oh yes, and some kids broke a pane in the front door." He paused only for breath, but Irwin jumped in.

"Broke a window!" The delicate diaphragm reverberated in the receiver. "Norman, you've got to be more alert!"

"Alert," Norman repeated, smiling helplessly at his grotto.

"Yes, alert. I *depend* on you to take care of all those details. God knows *I* can't be bothered with that nonsense. You are supposed to run just those four houses, collect the rent, take care of the few managerial details. I am involved with much more complicated transactions—*I* certainly can't take time out from these much more important things to worry about cockroaches and toilets, now can I, Norm?" He was so reasonable that Norman was tempted to kiss the mouthpiece.

"Certainly not, Irwin."

"Now I'm not saying that I *invented* the job for you, but there certainly wouldn't be any point to my keeping the houses if you weren't there to handle it. I'm not being unreasonable now, am I, Normy?"

"Who ever said . . ."

"It isn't too much for me to expect you to free me from those little things, is it?"

"No, Irwin." He tried it again silently, exaggerating the movements of his lips.

"I mean, I deal in transactions that run upwards of six figures. I carry my work home with me. My work is never done. The pressures on me are rannana."

Norman smiled at the slip into sermon.

"How in the world can you allow windows to get broken, Norman?"

"Allow?"

"It aggravates me no end."

"Tell me why you jumped at the window? I told you the whole building is . . ."

"Some things cannot be helped. Call them acts of God."

"So why not windows too?"

"Norman, I have no time to quibble. Just take care of those petty things without calling me. Don't you have *any* initiative?"

"Initiative I could perhaps dig up. But, Irwin, for the roof,

5

the banister, the plumbing, the electricity, for those things I need money."

"You know you have complete freedom to write checks on that corporation's account. I give you complete freedom of action on that. It isn't necessary to call me every time you want to buy a bulb."

"Blood from a stone, Irwin. The cupboard is bare, empty, depleted. In fact, it is below zero—I owe a two-dollar fine for overdrawing."

"Oh *Norman!*"

"I know, I'm a crazy spendthrift, I spend on blondes and the race track."

"I'm not saying that. But you *are* a poor manager."

"And I owe Gaylord."

"Gaylord is a shiftless *shwartsa*. He's not worth anything."

"That is irrelevant. For forty dollars a week you don't get a professional to take care of four buildings."

"Do you realize that my time is worth fifty dollars an *hour?* This conversation must have cost thirty-five dollars."

Norman waited a few minutes out of respect. Then in a gentle voice he continued. "Now, on Seventieth Street the elevator didn't pass inspection and the water is rusty in all the kitchen faucets. On Second Avenue the wiring is so bad that the inspector wouldn't take a bribe, said he drew the line at murder."

"Stop it, Norman."

"On Mott Street there is imminent disaster. The wall is swelling next to the toilet—it's going to collapse on poor Basellecci. Also, the grace period on the insurance is up at the end of the week . . ."

"God damn it, Norman!"

"Then there are the appliances on Seventieth Street. Ja-coby's—no, it was Hauser's—I think. . . . Anyhow, there are several stoves that don't work, and one . . ."

"Just shut up! I'll put five hundred dollars in the account tomorrow morning, and then do not let me hear from you for a long, long time!"

The tiny click in the receiver couldn't begin to suggest the force with which Irwin must have slammed down the phone. Norman felt a certain sense of nobility in putting *his* phone back on the cradle with exquisite delicacy. Then he had to smile wanly at the dusty, secondhand sunlight and the misspelled obscenities chalked in the well his office rested in.

"Five hundred dollars," he said in the tone of a man echoing his doctor's grim prediction. "Five hun-dred dollars." Still, it was only a minor plaint; he was not prone to self-pity but did allow a certain humorous sympathy for himself. He opened his palm as though testing for rain. He shrugged. Finally he took out one of the several ball-point pens in his shirt pocket and began trying to assign priorities for the things he had to do. Ten things were tied for first place, and he approximated the estimated costs.

A few people put on heads and peered down at him from the sidewalk above. They were attracted by his being behind glass, but more, perhaps, because they were drawn to the black letters on the window, letters that struck the ear of the eye with a softly melancholy and alliterative note.

I. MOONBLOOM REALTY CORP.
Norman Moonbloom—Agent

From his side of the glass, Norman always saw in the letters a resemblance to the Russian alphabet, and noticed too how the family name was almost symmetrical, with the same OO on either side of the terse NBL—like bookends. But right then he was not inclined to muse. He was trying to divide a huge number into a tiny one, and the sweat stood out on his small, gambler-white face with its blue-tinted cheeks and chin, its large pregnant-woman eyes. The effort was painful, and he bit his thin, childlike mouth. Suddenly the obvious simile occurred to him, and he put down the pen to laugh wretchedly. "Like an elephant trying to make love to a mouse," he said aloud. His humor made him close his eyes, as against the splashing of some caustic liquid.

The watered-down sunlight laid the window letters in a ribbon of shadow over floor and desk and man. One of the many O's made a daguerreotype of his blinded face. There had been no horrors in his life—only a slow widening of sensitivity. But he anticipated reaching the threshold of pain one of these days. It was like the fear of death; he could ignore it most of the time, although it was implacably there, to touch him with the very tip of its claw in moments of frustration, to bring dread to him during the 4:00 A.M. bladder call. The claw withdrew after just a touch, leaving him with a chronic, unrecognizable din that he did not think about; he was like a man who lives beside a foaming cataract and comes to take its roar for silence.

The thought came to him that he might find solutions if he changed pace. He resolutely opened his eyes. "I'll get a head start on myself, I'll start with the rents tonight. Yes, the rents," he said. He stood up to five feet seven inches, and the O now made a target of his chest.

His eyes crept over the small office; as always, he was slightly chagrined at the realization that his occupation had no real equipment beyond the receipt book and the ball-point pens. Still, his rather sad expression held no trace of bitterness. He had been a student until his thirty-second year, mainly because both he and his brother had been unable to see him as anything else. But a year ago he had closed the podiatry book with quiet finality: his last major after accounting, art, literature, dentistry, and the rabbinate. It had become clear to him that whatever talents he might have, he would never learn a special skill. Irwin had taken a grand-father's inheritance in cash; Norman had taken his in an unbroken string of semesters, fourteen years long. Now he worked for his brother at a small salary. Yet he sensed that justice had been done, and, optimistically, he wasn't convinced that *his* use of the money mightn't pay off in some oblique way. He worked too hard, even sharing some of the menial labor with the roving superintendent, Gaylord Knight, yet he felt that it would take a lot to extinguish him.

Wandering over to the file cabinet, he wrote "Astolat" with his finger in the dust on its top. The finished word made the shabby showcase of an office into a queer place; the sheafs of bills and receipts, spiked or corralled in several "In" boxes, became cryptic symbols. He smiled, creasing his blackish eye-lids and lifting his long-lobed ears (he could wiggle them at will). The walls were a fleshy pink and made of embossed tin like a cooky box. The linoleum was worn to a dirty hair color and was patched here and there with unevenly cut rectangles against the inroads of mice.

He spent a minute touching a few things on his desk. Then he put on his hat, a pearl-gray fedora with an immense crown and brim that made him look like a child imitating a gang-ster. He put on his suit jacket (also too large for his thin, slight body) and tucked the receipt book in its breast pocket.

Outside, in the pungency of the worn air, he sighed with premonitory tiredness. He locked the door, went up the steps, and headed for the subway that would take him to the upper West Side of town. He walked lightly and his face showed no awareness of all the thousands of people around him because he traveled in an eggshell through which came only subdued light and muffled sound.

TWO

HE WENT INTO the lobby and frowned at the new markings penciled on the walls. The refectory furniture disapproved, too, and the phony arches seemed threatened by the reality of the present. He kicked testingly at a loosened octagon of tile, peered up at the one bulb in the manorial chandelier. In the elevator he listened to the noisy motor and tried not to read the notice that said the elevator had not passed inspection. Rising in the slapping whine, he settled as usual for that modest ascent; he considered his ups and downs insignificant. Someone had scratched "Emperors" on the spackled wall next to an old, already rusting drawing of male and female genitals. He sighed and looked upward. The life in the building moved dimly around him like the pulsing movement perceived through new ice.

"The rent," he said in no particular way when the anemic-looking youth opened the door.

"Oh yeah, just a minute," Lester said, half letting him in and tucking back his long pompadoured hair. "Aunt Min, the rent," he called over his shoulder.

"Right in the middle of everything," Minna said in an undertone; her mottled baby face was spongey under the powder and rouge. "Come in, come in. Sit down. I'll have to get the . . ." She took the rest of the sentence into her bedroom as her sister, Eva, stepped out of the kitchen with a dish towel.

"Hello," Norman said to her.

10

"Does that sign on the elevator mean it's not safe?" Eva had the face of an old squaw and beauty-parlor blue hair. She squinted, deepening her self-made wrinkles.

"Just a technicality." Norman sat brightly institutional, his gangster hat on his knee.

"I'd hate to fall into the basement on a *technicality*," Lester said, raising an eyebrow. As Beloved Nephew, he knew his audience.

His aunt Eva laughed with her hand up to her mouth; there was a sex shyness in her attitude, the look of a young woman with her lover who suddenly finds her situation excitingly altered by the presence of a stranger. It was not at all funny with that rugged Iroquois face of hers.

Her sister came back into the room with her pocketbook. "What's funny?" Minna asked, looking to choose sides. And then seeing that it had to do with Lester, she threw aside reservation and made ready to laugh wholeheartedly.

"Mr. Moonbloom said the sign on the elevator was just a technicality, and Lester said, 'I'd hate to fall into the basement on a *technicality*.'"

Minna smiled, and her feeling was so strong that she had to pat down a stray tuft of hair on her nephew's head. "*Lester*," she said.

The two sisters ran their eyes through the head of the reedy, soft-soaked-looking young man, who stood with apparent insouciance between them. Norman could see, however, that the angle of his weak head was determined by the line of their common glance. Lester stretched like a pet cat. The light came through a bulb-burned lamp shade and cast old-penny color over the three of them. Norman checked the ceiling for falling plaster amidst their antique silence. A tiny mark showed on the shell of his consciousness. His big hat moistened in his hand.

"Well," he said in subtle consolation.

Minna took a breath that seemed to make a snapping sound. "I suppose we'd just better pay the man," she said.

"That's the idea," Lester said, jabbing adorably at his older aunt.

"Oh, *Lester*," Eva said. Like her sister, she could not say the name without feeling.

The light in there was like a smell, and when Norman got out into the hallway he took a deep breath and let it out a little at a time.

"Come in, young man. Make yourself at home." Arnold Jacoby had a soldering iron in his hand. Toylike and small, he seemed heated up by the tool, and his old face was rosy. "Setting up for supper. Maybe you'll join us? Betty doesn't fuss. At our age, Campbell's soup fills the bill. It's just a question of opening another can. Nothing to it. Love to have you."

"Well, that's very nice of you, but I have a lot of calls . . ." For some reason he pictured himself on errands of mercy in the midst of a plague. He patted the breast pocket, checking or indicating the receipt book there.

"Nonsense. Cup of instant coffee? Young fella like you can't be in all *that* much of a hurry!"

"Well I . . ."

"I mean you get to *our* age . . . you *should* hurry then. I mean, to put it in terms of *your* profession . . . I like to talk the other fella's language—kind of indicates a little interest in what the other fella does, you know? Like I talk to the kids, I try to throw in a little of their talk. Cool, man, like crazy, hah? Well, you know what I mean. So to get back to your profession, I'll put it in your terms. At my age you have to think in *short-term leases*. . . ." He chuckled modestly. "Yeh, yeh, *short-term leases*."

Norman heh-heh'ed politely, his hands out in an inconspicuous breast stroke.

"Oh, not that we let it get us down. We keep busy. *Betty!*" he roared suddenly, making Norman feel for a moment that he had walked into a trap. "For instance, I'm a modelmaker by trade—work for a big outfit, doing all their model work. But on my own time I do a little puttering." He looked up with a coy, provocative expression.

"Puttering?" Norman said.

Apparently it had been delivered in just the right tone of voice. The old, toylike face colored pleasurably. "Ah, ah hah," he said, waving a finger, arch now, convinced he had Norman panting with curiosity. He was something of a tease, but his teasing had been dragged a long way without getting rough, so you knew that it had never been cruelty.

"*Betty!*" he roared again. This time Norman only twitched slightly. Arnold Jacoby pushed him into a flowered armchair that embraced him like quicksand. "Well I'll tell you what I putter with. I *invent* things. I'm an inventor!"

"My, my," Norman said, furtively drawing the receipt book out. He waited a courteous few seconds and then, just as Arnold's mouth started to fit qualifying words, said "One of these days you'll have to tell me more about it. I'd love to hear about it now, but I have a few things to take care . . . Let's see, I make it out to be sixty-three dollars and twenty cents, right, Mr. Jacoby?"

"Call me Arnold—makes me feel more part of things. I'm seventy-three, but 'Mr. Jacoby' still sounds like my father. Dead a half-century this February. Oh, fine man, fine man. Great respecter of the human mind and spirit. Nothing crass about that man. 'Course it made him a failure—same as me. But then, I don't think you're a failure if to your own self you're true."

"Shall I make the receipt out to you or your wife, I forget, Mr. . . . ah, Arnold?"

"Doesn't matter really, does it? Not *that* receipt. But you just sit tight—have some instant java. *Betty!*"

"Don't shout so, Arnold," the old woman said, shuffling in with a bridge table. "Hello there, Mr. Moonbloom."

"Mrs. Jacoby." He tried to get up, but Arnold pushed him back into the billowing upholstery.

"Of course you'll have coffee, a little soup too," she said. She appeared somewhat older than her husband, already in her eighties. She was extraordinarily beautiful in the dim light they maintained there. Her face was not much wrinkled, only whitened like a sun-bleached painting. In the soft light they lived by she might still appear desirable to Arnold. There was something odd and exotic about her and about what was between them: a constant commemoration of passion, a special clause in their relationship which created a tension unusual between people of their age.

"Why'd *you* have to drag that table in, Bet? Could have asked me." Arnold stood in a rather ludicrous pose that Norman puzzled over for a few minutes, until it struck him that Arnold was holding his aged, paunchy figure like a man in the initial stages of courtship. Arnold squared his shoulders and bounded over to take the table from her. "Here, let me do that." His voice was an octave lower, the meandering ease of an old man strained out. He put the soldering iron down, flipped the table over dexterously, and opened the legs. Then he set it down in front of Norman's chair, blocking him in. "There we go," he said crisply.

His wife brought in three bowls of soup, a lover-like and secret smile on her face. Norman sat rigidly, clutching his ball-point pen and receipt book, staring at the steaming soup and the two old, deceptive faces. Arnold stood behind his wife's chair as she sat down, and then he sat down himself. The old woman folded her hands and moved her lips soundlessly. Arnold stared defiantly at the wall. When he caught Norman's bewildered eye, he said, "I'm a freethinker."

Norman nodded. Then, with a quick, desperate look around, he bolted up and over the arm of the chair.

The two old people looked at him with make-believe surprise. He was not part of their peculiar charade, and they seemed to see him dimly now.

"I have to rush along," he shouted. "Business waits for no man."

"Oh well, certainly," Arnold said. "Got to be on your toes."

"Every waking minute," Norman said, walking away on his toes.

"Oh, the rent," Betty said. "You forgot . . ."

"Be back for it tomorrow. Got to run," he called from the doorway.

"I'll look for you," she said.

"Yes, thank you, okay." He stepped into the hallway. The window at the landing showed the color of ice, and the hallway was made lonely by the muffled sounds of supper dishes and the fugitive smells of cooking. It was a time of constant movement for Norman. For some reason, he could not bear to eat alone at that hour; his loneliness was compressed to diamond hardness by the meeting of day and evening. Later, in his own apartment, he would be able to eat, and read as he ate. The darkness and the totality of night would make his solitary condition familiarly comfortable, and he would be able to convince himself that he was set in his ways and desired no change. Only the traditional supper hour of families recalled old hopes whose shapelessness had been glorious in prospect but which were unbearably irrelevant in retrospect.

Landlord-like, he squinted at the rough-stuccoed walls, peered up at the brown shine of the bulbs, to check their wattage. He performed actively as he walked the length of the hall, allowing no gleam of want to invade him. He rang the bell marked "M. Schoenbrun."

Marvin Schoenbrun said nothing, but stood aside for him to come in. He was dabbing at a small red hole nicked into his cheek by shaving, a morbid expression on his exquisite face.

"Won't take but a minute," Norman said, sitting down and writing out the receipt in his small, considerate handwriting, which was too well formed to reveal character.

The room showed too much *décor*. Lamps and pictures were faultlessly and artfully arranged. A cluster of sea shells lay on a low round table and several others hung at varying heights on almost invisible wire, giving the desired effect of streaming down. A Biedermeier chair paid conversational attention to a Spartan couch covered in black sailcloth. The walls wore black-framed prints. You sensed the thought that a breach of taste might precipitate a more disastrous cracking.

"There you are," Norman said.

"While you're here," said Marvin, as careful with spoken consonants as Norman was with written ones, "I was wondering whether there would be any difficulty about my having an air conditioner installed." His face would have been beautiful in some other age; now it was embarrassing.

"In *October?*"

"Mainly I want it for the filtering action. I have a sinus condition. And besides, with the windows open, the soot is dreadful." His after-shave lotion was too strong and sweet, and Norman wondered why he felt uncomfortable looking at him. I can no longer stand anything too immaculate, he thought. Dust is my destiny. He smiled at his silent pomposity.

"Well, I'm afraid there *would* be a problem," he answered. "See, the electrical system is kind of antiquated. *Antiquated* . . ." Norman shook his head. "What it is really—it puts a severe strain on the wiring when you turn a toaster on."

"What *is* the voltage?" Marvin asked, looking at the tissue he had been pressing against his cheek.

"The voltage?" Norman echoed.

"Yes, what is it?"

"Uh, well, it's very low," he said in the discreet tone of a doctor preparing the loved ones for an imminent death.

"Not one-ten!"

"Worse," Norman said darkly.

"It can't be."

"It is," he sighed regretfully.

"Well what *is* it?"

"What's worse than one-ten?" Norman asked cagily.

"Nothing!"

"That's what we've got."

"I don't understand. You wouldn't even have lights. How do the lights work?"

"I've asked that question myself."

"Oh, it's too silly. In any event, it probably wouldn't take an air conditioner," Marvin said bleakly. "Everything is just too ridiculous for words."

"I know the feeling."

"*Do* you?" Marvin looked at him from a cage of scorn.

"Every time I look in the mirror," Norman said cheerfully. "If you knew *my* history . . ."

Marvin looked inconsolable.

"You've fixed this place up beautifully," Norman said, standing. "I would imagine young ladies were quite impressed."

Marvin made a face of distaste.

Oh, Norman said to himself, suddenly reaching a total. Like that, of course. Poor fella, how can I compete for ridiculousness?

"Sorry about the air conditioner."

"Yes, yes," Marvin said. "All right."

"Good night."

"Good night," Marvin answered, frowning at the red-dotted Kleenex.

"Come in, come in," Stan Katz said from behind a wide shine of smile. "Don't just stand there, don't be strange."

Norman barely smiled back. The first time he had been faced with Katz's grin he had thought it expressed gaiety, but after long exposure to it he had recognized that what he had considered dimensional was really only painted on with clever fool-the-eye shadows. Now he felt no obligation to return it.

"Have to forgive the appearance, Moonbloom; we're in the midst of our fall house cleaning." He waved a trumpet at the littered room, which, as usual, showed signs of recent orgy. From the other room the sound of loud singing cut off suddenly.

Norman nodded and sat gingerly on a chair strewn with cracker crumbs. "I *would* like to ask a favor of you, Katz."

"Name it, Moonbloom, you have but to ask," Katz answered, his smile intruding on his speech so his M's were closer to N's.

"Well I've asked you before and I really . . ."

"Moonbloom-moom!" a skinny, black-haired man shrieked ecstatically from the doorway. He was stark naked except for sunglasses and a towel Arab-fashion over his head. "Is it Moonbloom of the Broom Street Moonblooms? Or Bloomin' Moonbloom of Coon Lagoon?" He had a pencil-thin mustache and a long, swanlike neck, and would have been quite unbelievable to anyone seeing him for the first time.

Norman smiled tiredly. "Hello there, Sidone," he said.

"And hello *there*, Moonbloomin' Moonbloom!" Everything was delivered with the fervor of a man who laughs harder than anyone else at his own jokes' punch lines. "How they hangin', Moonbloom? Look at him, Stan, how peaceful he looks, how *natural!* You would almost expect him to move. Ah, those embalmers, are they experts."

"He has a favor to ask, Jer," Stan said, slouching in a battered armchair and running his fingers dotingly over his horn, tracing the intaglio cartouches on its body, depressing the valves with feather touches, his smile revealing its structure as a multitude of minute quivers and electrical arcs.

"For Moonbloom—the *moon!*" Sidone declaimed ardently.

Norman sighed, waiting for the intensity of idiocy to recede at least enough for him to be faintly heard. The room *was* messy. There were cigarette ashes still in their original, cylindrical shape and lying in the grooves they had burned on tables and counters. There was a smell of spilled beer and unemptied ash trays and an odor like bitter punk. A plumber's candle stood in a saucer; a woman's stocking hung from a wall fixture; a drumstick rose mastlike from an empty whisky bottle, capped with a prophylactic.

Sidone put a cigarette into a long holder and lit it.

Norman sat forward. "Now I know you fellas are musicians and . . ."

"The secret's out, Stan," Sidone said. "Moonbloom's on to us."

"All right," Norman said with some impatience. "I know you have to practice, but you *could* practice during the earlier evening. Some of the other tenants . . ."

"Say no more, Moonbloom," Sidone cried. "I know your problem. We are annoying people. Well we *are* annoying *people*. Stan, you must buy a mute for that horrid horn."

"And you, Sidone, must buy a pair of those new sponge-rubber drumsticks," Katz replied.

"Now really, fellas . . ."

"No, no, don't thank us," Sidone insisted. "It's little enough we can do. I mean, what kind of world would this be without a fella helping the next fella. A little love goes a long way, Moonbloomm-m. Love, I say. *Amo, amas, amat, amamus, amatis, a tata, a zeyda . . .*" Sidone exploded into maniacal laughter and covered his privates with both hands.

Norman sat in the howling, writing out the receipt. Katz handed him the money, and Norman took it from him without expression, quite able to bear the mad volume of laughter. But then he was struck by the odd lack of smile on Katz's face; Katz looked naked and almost helpless without it. There was the feeling of conspiracy, as though he had crept around into Norman's hiding place and sat down there with him.

"We'll try to be more quiet," he said under the cover of his friend's wild laughing. Norman stared at him, wondering what he saw. And then Katz's lazy-looking tromp l'oeil smile was there again and the small barb of curiosity was cut off from the surface and left lodged in Norman.

In the hallway he heard the brief refrain of the trumpet playing the traditional bullfight theme, a machine-gun riffle on a drum, and then silence. The back of Norman's neck

20

began to ache as he went to the next door and rang the bell.

"I still don't know why you have to collect the rent every week," Carol Hauser complained. The Hausers were new tenants.

Her husband, Sherman, hissed by habit.

"Well it *is* a damn crazy thing," she said, turning her carefully wrought head to him. "Like a rooming house. I mean, this is an elevator apartment. It's ridiculous."

"The man told you all about it before we took the place. What are you bitching about it now for?" Sherman ground the words to small pieces and fed them to her. Large and bony, with heavy horn-rimmed glasses, his hair meticulously pompadoured, he had the look of someone ready for sudden death and concerned that it find him at his best. The girly magazine he had been looking at earlier lay in the crevice between the chair cushion and the arm. "What do you have to keep on for?"

"I'm talking to him." She moved her head slowly back to Norman. "And *cash*—why cash instead of a check? It's inconvenient." Even though she faced Norman, she seemed to be speaking to Sherman. Indeed, both of them ignored the agent; he was merely the catalyst that evoked their perversely pleasurable bitterness. Norman accepted the fact and kept his eyes fixed on the artificial fireplace with its artificial birch logs glowing in a red-bulb fire.

"He *told* you in the beginning. It's *their* business. The rent was reasonable, there was nothing under the table. You were happy enough to get it. Now you have to keep asking dumb questions."

"Can't I open my mouth without . . ."

"Ah, crap."

"Animal," she snarled, keeping her pudgy face and Du Barry hairdo absolutely still. She wore a beaded dress and high heels; with her thick, plump body, she seemed dressed for some pornographic purpose.

The lamp shade had a device that gave the effect of a river flowing. Norman studied it and came to the conclusion that the water on the lamp shade was real enough to put out the red-bulb fire.

"Well pay him, for Christ sake," Sherman said.

"Why don't you?"

"Because you have the goddamn money and you know it."

"It isn't necessary to use that gutter language."

"Hah!"

"What do you mean, 'hah'?"

"I mean you've heard worse."

"And what is *that* supposed to mean?" she said, welcoming savagery.

Norman stood like stone, half hoping he would be taken for an artificial figure in the room with artificial fire and water. He held his breath as the man and woman leaned redly toward each other.

And then the child came in, all blond and gold in Doctor Dentons, blue-eyed, shapely, beautiful. Slowly, Norman let out his breath, wondering whether the small boy could be an even more cleverly made artifact.

"I want ice cream," it said convincingly.

"Come kiss Daddy." Sherman's voice revealed another octave. His homely, groomed face dissolved to reveal a particularly intense ugliness.

Carol fussed with the shining yellow-white hair, her heavy lips slack with a febrile delight. "Bobby wash his face?" she said with babyish enunciation.

"I don't wanna. I want ice cream, a whole bunch."

Norman had the uneasy feeling it was a real child. He cleared his throat, surprised to find real phlegm.

"Oh yes," she said, walking toward the doorway to another room. "Sherman, wipe his nose."

For a second Norman thought she referred to him and he quickly pulled out his handkerchief. But Sherman dabbed at the boy's nose and Norman put his own handkerchief back. He laid the receipt on the leather-topped, gold-bordered table next to a china swan. The mother, father, and child were hooked up now, their circuit temporarily completed. Grouped next to the revolving river of the lamp shade, they could have been a subtle caricature of a holy family. From their positions around the little boy, they could not see Norman, and the last thing he noticed before leaving was the man's hand, creeping with animal accuracy up toward the woman's buttocks, and the woman smiling with unconscious lust while the child stood between them in drowsy boredom.

As he went down the stairs for his last two calls, he noticed that the window was dull with night. Like a blackboard, it waited for something to be inscribed upon it. Gradually, tediously, he was working toward his own time. Tomorrow he would take care of Mott Street and Second Avenue, and the next day Thirteenth Street. Only two more tonight, and then darkness and the vague lazy corral of his freedom. He shuffled and almost tripped over a raised tile. He raised his feet more carefully until he was before the door of the Lublins. He pushed the button and wondered whether the buzz he heard was a signal to them or something that existed only within his own head.

They were just two rather short, dumpy people, not American in feature or stature. Their children, a boy and a girl, had been vitaminized into somewhat better color. The room

23

was neat, slightly dowdy; it had the air of having been furnished according to the taste of several other people, as though *décor* were something the Lublins paid no attention to.

"The kitchen sink drips, Mr. Moonbloom." Sarah Lublin's tone was hardly one of complaint. She might have been commenting on the climate—something you really could do nothing about. Her face was so full of character that she ignored it. She had a large, rather hooked nose, full, wide lips, deep-socketed eyes of a sort of Wedgwood blue, and clear, smooth skin. "It keeps me awake," she said. "I wait for the next drip, I hold my breath and wait."

Her husband, Aaron, had similar skin, faintly yellowed, and his hair was black and false looking, combed flat to his skull. He sat with the girl and the boy on his knees, his hands on them with an impersonal reverence. He shrugged at Norman, asking for tolerance for a woman's foolishness.

"When *my* head is on the pillow, there is nothing," he said. "No drips, no creaks, nothing. I learned to sleep, long ago, as though there might not be time to again. Women cannot be that way. They are *curious* beyond everything else. It kills them to think that they might miss something. She must know if it will drip one more time, one more time. Even if it kills them, they must know."

Sarah's slight smile stayed on one side of her mouth. "The way *he* sleeps . . . before even he touches the pillow—in mid-air."

"A washer it needs perhaps?" Aaron touched the large-faced girl's ear as though looking for something.

"I'll send the superintendent to take a look," Norman said, idly watching Aaron's hand, half consciously waiting for it to stop moving so he could read the numbers tattooed on the forearm.

"*What* superintendent?" Aaron said, his sarcasm as bland as his wife's complaint.

"He's got a lot to do," Norman answered. "He takes care of three other buildings."

"I have never seen him, not once," Aaron said, his voice just that much lighter in tone to indicate what was probably humor for him. "He is like a myth to me. There are rumors of him; I see ash cans on the sidewalk. Once in a great while there is evidence of someone having washed the hallway. But the actual man—never."

"*One* superintendent for four buildings?" Sarah said, counting out the rent money with fingers that appeared sensitive to the feel of currency.

"It's an economic problem," Norman explained smilingly. "We're practically a nonprofit organization."

Aaron smiled slightly as he recognized deceit. His arm rested on the arm of the chair.

Norman lip-read silently, 3241179, not really sure of the last number.

"But the receipt is always for less than we pay," Sarah said mildly.

Norman smiled a little chidingly. "The rent is reasonable?"

"No complaints," Aaron said quickly, his alacrity indicating an old, well-developed talent for self-humiliation. "We are merely having conversation."

"I understand," Norman said, putting the money into his wallet.

The girl got off Aaron's knee and went into another room. The boy, more delicately built, waited a discreet minute to assert his independence, then followed her. Aaron watched them go with hard, vigilant eyes. Sarah watched him watching them. Her arm was white and unmarked and yet Norman sensed numbers there too.

"We'll see what we can do about that faucet." Norman stood in his large, dusty-looking blue suit. "I'll make a special note of it."

"Yes, a note," Aaron said, and went to check on the children, who were too quiet.

Sarah sighed. "*He* sleeps better, but *I* get more rest." She looked at Norman intimately. The furniture was their own, yet the place looked like a furnished room. Even the family photograph on the dark, clubfooted table had the quality of a hotel-room reproduction. There were things that Norman did not want to know.

"Good night," he said.

"Yes, sure," the woman answered.

The Spragues threatened him with that drowsiness he had felt with Arnold and Betty Jacoby, though less dangerously. Had he been actually less tired, he might have been amused by them. Instead, he felt a kind of vertigo.

Jane had huge, semiconscious eyes and irrelevantly voluptuous lips. Each time she moved and noticed her pregnant body, she expressed faintly annoyed surprise.

"He wants the rent, Janey," Jim Sprague said in a bewildered way. He had a lean, Lincolnesque face, and every word he uttered seemed like the beginning of a maze.

"The rent!" she exclaimed.

Jim frowned. "Well why don't you have a seat, Mr. Epstein?" he said.

"Moonbloom," Norman corrected, sitting down.

"Epstein is the delicatessen man," Jane explained, sitting with a ball of yarn.

"Have a drink?" Jim asked.

"I'll have a glass of water, if you don't mind," Norman said.

"Sure thing. Janey, what do you want?"

"A teeny bit of Scotch," she answered.

Jim nodded and went into the kitchen, where he clinked and poured and bumped around. Jane smiled at Norman, and he smiled back.

Jim stuck his head around the doorframe. "What was yours again, Mr. Moonbloom?"

"Water," Norman said. "Just water."

Norman and Jane tried a dozen different smiles while they waited. Occasionally she made gestures he couldn't understand.

Jim came out with three glasses and set them on a table across the room. Then he sat down. For a moment he studied the situation, made a silent little "Oh" of correction, got up and brought the glasses back. He gave the amber-colored drink to Norman, the plain water to his wife. Norman didn't bother to correct him.

"Jim is in dental mechanics," Jane said, licking her luscious mouth.

Jim agreed with a solemn nod.

There was too much silence. Finally Jim sat forward with an intensely interested expression. "Just what can I do for you, Mr. Moonbloom?"

"The rent," Norman said, afraid to speak too loudly.

"Oh, of course." Jim chuckled and sat back.

The two of them laughed politely and did nothing.

"I'll make out a receipt," Norman coaxed.

"Oh Jim, the *money*," she said.

Jim went into the other room and came out with some bills in his hand. Norman took the paper clip off, handed back the post card from Capri, and put the money away in his wallet.

Neither of them said good night to him. Jim was frowning

at the pink houses on the post card; Jane was gazing at her swollen belly, trying to recall how in the world it had come to be there.

Norman closed the door quietly, afraid to alarm them.

Gaylord was studying the ash cans in the cellar, and when he heard Norman, he put on his Caliban expression. His round, clever face became slack and oppressed, his eyebrows brooded.

"With *my* back," he said sadly, kicking at the heavy can. "It's a crime, but what can I do? I never learned a decent trade, never had no advantages. I'm a hewer of wood, I accept my lot."

"I'll help you with them," Norman said. "Don't overact."

"What do *you* know of the black man's burden?" Gaylord said contemptuously.

"I share it," Norman answered sourly, lifting his side of the heavy can.

"And you think any of them give a man any gratitude?" Gaylord said, waving his free hand at the ceiling, above which all the tenants boiled in their strange elements. "Hah! Not them. Just, 'This leaks, this broke, that broke.' All they got to say to a man is 'Do!' "

"A lot of doing *you* do," Norman said. "You're too busy philosophizing."

"See, you too. You got no gratitude either."

"I'm an ingrate," Norman said.

They went up and down the cellar steps a dozen times with the heavy cans, grunting together, coughing occasionally from the stirred-up dust of the ashes. A well-dressed man and woman looked curiously at them as they walked out to the sidewalk, joined to the heavy can, their outer arms extended. Norman was particularly strange to them, his oversized fedora square on his head, dwarfing his delicate face, his dark suit and neatly tied tie making him look like a picture in someone's attic. Together, with their flapping arms and grim hold on the can, the two men looked dedicated to an Icarian dream. Sweat and effort silenced and joined them. They hefted and groaned, and favored each other on the steps. The last can made Norman's legs tremble, and he dropped it so heavily that a cloud of ashes rose into the cool air.

They stood for a few minutes, catching their breath beside the squad of ash cans, looking at the city night.

"Smell like fall all right," Gaylord said. "Smell like apples."

"It's October," Norman said. "Even in the city you can tell."

"Stars gettin' clearer," Gaylord observed, scanning the building-jabbed heavens.

"The air is better," Norman said.

"Breathe better," Gaylord qualified.

"Autumn," Norman said in a long, weary voice.

Then they parted without farewell, and Norman went through the city to where he lived.

THREE

HE STEPPED INTO his own apartment, and his deep, relieving sigh was that of a man to whom hermitage is an ever-present temptation. His brother, Irwin, who was prone to guilt pains, had claimed many times that the reason for Norman's failure, the causes for the blandness in Norman's relations with people, stemmed from a love of being alone. Norman, divesting himself of his large, dusty clothes and running the hot water in the tub, wouldn't have argued the point. He didn't know why he was the way he was. His passions had always been dim to him. As a child he had seemed to be mostly happy. He had daydreamed a lot, conventionally romantic daydreams. He still did. The stretching inside himself had seemed like ordinary growth until his manhood, and after that had puzzled him somewhat. Now, of course, he sensed the imminence of pain but could not imagine how it would affect his personality.

He got into the tub and ran a little cold water. Then he lowered his thin, hairy body into the just-right warmth and stared at the interstices between the tiles. Sadness—he had experienced that emotion ten thousand times. As exhalation is to inhalation, he thought of it as the return from each thrust of happiness.

Lazily soaping himself, he gave examples.

When he was five and Irwin eight, their father had breezed into town with a snowstorm and come to see them where they lived with their grandparents in the small Connecticut city.

Their father had been a vagabond salesman and was considered a bum by people who should know. But he had come into the closed, heated house with all the gimcrack and untouchable junk behind glass and he had smelled of cold air and had had snow in his curly black hair. He had raved about the world *he* lived in, while the old people, his father and mother, had clucked sadly in the shadows. And then he had wakened the boys in the night and forced them out into the yard to worship the swirling wet flakes, to dance around with their hands joined, shrieking at the snow-laden branches. Later, they had gone in to sleep with hearts slowly returning to bearable beatings. Great flowering things had opened and closed in Norman's head, and the resonance of the wild man's voice had squeezed a sweet, tart juice through his heart. But then he had wakened to a gray day with his father gone and the world walking gingerly over the somber crust of dead-looking snow. It had taken him some time to get back to his usual equanimity.

He slid down in the warm, foamy water until just his face and his knobby white knees were exposed.

Once he had read *Wuthering Heights* over a weekend and gone to school susceptible to any heroine, only to have the girl who sat in front of him, whom he had admired for some months, emit a loud fart which had murdered him in a small way and kept him from speaking a word to anyone the whole week following. He had laughed at a very funny joke about a Negro when Irwin told it at a party, and then the following day had seen some white men lightly kicking a Negro man in the pants, and temporarily he had questioned laughter altogether. He had gone to several universities with the vague exaltation of Old Man Axelrod and had found only curves and credits. He had become drunk on the idea of God and found only theology. He had risen several times on the subtle and powerful wings of lust, expectant of magnificence, achieving only discharge. A few times he had extended friendship with palpitating hope, only to find that no one quite knew what he had in mind. His solitude now was the result of his metabolism, that constant breathing in of joy and exhalation of sadness. He had come to take shallower breaths, and the two had become mercifully mixed into melancholy contentment. He wondered how pain would breach that low-level strength. "I'm a small man of definite limitations," he declared to himself, and relaxed in the admission.

He dried himself with towels stamped with the name of a hotel his brother had owned for several months. Dry and warm in pajamas and an ancient flannel bathrobe, he went into his kitchenette and opened a can of chili. He heated it in a saucepan and stood moving a spoon around, humming absently. His alarm clock ticked in competition with the silently efficient electric clock on the wall. Dimly there came the sound of the traffic on Lexington Avenue, four floors below. He hummed and kept out the larger din of remembered voices. The spicy smell of the chili pricked his nose. But suddenly his humming oppressed him. He felt an unusual self-disgust, which puzzled him, and as he ate with the newspaper opened before him, he pushed down the faint disturbance. When he washed the pot and the dish, he had an image of himself, thin, dark, idiotically placid, sealed into a hermetic globe whose thinness gave him only the flickering colors of the outside.

For a while he browsed through the books on his shelves. There were the remains of his many pursuits: books on Hebrew theology, textbooks on the anatomy of the human foot, orthodontic techniques, an illustrated history of Byzantine art, collections of English poetry, an anthology of twentieth-century short stories. He decided on a soporific. Pulling a large, wine-red volume out, he took it to his bed and opened randomly to the chapter on the Metatarsus.

Buses and cars bleated, honked, and roared, with subdued violence; occasionally a human voice rose almost to his window, then fell back down without quite reaching him. And all of it was like silence to him. Though his home city had been small, he was a city boy from way back and he remembered his crying out "What's that?" at the bursts of silence when he had lived in the country.

When he was drowsy enough, he switched off the light and automatically turned into his daydream, which had to do with his father. He knew this was not his real dream, just as he knew his real dream was something obscure that he nevertheless felt was deep and profound and often confused with the beating of his heart. No, the favorite fantasy was only another soporific, one that parted the curtains of sleep for him. Like a boy's night story, it made him smile in the dark. He put himself into the huge form of his father and imagined the world as his playground.

As usual, it got him to sleep. But all night long he seemed aware of the din and sensed familiar voices. One tiny crack appeared in his shell, and he wore himself out trying to patch it. In the morning he was very tired and didn't look forward to the day at all.

FOUR

THANK GOD FOR a day like this! Even Mott Street was bearable in the clear, liquid air. The dingy grocery shops, the vegetable stand with its overflow of crates and scattered greens, the gutters wedged with paper and orange peels, even the crowding, crooked, narrow buildings, all had a rather exotic appearance in morning sunlight and shadow. Doorways were intriguing, and the air moved lightly over the shoulders of mothers wheeling their children and their groceries. Norman almost was convinced he might get through the day.

He turned into the turtle-green building and walked past the rubbish cans and the abandoned, one-wheeled stroller, and began the climb.

Basellecci was a man in a long interim of age.

"Good morning, Mr. Moonbloom. A lovely morning, is it not?" His colorless, fleshy face and curly gray hair, his sober hazel eyes behind glasses, combined to give him a look of extraordinary moderation. He beckoned Norman in out of the reeking hallway to where he had roasted the air with freshly ground coffee. "I am about to begin my brake-fast. You will perhaps have with me some good Italian coffee? I find it to be the most beneficial for the stow-mack after sleep."

"It smells good," Norman said, sitting in the cramped kitchen. Unfortunately his chair faced the little closet where the toilet was. With its heavy, wooden water tank above it, it looked like a seat in a torture chamber. On one side of it, the wall bulged dangerously, like an enormous contusion; it looked as though a great body of water were pushing at the wall, and Norman imagined Basellecci sitting on the toilet with his pants down and the water suddenly bursting through on him and drowning him.

"It is my—how you say?—'pick-it-up.' I must have my pot with me wherever I go. One must have some remmanant of graciousness, no? Here, it is the instant coffee, or the mud from unwashed tanks. I have transported my pot from Firenze to Cleveland, from Cleveland to Detroit, from Detroit to here." He fussed happily with cups and saucers. "I have several pots, like changes of clothes. They are of various sizes, of copper, pewter, alumimumum. Coffee is my vice. Harmless enough?"

"Perfectly," Norman answered, admiring the cleanliness of the apartment in a building so impregnated with filth.

Basellecci poured delicately, raising and lowering the pot so the steaming brown stream flexed in air. "Coffee," he said with a sigh of benediction.

"Mmm-mm," Norman said appreciatively as he sipped the roasty liquid that fulfilled the promise of its odor. He kept his eyes away from the terrible toilet. "You have something there, Mr. Basellecci."

"Some prefer with milk in the morning, but not I. Oh, sometimes in the evening I will add a drop of Strega or anisette, but normally . . ."

"And how does your teaching go?" Norman sat back and slowly drew the receipt book out of his pocket.

"Ah, *grazie, bene, bene.* Only that some of them, my *studenti,* do not work, they are sloppy. I do not know why some of them even come. They have no care, they pronounce—terrible! They have no respect for the way a word is made. A word, after all, has shape, texture, yes? Italian is a lovely tongue if it is *spoken.* They come, these second- and third-generation Italians, to—how you say?—brush up. Ah! Such tongues, such dialects, such accents! From Bari, their parents came—their Italian sounds like Chinese. Or Sicilians with barnyard accents. I say, 'Do not show off that you have some Italian. Pretend you never heard of it and come fresh to learn correctly.' No *grr-ratzy—grahtseeayy, grah-tsee-ayy*." Basellecci held his fingers aloft, curled in vowel love. His voice rang harshly. With the coffee cup in one hand, the other hand shaping his passion, he was between his sacred and his profane loves, and his neuter face was as near luminescence as it could ever be. "*Leem-pehr-may-AH-bee-lay . . .*" He looked tenderly at Norman, as though asking him to match such beauty. "Raincoat," he said modestly.

"The language of Dante," Norman said in payment for the coffee.

"Ahh," Basellecci sighed, shaking his head reverently.

Norman cleared his throat and took out his pen.

Basellecci came off his cloud, feet first. He peered guardedly into the snap-top purse he had produced from his pocket, "What about the wall?" he said, changing their relationship back to what it was.

Norman got up and walked over to the toilet chamber, a professionally skeptical expression on his face, implying that there might be something unreasonable in the complaint. He forced himself to press the swollen wall. It was soft and faintly damp; he repressed a gag. "Well, I don't know. . . ."

"I am constipated all the time," Basellecci cried angrily. "I sit there and watch that terrible swelling. I cannot relax. My sphincter is paralyzed with dread. Soon I will grow genuinely sick, and then I will sue in a court of law. You *must* attend to it!"

"It's an old building, Mr. Basellecci. However, I'll look into it."

"Look into, look into! What is to look into? There it is—one does not need twenty-twenty eyesight to see it. Go, try it yourself; close the door and sit there. See if *you* are capable of a movement!"

"All right, Mr. Basellecci, don't get excited," he said. The scalp around each hair of his head rose volcanically at the thought of his being closeted in there with his pants down. "I'll have someone up to look at it."

"I will sue for mental anguish as well as medical expense!"

"No, no, we'll take care of it. Just relax." This was the wrong word, he realized, grimacing with regret.

"Relax! How can I *relax?* My sphincter is paralyzed, I tell you. I ask little. I know it is a humble house. I am a humble man. I do not expect a doorman, an elevator, air conditioning, wall-to-wall carpets. I am equipped to do battle with vermin, I do not complain that only one window opens or that only one burner works on the stove. I am used to lighting candles for light in my bedroom. But I cannot, *cannot* go on this way. My system is already poisoned. I am cemented in. *I must have relief!*"

"Yes, certainly, Mr. Basellecci, I understand, I certainly will . . . Not another day will pass . . . Leave it to me." Norman backed out, nodding. "And thank you for the coffee. You don't have to worry, believe me. . . ." Over and over he expressed his assurances, his regrets, his concern, his compassion, his thanks. He barely stopped nodding before the next apartment door opened.

"Wung," he said to the young Chinese, bracing himself as always for contradiction.

"Whatta ya say, man, how's the world treatin' ya?" But his face *was* dynastic; his eyes were Orientally calm. The low, curving contours of a North Chinese face with that voice made it seem that a Ming vase had been wired for sound. "Like man, I'm gaffed—nowhere. These Village types deject me. Come in, come in. Oh but I'm hung over with talk! Ya-ta-ta, Ya-ta-ta. I mean, can't these pigs just lie down and do it?" He looped an arm through Norman's and steered him through the litter of beer cans, lingerie, and newspapers. "Park it while I take a reading, Pops. I'm spinnin'."

But he *had* hands like those Eastern painters who could twist out a bird with a single manipulation of a brush. Norman sat down with the memory of the girl who had betrayed him with a fart. "I've got a lot to do," he said from the edge of the malodorous couch.

"I know, man. But just let me work my way back. I mean it was almost blotto last night. She talked and talked. By the time I got her to a supine position, I almost didn't care."

"*L'amour*," Norman said, writing out the receipt.

"Oh, I *tell* you! You should have heard this chick. 'I feel the Oriental splendor of your hooded eyes. You are the East, eternally patient.' *Patient?* Man, I was *beside* myself!"

"The rent, Wung?" Norman said sadly.

"Let's see, the shirt came off here, then we wrastled past the bathroom," Wung said. He snapped his fingers. "Yeah, the tub, I left my jeans in the tub." He darted away and came back with a soggy wallet from which he produced soggy currency. "It's all coming back to me," he groaned, dropping down on a chair with his head in his hands. "Oh man, where am I going?"

"It's the spin of the world," Norman consoled indifferently. "See you next week."

Jerry Wung got up and bowed deeply from the waist. "Like *arrivederci*, most honorable Moonbloom," he said.

"Like *Shalom*," Norman answered, returning his bow.

Beeler, the retired pharmacist, had never had his own store, and his face was a silvery constant shrug. His bald pate led Norman into the room, whose furnishings had been the last word in 1924. His armchair was tubular, and the coffee table had rounded corners and parallel nickle grooves. Turning, he motioned Norman to sit on a tortured ottoman. Then he sat himself with a grunt and stared at Norman, a cigarette smoldering between his lips, the smoke closing one of his light-blue eyes.

"Sheryl," he called, without turning his gaze from Norman. "Pay the man," he said to the big blonde young woman who looked in from the doorway.

"The toilet doesn't flush," she said, running her eyes over Norman with dance-hall selectivity. She wore a silk kimono with a dragon embroidered and straining under the weight of full, slack breasts; it had been her mother's kimono, and seemed exotic to her because she still recalled her mother's secretive freedoms. She came into the room with a slow, heavy walk and bent over her father to kiss his bald head, her arm across her chest to keep her breasts from swinging.

"Totinka," Beeler said tenderly, plucking out his cigarette but keeping his eyes on Norman.

"I'll have the man up to check," Norman said over the receipt book. Knowing that Beeler was watching him, and knowing that there was no worth-while reason for looking at the big, fleshy form, Norman nevertheless found his eyelids pulling against their lowering. It was like telling someone to stand in a corner and not think of a white rhinoceros. He had to look up at the bulging dragon. Sheryl smiled.

"I'd appreciate," she said. "A girl kind of depends on the john, you know."

Norman licked his lips and remembered that his life of continence could result in a congested prostate. "Of course," he croaked. He cleared his throat. "Of course," he said more clearly.

"This is my Baby Girl," Beeler said, pointing first over his shoulder to the big blonde woman, then moving the bony pointer toward a silver-framed photograph of a fat little girl with Shirley Temple curls. "She hasn't changed, has she?"

"Not a hair," Norman said, taking the money from Sheryl, who smiled a little defiantly at him. She turned and walked out of the room, letting Norman see the breadth of her hips and the faint declivity of the silk over her buttocks.

"An angel, that child," Beeler said, lighting another cigarette and setting it between his lips to torture his eye again. "You should have seen how her mother dressed her. Pink dresses, big bows, all starched. People used to stop and stare. My wife loved it."

Norman got out when the old man turned his blue, indecipherable eyes toward the photograph. As he closed the front door, he heard Sheryl singing the blues in the bathroom, her voice off key and coarse.

Kram was immaculate, and his apartment had the sterile look of a laboratory. A cylinder of compressed air stood beside his drawing table, upon which lay the delicate, dragonfly shape of an airbrush and the photograph he had been retouching, a picture of a goddess in a foam-rubber bra. The hump on his back seemed only equipment for him, and so precise and certain were his gestures and his voice and his clear, dark eyes, that Norman often felt Kram was shaped correctly and other human beings, himself included, were mutations.

He handed Norman the money, his clear face unencumbered by any desire.

"Any complaints?" Norman asked confidently, noting the exactitude of spacing in the man's thin combed hair and the clean shine of his glasses, which did not have the faintest speck of dust on them.

"No complaints," Kram said, with the slightest shadow of a

smile. He was a man used to sleeping on his side and to the impossibility of perpetuating anything. "Everything is as it should be."

"I think you're the only person I know who has no complaints."

Kram chuckled softly. "I used them up long ago," he said. "There's nothing can happen to me, good or bad." He motioned Norman over to the drawing table where the brassiered goddess smiled indefinitely. On the small taboret beside the drawing board, his brushes and tacks and hard pencils were arrayed like surgical instruments. "You see what things are? They are flat and poor and they require my skill to have even a semblance of substance. You should see what she was before I doctored her up. Her skin was like a sponge, her neck was full of tendons, her breasts were so shallow that they didn't cast any shadows. Everything. Pictures of food come to me looking like garbage, and I make them look good enough to eat. Kids who look like little angels in the magazines—I take the snot out of their noses, the pimples from their cheeks; I make the glaze in their eyes look like a dewy shine. It's interesting work, isn't it?"

"It seems to have disillusioned you."

"On the contrary," Kram said with a smile. "I was *disillusioned* before I came to this profession. Retouching has restored me, though in a different way."

"Well, maybe I could take lessons."

Kram looked at him strangely, a little humor left in his eyes. "I don't think so," he said. "I think you're a different case altogether."

Norman looked at him, wondering at the inward shudder this caused. Then he smiled, because there really was nothing between them, and with a little wave he left the hunchback in his immaculate apartment.

Norman chewed the wadded paper that ketchup and onion defined as hamburger. Around him was the ground-up conversation of people on their lunch hour, interspersed with the clacking of thick plates and thin metal, and commanded by the cries of the short-order cook and the countermen as they called out abbreviated orders.

"BLT. Burn one. Grade-A shoot. Lemme have a number three, light on the mayo . . ."

Norman sat amid the grease smells and the nerve-racking clatter, not at all deluded into thinking he was being nourished. But he was used to the terror of those luncheonettes where people swallowed mouthfuls whole, their eyes bulging, their mouths working painfully, as though they were chewing themselves. He was out of it, or had never been in it; an invisible placenta allowed him to move at his own speed. His stomach was used to food prepared for mass lack of taste. By lifelong habit, he heard but did not listen, just as he saw but did not look. Like a cautious mouse in an electrified maze, he remembered his few tentative sorties *toward* things, his few brief adventures into the barest hint of pain. He kept to a small circumference now, having experienced nothing that compensated for the discomfort of sensation. When he asked himself what his life meant, his invariable answer was, evasively, "It doesn't *mean* anything; it *is.*"

And *ding*, the act was consummated, his change flung down on a spiky rubber mat. He took a book of free matches for evidence that he had been there.

Out in the sharp sunlight, people were too numerous to notice, bits of face and wool. He belched up the condiments and the onion, gratefully; it covered the bland badness of the meat taste. For an after-lunch treat, he breathed the warmed, autumn air and thought about the fact that leaves were coloring someplace, and that the browned apple core in the litter basket had filled with juice on a real tree. There was no longing in his thoughts, only the condescending amusement of a man who allows no credibility to dreams except during a time set aside for dreaming. "I'm not more than half alive," he thought cheerfully, never considering that the state of being fully alive might be impending. "God forbid," he would have said to that suggestion, not believing in God or the threat.

The four-family house on Second Avenue was the "best" of the four buildings he managed. He looked at its narrow, brownstone façade with an almost boyish smugness. Now, thirty-three years on his way toward wherever it was human beings ended, he was "working" at gainful employment for the first time, and he savored the idea of it, much in the manner of a child who sucks on an unlit cigarette.

Wade Johnson opened his door and grinned dangerously, his hard, meaty, good-looking face searching for outrage. Norman said, "It's me," and flinched in anticipation.

"Come on in, Norman, you little Jew prick," Wade said lovingly. He was as thick-muscled as a stevedore, and his blue eyes were always just a flame width from either rage or merriment. With the treacherously gentle touch of a cat on a stunned bird, he took Norman's arm and led him into the apartment, which was walled with books. "Sit down and listen to that Limey Eliot, listen," he said ferociously, shoving Norman into a chair.

"... Only
There is shadow under this red rock,
(Come in under the shadow of this red rock),
And I will show you something different from either
Your shadow at morning sliding behind you
Or your shadow at evening rising to meet you;
I will show you fear in a handful of dust."

He kicked Norman lightly. "Hah hah, that Old Possum, hah!"

"'The Wasteland,'" Norman said. "I did a paper on Eliot at Michigan; no, no, I think it was when I was up at Bowdoin."

"Paper, paper, never mind the goddamned paper. Hear it, man, hear it! You and your goddamned *papers!*" He leaned over Norman, smelling of rye whisky. "'I will show you fear in a handful of dust,'" he snarled into Norman's ear. "Shit, Norman, don't start jabbering about your papers!"

"Such language for a schoolteacher," Norman said tensely. "And with your kid sitting right there." He gestured toward the tender-faced blond boy who sat on a bench, smiling sweetly.

Wade guffawed. "Teacher, who's a teacher? They don't want teachers; they want titties, wet nurses. They want people to chew up everything until it's a pasty gop and then push it into the little drooly mouths. 'In Flanders fields the poppies grow, between the crosses, row on row . . .' That's what they want, those c——s. Or, 'I think that I shall never see, a poem lovely as a tree.' They're like you; they want things that fit neatly on paper. Could I put darkness and light right there in the classroom with their hygienic little souls? Could I say:

". . . I flung her onto a basket of cushions and sailcloth in a dark corner. And I remembered nothing but her white drawers trimmed with lace.

"Then, O despair! The wall became dimly the shadow of trees, and I was plunged in the amorous sadness of the night."

He held Norman in the wake of his voice, grinning sadistically in the afternoon sunlight that churned up around him in dust motes. Finally he shook his head in mock despair. "No, no, it's no use; you're still on paper, Norman. You live in a dream, you know that?"

"Really?" Norman said, amused. "And how about you with your raving? What do you call that?"

"Hey, but I feel pain, I'm full of sensation. I've got an idea that *you* could watch a murder committed and just smile your goofy little shit-eating smile. You're like a body under water, you know that? Yeah, Moonbloom, that's the image, a god-damned Hebrew body wrapped in water. When you talk—glub, glub, bubble, bubble." He pushed Norman back into the chair when he tried to get up. Norman laughed helplessly and shrugged.

"Aw come on, Wade, I'm a workingman," he said.

"Never mind that," Wade answered. "I'm not through with you. I sit here spending my Saturdays correcting the toilet paper my students hand in, and the spring winds tighter and tighter. I drink and try not to yell at little Wade Junior, here. And then a pair of big Jewish ears comes in, and I can relieve myself." He turned to the smiling child, who gazed at his father adoringly. "Wade Junior, pal, be a good Joe and fill up another juice glass with Daddy's whisky. There's a good fella. . . ." He turned back to Norman, his eyes glittering.

> "Do not go gently into that good night,
> Old age should burn and rave at end of day;
> Rage, rage against the dying of the light . . ."

It took Norman a half-hour to get away, and at the door Wade said plaintively, "How do I get these bastards at school to let me really *teach*? I've been thrown out of five schools and quit two more. And why, *why?*"

"Because you're a bum teacher," Norman said tauntingly from a safe distance down the hall.

"I'm a *great* teacher!" Wade howled, his eyes red and laughing and mad. "I could get kids to feel with every square inch, I could get them to love beauty, as I do."

"God help them," Norman called back, going up the stairs,

relieved to be away from the wildman, his relief a purely physical, mindless thing.

"You skinny Jewess's get, you circumcised Uriah Heep! *You* know, you know damn well. . . ." His voice echoed through the corridors and in the stair well, and then was detonated by his door slamming.

"Hi, Norman," she said, the breath behind her voice either natural or learned, but natural now. She opened the door wide, smiling with her rich mouth closed. Her dark eyes were huge and beautiful, as is frequently the case with hyperthyroid, nearsighted people. Norman remembered drawings of the eye in cross section and went inside, his only apparent thought being that somehow his coming for the rent got him in there but that his entry made the one door seem like the back door.

"Leni," he said, his hand over his heart, as though in avowal; really he was only checking habitually for the receipt book.

"You're so regular," she said. "My son Richard's school hours and you—the only constants in my life."

"How's everything?" Little rivulets washed against him—not that he felt anything for her, but if he had been tempted to . . . He saw all the things that kept her from being pretty: coarse black hair, a little too thin at the front of the center parting, skin just on the drab side and vaguely rough, little crow's-feet leading from her eyes to thirty. She had a broad face, and her rather square, slightly jutting jaw gave her mouth a slightly savage look. Then, too, her teeth weren't anything to write home about and her . . . "Hope this isn't a bad time for you."

"Oh, I don't know the good times from the bad times. No, I'm not doing anything important. Reading a script for a microscopic part in a microscopic play. I wish I could afford to pass it up." Her smile purposely covered her imperfect teeth, and yet it brought out her abundant reality. "Do you think I'll make a good ingénue, Norman? Am I young and willowy enough?" She held her hands out in girlish gesture, her hips wide, her waist short and not too slim, her breasts full and past their early resiliency. The side of her slacks gaped to show a tiny patch of faded pink. "Could I pass for eighteen?"

Norman chuckled uncomfortably.

"Well you're wrong. I could. You're as young as you feel, arf, arf. I'm a professional ingénue. I don't look young enough, but I have the ability to prroe-*ject*. The limitation of parts is due to . . . Well, perhaps because that's the only thing I can feel strongly, a desire to be in my teens, indefinitely."

"And how's Richard?" he asked, sitting on the plastic armchair.

"You're changing the *sub*-ject," she trilled.

Norman looked innocent.

She grinned and flung herself down on the couch with one leg under her. "Oh that kid—he's a Method actor. Like mother . . . He's so convincing. I can't do a thing with him. The thing is, he wants a father without my having a man. Oh yes, I have problems."

"You were going with a young engineer, if I'm not mistaken?"

"*You're* not mistaken, Norman, *I* was," she said wearily.

"Another dead soldier?"

"Oh, you know . . ."

Norman knew. In the nine months that he had been making these rounds, she had indicated relationships with five men. Relations. He shifted dimly. There was quiet except for the sound of her son's pet white mouse scratching in his cage in the bedroom. Arrested with his hand in his breast pocket Napoleonically, he imbibed his slow, steady nourishment. He saw her pale full neck as she rested her head on the back of the couch-bed, her white-sweatered breasts, heavy in their rise and fall. Slowly, passively, he turned over and over, used to his own pulsing silence. From where he was, she was just weight and warmth.

"I tell you, Normy, I get low and tired. I feel like dropping the Muse and this kooky life and marrying a nice tired businessman."

"Oh, you'll probably meet some fascinating man and get your name up in lights," he said.

She laughed. "I don't remember ever thinking about that. As a kid I play-acted because I lived in a gloomy house with old parents. Now I'm just addicted to grease paint. Besides, I can't type or sell dresses, and it wouldn't be nice for Richard if I sold my body."

Norman said nothing, and she heard him. She looked at him quizzically for a moment. "And what about you, Moonbloom, what's with you?"

"Oh me," he said, shrugging. "I'm New York's most educated rent collector. I'm trying to make what I'm stuck with into a vocation."

"Somehow you seem too good for your job," she said.

"It would be the first thing I was too good for. Maybe that's what people should do, something they're too good for."

"I don't quite make you out, Norman," she said suspiciously. "Either you're some kind of a sneak or else . . . I almost get the impression that you're *sleeping*."

He smiled, ignoring the odd scratching sensation that he sensed, rather than felt, in his chest.

"Okay, take your rent and go before you distract me. I have enough things already. . . ."

"I'll give you a receipt."

"You know what you can do with that receipt," she said, escorting him to the door, her sweet smell just getting through to him. He looked at the wide white part in her coarse hair.

"So long, Leni," he said.

"So long, Moonbloom," she said in her breathless voice. It boomed profoundly and came through the deepness to his subterranean dwelling. He rolled restlessly and blood flowed warningly.

J. T. came to the door and made a tired, gentle gesture of welcome. "It's Moonbloom," he croaked, and then coughed a little; the phlegmy, shredding sound established his identity. He was tall and gaunt and bent, and the painter's colic was drawing him into an ever more acute curve, like an invisible bowstring; you sensed what the release would be.

"*Will* you please sit down, J. T.," his wife said, and then, to Norman, "That man just *has* to pop up every time the bell rings. Sure don't have to worry about this fella, J. T.; *he* wouldn't get discouraged and go away, would you?"

"No, Mrs. Leopold, you're right about that," Norman said.

"Well, come on in while I try to put together all my chicken feed." She led him into the living room, which was papered in ancient brown stripes. There was a glass-shaded lamp, circa 1911. Norman vaguely recalled seeing such lamps used cleverly in pictures of modern rooms. But here, surrounded by massive, clubfooted tables and highboys, it was being played straight, and the reds and blues of the lamp shade were part of the consistent picture from a dusty, old, commonplace album.

She rummaged in a pocketbook as big as a small shopping bag and covered with some sort of coral oilcloth, talking as she squinted at what she was ostensibly doing.

"J. T. feels that the hallway ought to be swept out once in a while," Milly Leopold said. Suddenly she made a silent "ah" and plucked out a wrinkled bill. "Isn't that right, J. T., honey?" She smiled, pretending to be animated by the gaunt, blue-faced man with the heavy 1890 mustache.

J. T. did a little something with his face that might have been his smile.

"And another thing J. T. would like to know is when you're going to take care of that busted burner on our stove. He's getting mighty impatient, aren't you, J. T.?"

J. T. wrinkled his face. Impatience?

"No, it doesn't do to arouse J. T. He's gentle and soft-spoken but you dasn't push him too far.

Pushed too far, J. T. coughed cavernously. The sound of splintering wood came from his chest, vague, buried leakings. Milly was briefly frozen by the sound; her eyes stared, and her smile became somewhat dimmer. She watched her husband's large, cracked-nailed hand grope over a book with numb, blind flexings. J. T. picked up the book and opened it at random; then he stared over the top of the book at the rug, as though convinced he had removed himself sufficiently by that act.

"The best thing would be to take care of those things," she said somewhat distractedly. Her face was round and aged in the pretty, unbelievable way of grandmothers in children's books. She wore septagonal, rimless glasses and had curly gray hair combed to account for each silvery strand. Everything about her appearance was naïve, except her eyes, which remembered everything despite her prettying effort.

"I'll have to get after the super," Norman said, decorously addressing the old painter. He eased the money from her hand and put the receipt into it. "The stove too."

She barely nodded, though she maintained her smile. The coughing had smashed something in her; patiently, she fitted the shards together and swept up the pieces too small to be saved. She stood when Norman started for the door, looking to see what effect that had on her husband.

But J. T. merely stared at the diminishing light of afternoon with a quiet rage; handsome in an old barroom way, he was bluish and perplexed looking.

"Well," she said with a deep breath at the door, "you look into those things, Mr. Moonbloom. We're people of very limited means—as you may know, I go to business myself, and Mr. Leopold is only eligible for minimum Social Security. The rent is a serious problem for us, and we certainly expect to get all that's coming to us. Now that burner has been broken since . . . well, my son, Carl, was here from Michigan in July —he's in TV repair out there—and the burner went on the blink then. Now that's, let's see . . ." She counted on her fingers, her eyes strained in a ridiculous attempt at concentration. The rumbling cough sounded softly in the apartment, and her counted fingers turned arthritic. "That's a good four months, and I've been after that colored fella a million times, and he just keeps telling me all the work he has with four houses, and I say well what about me and I'm a darn sight older than you and I manage to . . ." She talked to fill the brooding concavity behind her, and Norman slid away from her, nodding and moving his lips agreeably.

Ilse Moeller was an astringent termination to the Second Avenue tour of duty. Pretty, sourly smiling, she looked at Norman as she looked at everyone; she seemed to feel herself to be an ugly mold and saw all people as her castings.

"Here he iss," she said with nasty humor. "Fire, famine, flood, nutting stops the rent. So constant, my, my."

"Perhaps it's reassuring?"

She ignored that, turning her back to him to get the money. She was shapely, but her arms were almost grotesquely too

51

long and seemed to drag at her shoulders. "Do you not ever think beyond the rent? Does it not occur to you, little rent man, that the vorld is killing itself and that the bomb vill soon turn all money to ashes?"

"Sometimes it occurs to me," he answered pleasantly, his face too small and battened down for her clumsy anger to damage. "But I keep working and you keep working and somehow things go on."

"You evade like a coward. Or perhaps you don't like talking to me?" Her smile was scornful and knowing and bored.

"What a thing to say," he answered, holding out her receipt with an incorruptible smile. He approved of her immaculate apartment, which would have stood up to Kram's standards. Only, the hunchback's eyes were coldly serene, while hers were harsh and disorderly.

"You don't like Chermans, do you?" she said, her smile bitten into her good-looking, rather blotchy face. She held on to one end of the money, so he was forced to remain face to face with her.

He raised his eyebrows, in a kind of surprise that his face expressed anything.

"I mean, you are a Jew . . ."

"Oh, *that!*" He chuckled at her misapprehension. "No, no, that's silly. Why should I hold anything against you?"

"Are you perhaps a fool?"

"That possibility exists."

"Agh." She let go of the money and waved him off. "All right, go, go. You must excuse me. I have things to do. I must vash my hair," she said with a little gesture of mock daintiness. "I have a *date* for this eefning. I must be a cute, pretty little doll baby, so female, so stupid. Then the man vill like me and perhaps buy me a dinner another time. Ve vill dance and drink and then wrestle for a while in the hallway here, and I vill cutely refuse him to come in, hinting that maybe *next* time . . . So, that iss vat iss between me and my sleep tonight."

"Have a good time," he called over his shoulder without thinking.

"Stupid fool!" she said, and slammed the door.

He shrugged and went out of the building with all the money.

Outside, Gaylord was studying the building like a man planning to redesign the façade.

"Got a lot to do in that place," he said dolefully. "Don't hardly know where to begin." Orange sunlight gave conviction to his strong figure and dignity to his broad, dissatisfied face.

"Just study the situation for a few days," Norman said without stopping, wary of Gaylord's trapping him into manual labor.

"Oh you go ahead and mock."

"Don't be so sensitive. I'm not mocking."

"Nobody knows."

"Bye, Gaylord." He waved with a snapping motion of his wrist.

"Go on, go on. I'll take care of it myself."

"Good man, Gaylord," he called back from too far away to be caught.

The early dark began blotting the color of things as he walked down Thirteenth Street. Small, fly-specked luncheonettes alternated with wholesalers who dealt in narrowly specialized items. Here were costumes dusty and dated, there a place that was established in 1907 and specialized in shoe trees; next to a cleaner's was an outlet for doll's eyes—Only to the Trade. The street seemed to be avoided by the Department of Sanitation in memory of a forgotten feud, but the dirt there was not particularly repugnant, seeming to consist mostly of paper. The buildings, above the tawdry shop fronts, were noble in their antique cornices and dark green, scaly paint, and yet, taken all together, the street presented the gritty complexity of a broken rock. Norman smiled slightly as he walked, wondering whether or not the street depressed him. His doubt recalled Ilse's name-calling, and he tried to define to himself what, exactly, a fool was.

The house was squeezed breathless by two huge warehouses, and some of the windows showed the strain in quite apparent warping. As Second Avenue could be described as the "best" house of the four, so this one was obviously the "worst."

Today, the ground floor smelled of bananas. "Karloff," he said, wrinkling his nose. He knocked at the door from which the smell seemed to come.

"Vas vilst du?" The roar had a startling echo.

"Moonbloom, the rent." No echo at all.

"Gay in draird!" The door was flung open to reveal the mountainous ancient.

"Now, now, Mr. Karloff."

The man, still over six feet tall, was being tugged downward in a thousand places. It was as though a multitude of hooks tied to weights were snagged in the outer corners of his eyelids, in the flesh of his cheeks and the corners of his mouth, at his shoulders, his ear lobes, his temples. It gave him the look of a gigantic, extinct creature thrusting upward from the frozen mud. His skin was almost black with age and crumpled into so many short, intersecting lines that squinting slightly one would not see them at all.

"Vas vilst du mit mir? Ich hut nit kein gelt. Ich hut gornisht,

gornisht!" His carnivorous breath was bearable only because of the accompanying whisky odor.

"Come on now, Mr. Karloff, you tell me that all the time. But I know better. You have money. Why, you eat enough for a whole family. You spend four dollars a day for schnapps. You're richer than I am."

"*Ich nit vershtayen,*" Karloff rasped in feigned bewilderment.

"You understand fine." Norman slipped past the great hulk and went to the table, upon which were strewn pieces of bread and scraps of meat. A torn loaf stood beside a half-empty bottle of whisky. Roaches took their time on the walls, and the curtains were in tatters. The walls were so filthy and old and of such indescribable color that they seemed like recesses of murky air and made credible the echoing bellow Norman had heard from the hallway. On the hamstrung bed and the crippled, leaning buffet, there were broken-spined books with Yiddish type, and pieces of a Jewish newspaper were stained by fish heads. Under a cracked, filthy bowl of cold soup, Norman was surprised to see a copy of *Moby Dick*. His fingers pincered fastidiously, he removed the bowl and opened the book; it, too, was printed in Yiddish. He looked up at Karloff, visualizing an Ahab condemned by fate to live too long.

"How's the book?"

"Ah, *zayer goot,*" Karloff said, smiling to show the black stumps in his ravenous mouth. Disarmed, he fell into English. "It is story fuhn a fish, a *graysa*, big . . ."

"A whale," Norman said helpfully, rubbing his fingers together in request for the money.

"Yah, yah, a vale. And the *menchen*, the kepten . . . he has a *dybbuk, ehr gehven mashuga* fuhn duh vale. And the sea . . ." He waved his long, heavy arms, and his dark, rotting face shone with great excitment. He was one hundred and four years old, and his remaining strength was in his rage. His children were dead, and Norman had seen his youngest grandchild, a silvery-haired man already troubled by hardening of the arteries who paid rare, disgusted duty calls. Karloff consumed vast quantities of food and drink, had a vile temper, and claimed to be the oldest atheist in the world.

"The rent," Norman prodded.

"Such a *meissen*," the old man mused, stuffing a ragged chunk of bread into his mouth.

"And Mr. Karloff . . ."

The black face looked at him blandly.

"For the dozenth time, I'm going to have to ask you to keep the place a little cleaner. We keep having the exterminator, but it's a losing battle. You *must* not leave garbage around. People complain."

"*Ah shwartz cholerya offen zie—ahlamun!*"

"No need to curse. I'll have to insist."

"Yah, yah," Karloff said scornfully. "Go already."

"The money, Mr. K."

"*Nah!*" He pushed the crumpled money at Norman, obviously having had it in his hand all the time. "Take, take. *Du vilst mir tsu shtaben,* I should die, hah! Not me, not Karloff! I am strong, *Ich hut kayach,* Karloff *hut graysa kayach!* I don't die, I don't die!" He beat his huge, collapsed rib cage; standing in the filth of his room, he was like a gigantic, tattered plant grown from a compost heap. "GOWAN, GO!" He howled.

Norman went.

Sugarman paid him in small bills and a multitude of change taken from his previous night's candy sales. He was a candy butcher on trains going out of Grand Central, quite widely remembered by passengers for his entertaining manner of hawking his goods. Yet, like most clowns, he was at heart a dolorous person, resigned to predetermined fate. With no humor discernible, he had told Norman that his name had doomed him to his trade.

"Come in and get it, Moonbloom," he said. He was in his late forties and had a curly, florid face and a strong, thick body. "This money has character, so don't make a face at the small change. This half-dollar, for example. It changed trains at Peoria and again at Chicago. It took the milk run downstate to Cairo and was carried back up to Sandusky, Ohio, in a whore's garter belt. Quickly it lost the brief warmth of that intimate purse when she put it into a collection basket in a Catholic church there. A kindly felon in the audience took it in change for a zinc slug and transported it across two state lines to Utica, New York, where it changed hands in a game of jacks-or-better, draw poker, one-eyed jacks wild. The bean salesman who won it brought it home to Albany, where it went into his wife's pin money. She bought her boy friend a hand-painted tie with it, and the store rolled it with others of its kind and deposited it in the Third National and Mineral Savings Bank. The following day it was in a teller's eighty-dollar-fifty-seven-cent pay envelope. This man, a sufferer from Reynaud's disease—profuse sweating of the palms—took it on his visit to his father in New London, Connecticut, where he paid for a tankful of Esso premium gas with it. The service-station owner then took the New Haven Railroad to New York, leaving New London at seven oh three Eastern standard time. At precisely eight forty-eight, same time zone, he paid for a bar of Hershey's chocolate (nutless). I know the time because an air hose broke and we were stalled near Cos Cob." He sat down on his bed and looked at the patient little man with the receipt book. "And still it doesn't come to rest. It goes to Moonbloom, and I will not know its destiny hereinafter."

"I'll take good care of it, Sugarman," Norman said, writing out the fictitious receipt.

"No, no, you won't," Sugarman said sadly, the Pagliacci grief and self-disrespect coating his eyes. "You have something innately unwholesome about you, Moonbloom. In spite of all your busy handling of money and receipts, I sense a heedlessness that extends to a basic disregard even for money. Like me, you are essentially humorless and unalive."

"How can you call yourself humorless, Sugarman? You're known as the wit of the rails."

"I only cry out in the darkness as we rush through the countryside," Sugarman said, laying himself on his bed. "My jokes are merely wails; my sounds of humor are cumulatively a dirge. Hey, don't I know—humor is tragic; it sinks the knife far deeper than solemnity. The laugh is as elemental as a baby's gas smile, a reflex of pain."

"You're very eloquent, Sugarman," Norman said, as willing to kill time one way as another. He was near the end of his collections, and the evening ahead was just a long, embryonic period of time. As far as he could tell, he derived the same pleasure, or sensation, from this as he did from the coin-induced foot vibrator he had used the week before. "Is it possible you've missed your calling out of excess concern about your name?"

"No, absolutely not. My shoulders, my spirit even, are shaped to the strap of my candy tray as my father's arm and spirit were shaped to the phylacteries. I was born with my spiel and at an early age shocked my father out of his morning devotions with my heretic and profane cries. 'Last call for candy, ice-cold awrange drrink, peanuts, ham and cheese sandwiches, chocolate bars—male and female, chewing gum, delectable cookies. This train does *not* have a diner, ladies and gents. There will be *no* refreshments between here and Boston. You will be famished, parched, *and* debilitated. This is your last chance to nourish your bodies, to replenish the vital juices lost to sweat. These awrange drrinks *remain* cold for extraordinary lengths of time due to a special ingredient. There is *positively* no dining car on *this* train. I am your last hope for sustenance. Hersheys, Almond Joys, Milky Ways, ice-cold awrange drrink!"

"You'll sacrifice your professional standing, giving me that performance. I definitely will not buy."

"True, true, but what can I do? It's all busman's holiday for me. I'm like a sailor with eternal sea legs. I rock in my bed and wake in the dark expecting to see Bridgeport or New Haven floating past in the night like memories. There is no present for me. I am all past. I have spent my youth no place, in transit. I am a wraith, Moonbloom, I doubt my existence. When I enter a room, it is as though someone had just left. I have no social life, no friends. For sex I use women as I would a vending machine. All recedes from me, as though seen through the window of a train, and I see faces as I see the fronts of buildings in the hundreds of hamlets I pass, all overlain with my own ugly puss."

"Obviously you're lonely. Why don't you join the Y or some Over Thirty-five Club?"

"You are being deliberately cynical. Nothing reaches you but vague premonitions."

"Maybe some time we'll go into it further," Norman said as tedium suddenly began rising up over his ankles. He stood and put his money in order.

Sugarman stared at the ceiling. "Moonbloom," he said spitefully, "your clothes are too large for your body."

"Noo-o, Sugarman, I'm too small for my clothes."

"You are no help."

"Not even to myself," Norman agreed, reaching the door.

"This house is cruddy," Sugarman said petulantly.

"No question."

"Everything is cruddy."

"Now, now, Sugarman."

"I'm tired, Moonbloom. After I talk for a protracted time, I get weary unto death. Go, let me dream of that last big train of them all."

"Sounds Freudian," Norman said, opening the door.

"Drop dead, Moonbloom."

"I only wish you well," Norman said. And he closed the door on the figure of the candy butcher, lying diagonally across his bed, his eyelids down and fluttering.

As usual, Paxton seemed busy. He let Norman in with a little feminine gesture of irritation. "Oh heavens, *you* agayn." He smoked like one of those machines that supposedly test cigarette filters, but his black face was knobby and calm, removed from the nervous gestures of his hands and shoulders. "Well, come on in, baby, but I *am* in a sort of tizzy."

A Dazor lamp stood poised over his typewriter; beyond, the disorder seemed hostile to his attempt at work. The room looked frenzied. There were papers all around, and there was the feeling that the inhabitant of the room could not live without paper, that he was an odd species of creature who could be nourished by nothing else. Books did splits on the battered bed; magazines were piled against the walls and under the bed. Paxton minced to the bed, swept off some magazines and envelopes, and waved an invitation to Norman to sit.

"I'll be out of your way in a minute, Joe," Norman said, lowering himself cautiously on the uncertain seat.

"Oh, that's all right, love. I'm so disorganized anyhow. And *je suis fatigué;* I need a break. Have a drink, Norm?"

"A little soda, maybe?"

"Soda, soda," Paxton said, contemplating the debris and scratching his tightly grown hair with a delicate finger. He kept it cut short and did nothing to beautify it, using no grease or lotions. His mouth was classically thick, but his nose betrayed some forgotten Caucasian in the woodpile and was long and sharp. His eyes were globular and moved very rapidly. "I just *might* have some kind of flat quinine water."

"Make it water."

Paxton filled a jelly jar at the sink and dropped into it a melted-down wafer of ice. "Oh, I tell you," he said, handing the glass to Norman, "that old word-machine is a monkey on my back. Sometimes I don't know why I bang away on it. I don't even think about what is going onto paper and to my agent, penultimately to the publisher and ultimately to the ladies in the book clubs. It begins to seem as though I could just go on and on without even having a ribbon in the typewriter. The act of striking keys becomes the be-all end-all. I've just got to get out of this room soon or—*bughouse!*"

"How's this one coming?" Norman asked, receipt book in hand.

"Oh, *très bien,* but I'll get to hate it before I'm done. I'm rotting inside, lovey—it ruins everything. I start with hating the White Citizens Councils and begin hating citizens and wind up hating yours truly. Lamentable, but not hopeless." He looked at Norman with his prominent eyes, which struck out at people, their cleverness magnified, projected by the receding forehead and the smallness of his other features, so that his face was like an onrushing vehicle, its way lit by the eyes. "I'm just waiting for a royalty check, and then, *adieu* Thirteenth Street, *adieu* United States of Some Americans. I go to Paris, where the squalor is rosy, where mold is precious."

"Then you think one place is different from another? I've never been as far away as Europe, but I've had my head on the pillows of several states, not to mention six months at the University of Mexico and a summer session at McGill. The light was the same everywhere, and everywhere I displaced the same small amount of air."

"You, Norman, are an extraordinary case, not typical of Homo sapiens. They say elephants gestate for God knows how long. Without intending insult, let me say that I believe your sainted mother must have been a mastodon. The gook is still in your eyes."

"Enough," Norman said with a faint sliver of irritation. "I get a little tired of hearing people say that I'm in a fog. I think it's just misery loving company. No one can stand to see tranquillity."

"As you say," Paxton said with a shrug.

"Anyhow," Norman went on, mollified easily because his angers were never more than a few inches high, "you apparently don't like it here."

"Like? Man, I'm just tired of Niggerdom. I'm small and frail, Dad, small and frail. I can no longer stand to look at my brethren; they haunt me. I'm an artist—they need preachers and warriors. Joyce left home so he could see what he was doing. Lord knows, I've got more reason."

Norman digested that, sipping slowly at the water, which tasted of rust. Those pipes! On the mantel of the dummy fireplace were Paxton's three published books, literary successes all; but they had earned the author a total of forty-seven hundred dollars over the five years since the first had come out. Norman turned his eyes on the slight, black man, who seemed to be burning away in the clouds of his ferocious smoking.

"Maybe you should get married, Joe," Norman said innocently.

"Wow, that would be a *truly* spiritual thing—no confusion with lust there. Oh, baby, I *like* women, but that would be a perverted relationship. I'm a wholesome American faggot, lover; at least that part of me is somewhat orderly. That's all I'd need to louse myself up—a touch of bisexuality. Why, I'd never get any work done."

"Just so you're happy, Joe," Norman said, writing out the receipt.

"You're so *wry*, baby. I'll bet you're the wryest landlord in town."

"I'm only the agent," Norman said softly.

"Man, if I had time, I'd like to take you apart and see what's what," Paxton said, his ugly face suddenly metamorphosed by an incredibly beautiful smile. That smile was the secret of his charm; it seemed to forgive so much, that the beholder was forced to forgive him. "You have the makings of something, something. . . ."

"Black man speak with forked tongue," Norman said, handing over the receipt with one hand, the other out for the money.

"Don't be surprised if one day you open a *Paris Review* and see yourself flayed and pegged out in print."

"I'll look forward, Joe."

"Take a traveler's check?" Paxton asked, the flawless, warming smile fixed hypnotically on Norman.

"For you, Joe."

"Merci, chéri."

"You're welcome, Yussel."

And they parted, somehow both friends and enemies.

Del Rio studied drama on the nights he didn't fight. You could see the complexity of his regimen in the way he looked at you from under the battered folds of his eyelids.

"Rent time," Norman sang out.

"Hullo, Moonbloom," Del Rio said, somewhat Marlon Brando in tone; but his swarthy face, thickening under the small jabs of ring opponents (he was a good boxer and rarely absorbed heavier punches) seemed to Norman on its way out of eligibility for the lover roles.

Of medium height and superbly built, he moved lightly, guardedly. At a hundred and thirty-eight, Norman felt ponderous, and he sat quickly. The room was very clean and almost anonymous except for the several books and notebooks. The picture of John Barrymore on the wall looked like something that had come with the room. A red satin robe with DEL RIO in white lettering on its back hung on a hanger on the door to the closet. On the table an open book was guarded by a tall jar of wheat germ.

"There's cockroaches again," Del Rio said, taking his wallet from a drawer. "I'm getting fed up. I have to use that lousy can in the hall with those slobs Paxton and Louis. I clean it out myself every other day. I buy disinfectant and do the tub and the sink and the floor and the goddam toilet bowl. I sweep out the hallway on this floor and I keep my room clean. But I don't have a chance with those stinking cockroaches!"

"I spoke to the old man."

"Spoke! Get him the hell out of here. Put him in a home for the aged or something. He's extinct, that old nut. I swear I'm going to call the Department of Sanitation or the Board of Health!" His Indian-black hair picked blue lights out of the approaching dusk, and his face, which had seemed phlegmatic under its armoring of scar tissue, was stirred now by an odd-flavored anger, almost a passion; he might have been expressing a perverse love for that which provoked him.

"He's a human being," Norman said mildly, almost flippantly. He felt much safer with Del Rio than he did, say, with Wade Johnson. Del Rio never raised a hand to anyone outside the ring.

"Well, so am I! I can't stand filth. Besides, anyone who lives dirty like that is an animal, not a human."

"He's old," Norman said, filling out the receipt.

"I can't see how people can be so sloppy with themselves—their bodies and their minds. They're messy all the way through," Del Rio said with a twitch of disgust.

"Not all of us have your discipline, Del Rio," Norman said, waving the receipt, although he knew the ball-point writing dried almost upon contact with the paper. He thought wistfully how pleasant it must have been to write with a quill and then pour sand over the parchment.

"That's why the world is so messed up."

"Because we don't wash enough? Come on, Del Rio—the Germans are an immaculate race."

"*Inside* they're messy, they're full of filthy fairy tales."

"Well, it's an interesting theory. But how can you be an actor if you can't identify with all us untidy humans?"

Del Rio flushed like a prepubescent boy accused of having a girl friend. "That's something else again," he said harshly. "An actor can be like a scientist. When he performs, he is conducting an experiment. It's like he's using his voice and body as a microscope. I mean, I could even play that old maniac Karloff, probably. But I'm always me. A scientist doesn't have to *identify* with some gloppy tissue he's studying."

"Well, I don't know," Norman said, feigning thoughtfulness; he was playing an old, mild game with Del Rio. "It doesn't seem you could be much of an actor that way."

"You're wrong," Del Rio said intensely. "The passion should be for the craft, not for the subjects. It's like what I do in the ring. If I let myself get emotional, I don't fight well. But if I stay cool and watch everything I do and everything the other guy does, I come out fine."

"I wouldn't imagine you'd have many friends with your attitude," Norman said, counting the money slowly and arranging it in his wallet in order of denomination.

"Big deal. I used to have friends and family. They loused me up plenty. I'm better off now."

"Never lonely?" Norman asked, his pregnant-woman eyes faintly teasing.

"*Always* lonely," Del Rio said proudly, his lean, perfect body a testimonial to his ascetic triumph.

"I'm not convinced," Norman said.

"That doesn't matter to me," Del Rio answered calmly. "The thing is, I can always understand my pain—everything is clear to me."

"Maybe you won't always be so strong," Norman said, standing and wondering why he bothered with all the talk. He suddenly felt very tired. The something that had made him feel ill the previous evening must still be in him. For a moment he felt an idiotic panic at the possibility of something incurable, but it was gone with as little aftereffect as a single heart palpitation, and he smiled at Del Rio. "I'll see what can be done about the roaches," he said.

"Do that," the fighter said, standing in the bright loneliness of his room. "*I can't stand dirt.*"

"Only *dirt?*" Norman sighed with the faintest irony.

"Don't laugh at me."

"Is that another thing that bothers you?" Norman asked from the doorway.

"All right, all right," Del Rio said impatiently. "Look, I've got some reading to do and I want to catch a little sleep—got a fight in Newark tonight."

"I'm going, I'm going," Norman said in mock panic. "See you next time."

Del Rio didn't answer. As Norman closed the door, he seemed to be narrowing the frame on a picture of the fighter, sitting at his table over the book, his large knuckled hands laced over his forehead, completely motionless as he read. His immobility made apparent the furtive movement of a roach on the molding over his head. Norman grimaced emphatically for the insect's danger as he closed the door with a little click.

Louie, a Jewish gnome, lived under the roof.

"Hi ya, Norman, whatta ya say? Hey, nice day out, hah? Suppose to be fifty-five degrees, but I don't know. . . ." He was a messenger for a photoprint company and he had large photostats of farm scenes on his wall. There was a small television set with a screen the size of a playing card, a two-burner stove, and a large store of canned foods. Often he was happy. But Norman had seen him lying on his bed with a corner of the pillow in his mouth, frightened and ill looking. "But I got this sore shoulder. Doctor said it's bursitis . . . yah . . . bursitis. . . . You think *they* care, down to Delmore Photo, that my shoulder hurts. Nah, whatta they care! One of these days I'm gonna walk out on them. I'm not fooling. Oh, I had a offer from Scarpo, over on Eleventh Avenue—pay three bucks more too. I said, 'Well I'll see.' You think Delmore appreciates I'm loyal? Hah!"

Norman nodded his way in and took his receipt book out

for the last time that week. A Western was crepitating softly on television; Louie's canned supper bubbled cosily on the little stove.

"Think I'm gonna go out by my sister's next week. She's got a house out to Longuylin—Massapeeka. Think I'll go out there and sit in the sun there. She got a pretty yard and kids. The kids call me 'Uncle Louie.'" He chuckled meltingly. "Them kids! I bring 'em out balloons or candy, cheez. . . . Yeah, think that's what I'm gonna do."

Norman wondered if Louie talked to himself when no one else was available. The words came out so fast and irrelevant to sensible response that only nodding and smiling were possible. He nodded and smiled at the little man. Louie was fifty-one years old, but his hair was still all black and combed flat to his monkey head like gleaming skin. His ears were simian too, and he had a large nose and small dun-colored eyes.

"I'm gonna catch that picture down to the Apollo. It's about this monster from the North Pole. Manucci, fella what I work with, seen it. Says the monster comes to New York and knocks over buildings and they bomb him and all. Supposed to be very interesting. I don't know though—I think maybe I need glasses a little. . . ." He rested his hand on his nose. "But anyhow, next week I'll run out by my sister, I think. Yeah, visit them, have dinner. I sit with the kids while they go out dancing and like that. It's nice there, big house— Early Colonial split. She keeps a special bed for me in the playroom, foam-rubber mattress. She's a good cook, my sister. And they like for me to come out. 'Uncle Louie,' they call me—ahh-hhh. . . ." He shook his head wonderingly.

Norman slipped into his wallet the money that Louie had had waiting on the table. He wedged the receipt under Louie's floral plate and stood up.

"Ah, but them guys over Delmore—wise guys, they make fun, you know? Smart guys, mock me—hah ha ha. Some time I'm gonna . . ." His face darkened and twisted, weird emptinesses rolled behind his eyes for a moment. Then his dullness laved him. He squinted at his supper boiling, and looked blankly at the Western, which faded into a commercial for cocoa before his eyes.

"Yeah, but I'm gonna see that picture over to the Apollo. Manucci says that monster is bigger as the Empire State. I don't know though—I think I need glasses a little. . . ."

Norman left unobtrusively, while Louie was talking.

He walked through the evening streets to the subway at Fourteenth Street. The sky arched into superfluous immensities of distance; for Norman, the distance between him and the nearest passer-by was infinite. He felt dull and weary. There was a ringing in his ears that he attributed to a "bug" that must have attacked him the previous evening, and he defended the pulling, pushing sensation in his body, diagnosing a low fever and focusing on his perfect abode some concrete miles ahead. He looked forward to the comfort of doctoring himself. The wind, which had been autumnal during the day, now had the cold, death-damp smell of winter. He couldn't go around without a coat any more—this treacherous, changeable weather. He mused on the possibility of thermostatically controlled clothing that would keep one's body at a constant temperature, and didn't see the drunk vomit hideously, although he passed within a foot of him and was splashed slightly.

When he got home, he put a pot of water to boil for a spaghetti supper and sat down with pencil and paper to recalculate the things that should, but which he knew could not, be done. And each time, as he prepared to write that which seemed to require first priority in his fictitious plan, another face appeared to him and he remembered another complaint. The sisters Minna and Eva reminded him of the elevator; he tried to recall whether it was an Otis or a Westinghouse. The Lublins' dripping sink plunked into his consciousness with its irritating persistence. Merely a washer . . . But the pencil was arrested at the point by the swelling tumor of Basellecci's wall. And then there was J. T. Leopold's stove and the wiring on Second Avenue. . . . The slow crawl of a doomed cockroach made a distracting track across his mind. Leni Cass leaned into his eyes, and he tried to recall her complaint. Had she had a complaint? He got up with a hiss of exasperation, dropped the spaghetti into the boiling water, and stood watching it soften and slide down limply into the pot. He was feverish; there was no sense trying to think straight.

He set the timer at nine minutes and wandered over to the window, brushing absently at imagined lint on his trousers. Suddenly he caught sight of an unexplained stain on his pant leg. He bent down and scraped at it, imagining a foul smell. Straightening, he stared through the window, trying to relive the time, to pinpoint the moment when that filth could have touched him. And staring vacantly at the buildings outside, his lucidity impaired by the low-level fever, he imagined he saw the Monster from the North Pole looming over the skyscrapers downtown.

FIVE

THE FEVER PUZZLED and intrigued him. He sat in his little office, the phone held a few inches away from his ear to mute Gaylord's aggrieved shouting, examining the sensation of fragility. His limbs could have been made of glass, and although he was not aware of discomfort, pain seemed imminent. His skin felt *susceptible*—there was the ghostly sense of knowing pain without feeling it. The closest he could come to an example was the silent statement, "My hair hurts."

" 'Got no pressure,' they yell to me, 'got no pressure.' " Gaylord brayed from the phone. "What am I suppose to do? Top floor they got no water at all, rest of the house just a trickle, like a baby peeing. I say, 'I'm no plumber, got to call the agent.' They say, 'Well do *something*,' all mad at me, like I took their water away. I get the brunt, they pick on me, probably figure *him*, that *swarsa*, he's to blame. You better get on over here, Moonbloom, get this straighten out 'fore I lose my temper and tell them times change, slavery gone out, man got to be treat with a little dignity."

"You're too sensitive, Gaylord. Take it easy, I'll call the plumber." Sensitive—the word made the tiny hairs on his forehead stand up. He gave a slight shudder at the thought of bumping his arm against something hard.

"Sure, you're there, you say, 'Take it easy.' You come *here*

71

and get abused like I get abused, see if you take it easy. 'No water, no water'—you think they dying of thirst middle of the desert. I'm going over Thirteenth Street; got plenty to do. I'm not about to stand here and listen. . . ."

"All right, Gaylord, all right."

He hung up, and put his hand to his head to check his temperature; but he could feel neither his hand nor his head. Before him, the letters on the window were haloed by the noon light.

"tnegA," he read aloud. "tnegA—moolbnooM namroN." But there was this pressure on his heels, something forcing him to stand on his head and crash through a hoop of pain. "Okay already . . . plumber, plumber . . ." He held his finger poised over the buttons of the memo pad. Bodien! He pressed the B, and the device popped open to a page of names. Delightful. He looked at the swim of calligraphy, blinked, and read names.

Binkerman
Boroff
Battapaglia
Brass Pipe & Foundry
Xotichitl
Beerbau . . .

"Xotichitl?" What in the . . . Oh, but stop this, Seventieth Street was without water. He put his finger on each name, intent, not fooling now. His ears rang.

He told the plumber to meet him at the Seventieth Street house and made ready to leave the office. He took the check for the insurance company and put it in an envelope, made a note to himself to look at the name on the elevator so he could call the repairman, wrote down the name and number of the electrical contractor, the exterminator, the roofing company. He tried to think who would take care of the swollen wall, ended up just writing "Basellecci." He went out patting his pockets.

A delegation of women was waiting in the lobby, aproned, together in accusation but not speaking to each other. Eva Baily was more than ever like a fierce squaw; Carol Hauser merely looked peevish under the burden of her bleached hairdo and the tugging of the blond child; Sarah Lublin stood with melancholy serenity. Betty Jacoby was there, too, but in the artless light of the lobby, she seemed to be fading away.

"Well?" Carol Hauser said menacingly.

"It's two hours now. I was right in the middle of . . ." Eva suddenly preferred to leave it at that.

"The plumber is on his way. Don't worry about a thing. We'll take care of it," Norman assured them. They were no more than pasteboard figures, and he smiled at how harmless they seemed. They went away as though a gust of wind had taken them.

Bodien, the plumber, came ten minutes later, just as Norman was beginning to imagine the fake manorial motif of the lobby was real. They tried to go down the narrow steps abreast and then spent almost two minutes, jammed between the rail and the wall, arguing politely about who should go first. Norman, not himself, said brusquely, "Okay," and pushed out of the impasse. In the cellar he trained Bodien's flashlight on the dust-furred pipes while the plumber tapped and felt them uncertainly. Norman waited patiently; for what he was permitted to pay he didn't expect great professionalism. Bodien was a sort of amateur, a handy man, an unfrocked plumber whose only qualification for the trade was a where-angels-fear-to-tread audacity.

He took a Stillson wrench out of his toolbox and began to unscrew a particularly large and menacing-looking pipe.

"Don't you have to turn something off or something?" Norman asked, noticing an ooze of water around the threads.

"Oops, heh, heh, that's right," Bodien said with a wink. His face was mangy, there were bristles on his nose, and he never took offense at constructive criticism. He turned off the main and went back to his wrench. A little squirt of water struck Norman's face and startled him disproportionately.

"Whaa-a . . ."

"Better step back there," Bodien said sternly. He finished detaching the pipe and stood looking at the slow trickle with the gravity of a doctor examining a biopsy. "Mmm-mm, yeah . . ."

"What's wrong?" Norman asked, feeling chilled in the stony dampness. His hand brushed against the thick dust of something, and he shuddered.

"Don't seem to be anything . . ."

Norman felt like whispering; he was reminded of clandestine games.

"Bodien."

"Yeah?" the plumber asked.

"There *has* to be something. The people upstairs have no water. This is not hypothetical. Something is clogging."

"Well," Bodien agreed, "there should be *something*." He looked warily at the maze of pipes, then made a decision again. "I think that one there, the real thick one . . ."

"You're the doctor," Norman said, following the wrench with the flashlight. His head began to hurt, and the light became heavy in his hand. Something is happening to me, he thought. He had never felt quite like this. All his life he had been subject to colds and the minor illnesses, and he remembered the dark colors of his daydreams in his grandparents' house on those winter afternoons when he had been sick in bed and had seemed to fill the room with the anticipation of another dimension. He could not remember *what* the illusions had been. In a way they had been purely sensory; his whole body had awaited some unimaginable experience. There had been a delicate salting of pain on his skin, a hollow, breath-taking spasm that involved him from heart to groin. Familiar sounds had broken through to brief and unbearable clarities. But always there had been the security of knowing he would sink back, that he would recover and go on as before. Now, for some reason, he felt the threat of permanent eviction. What, what is this?

Bodien leaned on the shaft of his wrench. Slowly it turned metal against metal. There was a fertile smell of refuse and water and the odd silence in the pipes. Bodien grunted. The pressure on Norman's head grew. He looked around at the darkness with a frightened longing. No, no, he would just go right home, undress, pull the shades down, and get into bed with a heating pad. The thought of pain terrified him for the first time. Could a doctor help? He thought not, felt right then that the doctor would somehow be working against him. Bodien's grunt was final. The pipe came apart with only a feeble trickle.

"'et's see now." The plumber put his hand cautiously into the pipe. His face showed a squeamish expression that gradually evolved into complete revulsion. "Echh," he said, drawing something toward him. His hand came out black and slimy and swollen four times its size. No, it was something in his hand, but you couldn't see where hand left off and catch began. The pipe belched and gushed about a gallon of water onto Bodien. He gasped, cursed, then held the slop up triumphantly. "'ere we are, Moonbloom, 'ere's the culprit."

75

"What is it?" Norman asked weakly.

Bodien shook his head; that was not his concern. "Gook," he said.

Norman held the light while the pipe was put back together and then tracked Bodien over to the main and illuminated the operation of turning the water back on. There were thuds and crashes and then the terrifying rush and flow. Norman could feel an impulse to fall and be carried along by it. He ran the light over the pipes and found it shocking to hear all that violence of movement while everything in sight remained motionless.

"Yessir," Bodien said smugly, putting his wrench in his toolbox. "They got water now." Norman looked up with him at the dark ceiling of the cellar, as though he could see the metal veins carrying the flow through the body of the house, and pictured the sudden resumption of things in all the apartments.

He went directly home and closed the door of his own apartment like a man pursued. The wind had left gashes on his tender face, and his eardrums felt pierced. With trembling hands he got undressed and burrowed into his bed. Brain fever, he told himself, trying to joke his way out of it. The daytime noises of the street were huge and hideous, and his limbs felt wrenched. He wondered whether he dared get up to take something, thought better of it, and lay where he was, conjuring up the figure of his crazy father and trying some unclear folk dance with him to the tune of imagined string instruments. But the city would not release him to daydream, and he dove desperately toward his usual dreamless sleep.

But it was occupied, filled like a vast hall with all the tenants. Katz tootled his trumpet in greeting, and a gelatinous note fell *splat* on the ballroom floor. Basellecci aimed a wide-mouthed cannon at him and smiled with his canonical face. Two people were screaming. He was screaming, and he woke up filled with embarrassment and fear and lying in a drenching sweat.

He tried to question but failed halfway, and all that came from his gaping mouth in the truant hour of afternoon was a long "Whaaa-aaahh . . ."

SIX

FOR FIVE LONG days he resided in the vessel of his bed, tied to the shore by the most tenuous mooring of consciousness. Feebly he trod the precarious gangplank to the bathroom and the kitchen and then back to the somnolent, rocking bed. He didn't remember calling a doctor, but one came and gave him two kinds of capsules. Once Gaylord called about something, and he apparently made clear his situation, because the superintendent left him alone after that. He had some recollection of a silly conversation with his brother, Irwin, out of which he retained only a series of disgusted *rannanas*.

The rest of the time was a long dream that bore a simplified resemblance to what he would have called his *life* up to that time, but it was disturbingly more appropriate to dream than life should be. He went back in time and found that his direction was more lateral than recessive. In his bed he was bruised by what turned out to be only a series of flat pictures, and he had the desperate feeling that he observed them from a position on the edge of a cold immensity and that the completion of his hallucinatory reminiscence would push him off into God knew what. And if there was pattern to how he observed that comic-strip chronicle, it was lost on him. He read in the manner of all the languages; left to right, top to bottom, right to left. Succeeding frames had him a reedy adolescent, a toddler, a blanket-sucker of seven. His eyes fixed on the ceiling or on the rumpled cloth of bedclothing, as though any surface could reflect the pale projection. "Norman Moonbloom," he said from time to time, animating the machinery of memory. The city went on in its outside time. There were the sounds of the days rising to climax and settling back to half-sleep. Dimly came the footsteps of his neighbors going up and down the stairs and the voice of the endless belt of traffic. "Norman Moonbloom," he said in incantation, and he studied hard the pictures of himself, wondering what had taken so long to leave him at this point of virginal terror.

Four years old on a rainy, preschool morning, sitting at the piano, playing delicate discord and pretending to be reading music with an opened dictionary on the stand. Under him, inside the bench, were all the mysterious songs locked into sheets of notes. Rain so sweet on the windows, and his grandmother humming "Melancholy Baby" from the kitchen.

Twelve and drawing an imaginary map of an imaginary continent, armied with split peas. On the edge of his game a scornful face—Irwin? He was seen as vaguely obscene, with the black down on his cheeks, still maneuvering those miniature armies.

Going on ten and happy in the radio light, snug in the sound of a man talking about such vivid horrors in Europe. A fairy-tale ease opens his mouth, his grandmother clucks behind him, he sees crayon colors, the blood red a little too waxy to believe.

Fourteen, standing in a summer evening and looking deliriously at a girl while a dangerous boy insults him, reduces him to a bed-wetter. He smiles, offering no target, the girl laughs, tree leaves move hauntingly, a summer night as huge as heaven, smells of warm pavement. He touches his hurt but feels no pain. The other boy and the girl move off laughing, and he is a straw figure with a painted smile.

Something eludes him and he goes home and to bed while everyone else is still outside.

He is three and strawberry ice cream is New Year's Eve. His grandmother drops tears on him and holds him close. He licks the sweet pink cold. She wraps him in something light and soft and very strong. In the morning he will find it has become his skin.

Eighteen, he writes on the form, though he feels the same as he did at eight. He picks up his suitcase and goes out onto the campus, directions clasped in his other hand. He is in a room with a desk. This is college, but when he opens the book it is as always; he expects momentarily to hear his grandmother humming.

His age not clear, he sits on the dusty ground, the king of the ants. He builds walls and prisons and murmurs edicts. Far over the fences he hears Irwin in a ball game. The afternoon is milky with heat, and he abides.

They are at the funeral chapel, with its electric-candle flames and maroon carpeting. His grandmother lies, beaky nose above the rim of the coffin, while the rabbi says some things about her that don't seem familiar. He feels nothing painful, only a sort of nervous sadness, as though a disaster he cannot remember has happened. He looks at his brother, who is crying. His skullcap keeps shrinking up on his head, threatening to fall off. He takes a deep breath of the sweet-ened air and cries a little too.

He and a girl named Monica Alpert are sitting beneath the oldest tree in the Western Hemisphere, or the fattest. Mexicans are moving in the sunlight beyond the immense shadow of the tree, and Monica is talking to him, offering, it seems, some great loveliness to him. She looks like a younger Edith Sitwell, and he is aware of the fine romantic quality of the setting. But all he can do is observe the motions of her lips and think about the flow of the blood through his own body. He realizes that she is slipping away from him, running down like water in a drain. There is only a small puddle left, and he feels he should reach out for her in some way but doesn't. Soon he is walking through the foreign town with a book under his arm. He is alone and searching for a regret he cannot feel. The town feels like his home town.

There are line drawings of teeth and jaws, skeletons of feet, engravings of Old Testament passions, the flayed Vesalius figure, ". . . and drew him down to me so he could feel my breasts all perfume yes and his heart was going like mad and yes I said yes I will Yes." Outside this dormitory window or that one (leaded panes or honest wood) snow is Christmas-card pretty, and there are very few tracks, because most students are away for the holidays. He supposes melancholy but achieves only that numb cosiness. Moonbloom on campus concentrates on psych.

And, most profoundly, he is being soaked in the words of his grandmother, marinated in the membranous belief she lives by. They sit, just the two of them, on the thousand and one Connecticut nights, listening to the radio and talking during the commercials while winter wind or summer mistral tumbles husband, wild son, arrogant older grandson. And he is all she has, so she preserves him in a shell of *moderation*, warns him against pain, and tells him how he can crawl beneath it and dwell in warmth and safety. . . .

He opened his eyes on the fifth afternoon to see his window shade aflame with sunshine. His beard scratched on the pillow, and his sheets were gray with sweat. Weak as a newborn, he nevertheless realized that he had no way of avoiding whatever it was that had happened to him. Timidly he got up, and found that something had been torn away from him, that all the details of the room made deep impressions on his eyes. There was a blistering of plaster at the junction of wall and ceiling, the doorframe had a painted-over cut, the window shade was like worn skin, and he shuddered for it. He went into the bathroom and adjusted the water in the shower, solicitous of his frail, skinny body. The water drummed on him, wakening all his nerves.

He dressed carefully in clean clothes and then wondered whether he would dare the outside. It was Thursday; tomorrow he would have to start collecting the rents again. And what further deterioration had set in in the houses? How high were the bills piled in his basement office? Dread of the familiar routine filled him. The illness had done something to him. For some reason, he had no idea what to expect from himself. Even walking was new to him, and he found himself estimating his weight distribution with each step. Shaved, swaddled as warmly as possible in suit and overcoat, he put his hand on the doorknob. God help him, he was not prepared for this. And he went out into a strange city.

SEVEN

ON THURSDAY MORNING, during the time Norman was crawling out of the last of his hallucinatory illness, Lester exploded at the final soft probing of his aunt Minna.

"You want to know what's bothering me?" he screeched, shaving soap still on his earlobe and Eva extending a tentative hand to wipe it off as well as to gentle the high-strung (how the two aunts loved that word on him) boy. "Well I'll tell you, I'll tell you why I been looking so down in the mouth. Your little nephew Lester has gotten into man-sized trouble."

"What, what?" Eva moaned. She and Minna were together in the pummeling of fear while their nephew's fresh-squeezed orange juice settled in the glass and his Cream of Wheat turned cool. The oil of the vitamin drops would show on the top of the juice, Eva worried, like evidence of evil intent on her part. "Don't get all worked up, Lester dear. Just tell me."

"Let's just sit down and talk it out," Minna said with her usual attempt at psychological resolution. "There's nothing that can't be talked out." But she knew she would be going to the office with a stone in her stomach, and she hated to throw up in that tiny lavatory where everyone could hear her. "There's no sense in just . . ."

"It's a girl!" Lester said grimly, studying the orange juice.

"Drink it," Eva said.

Lester pushed it away with disgust.

"A girl." Minna seemed to gargle the word. "What do you mean?"

"What do I mean? I mean that I've gotten her in trouble." He chopped at the cereal, his weak, youthful face raked by misery and anger and fear. "She's pregnant, she's pregnant."

"Oh God," Eva said, clapping her hand to her heart.

Minna bolted for the bathroom, and Eva and Lester were motionless in the sound of her vomiting, guilty, anguished, and resigned. Finally Minna came back, chalk colored, her lipstick and rouge like embalmer cosmetics on her face.

"All right," she said in a dead, purged voice. "Tell us about it."

And Lester proceeded to narrate the tedious details they had enjoyed smugly in books and on television programs for years. A girl who worked in the same office, someone he had been dating for some time. They had gotten to that point where . . . Yes he liked her . . . yes she was a decent girl in spite of . . . She had missed two—you knows . . . her family would be wild. . . . No, it didn't show. Yes he was sure he was the one—she hadn't seen anyone else since. No, of course he didn't want to get married, he was too young and hadn't found himself. . . .

Strangely, the more he talked and the more his helpless misery was revealed, the more animated the two aunts' faces became. Minna seemed to get some color back, Eva became sly and strong looking and more Indian than ever. Occasionally she touched her sister to mark a certain detail, and Minna nodded knowingly back at her. What was common to both of them revealed a side of their old, deformed love for each other. If Lester noticed a perversity in their rekindled faces, he didn't know what he felt about it—gratitude for their protection or resentment for their finding strength in his fiasco. In any event he did achieve relief in resting part of the burden on them. They were at least mothers, perhaps more; to date they had not let anything irrevocable happen to him. Once he had stolen a piddling amount and they had taken care of it; another time he had cheated on a school examination and they had smoothed that over. He had come home sick and drunk and frustrated, feeling like an exile from the world, and they had warmed him and reminded him that he was important there. He was stuck together with the adhesive liquid of their love, and in their presence he could never come undone. After a while he was smoking peacefully and sharing their solemn study of the problem.

"Drink your juice," Eva said in a tone of renewed command. And Lester, temporarily knowing his place again, drank the juice and imagined a bleak peace for a while.

"There are several things to do," Minna said, smoking so quickly the cigarette was down to a stub in no time. "There are *doctors* . . ."

Eva looked at her with a thrilled revulsion. Lester sat open-mouthed before their old powers. Minna nodded sternly, her face filled with unaccustomed strength. "And there are medicines . . ."

"And if those don't work?" Lester whined, on the verge of nervous laughter because of the deep relief he felt.

"Well there are homes where a girl can have her child without anyone knowing. They put the child out for adoption. It probably won't come to that, but just in case, I will look into it. We can speak to her family and no outsiders need know."

"See, you get out in the business world and you know so many things," Eva said in grudging tribute to her sister.

"Oh my God, *everyone* knows about those things," Minna said, taking the tribute loftily.

Lester finished his breakfast, taking deep breaths and letting them out in sighs after each mouthful. When he was finished he kissed each of his aunts and told them he didn't know what he would do without them, and they just nodded sadly, full of their beloved cross, doting on the sweet sorrow he brought them. They sent him off to work and then looked at each other over coffee.

"Did you expect anything like that?" Eva said dolefully.

"Lester is . . . is susceptible. He's high-strung, emotional. It was something I had considered."

"Well I never . . . I mean, it's terrible," Eva said into her cup.

"Yess-s," Minna said dubiously. "When you have a boy . . ."

"They're hard to bring up. But he has good things. It's just a question of finding himself."

"That's all it is." Minna stubbed out her cigarette, drank the last of her coffee, and stood up. "I'm going to have to make some phone calls, speak to some of the girls in the office . . . you know."

Eva nodded. "Don't forget your sandwich," she called after her sister.

Minna held up the bag to show she had it. "Don't worry," she said.

"No, no, I won't worry."

For a long time after her sister had gone she sat at the kitchen table examining a little corner of ironic life. She had been married for three years, and she and Joe had tried to make a baby all the time. All she had left from that brief wedlock was an official married name and a weapon to use cruelly in her fights with Minna. Lester had let himself go just once perhaps, and look at the trouble. And where had Minna learned that ugly wisdom? Had she perhaps herself been . . . No, not Minna; she was too fastidious to have been kissed by a man. Wasn't it all strange? And yet wasn't it a consolation to know Lester still needed them? With a sigh that was a good deal sadder than she felt, she got up and did the dishes.

When she took the rubbish out to the hallway dumper, she met Betty Jacoby, and they stood for a while in that brief neighborly attitude of exchanging talk.

"A young boy like my nephew has problems. It's hard for us old ones to remember what things look like. He gets involved—it's the enthusiasm of the young."

Betty couldn't stand up straight for the tug of arthritis and yet she almost relaxed because she didn't have to pretend it wasn't there. Only in Arnold's presence did she keep herself erect and let the dim light efface all the time in her face and body. "They're the same at seventy," she said, "just older boys. Arnold is trying to keep some kind of trouble about his job from me, but I know. They're so transparent, so foolish. You can't be honest with males, you daren't."

"I know," Eva said. "They'd be lost without us."

And two blocks away, at the edge of the park, Arnold was surprised on his bench by Marvin Schoenbrun. "Just getting a little air before I go to work," Arnold said cheerily.

"Well it's at least a place for a little peace and quiet," the handsome young man said, sitting on the end of the bench. "This city is so crowded with crude people, noisy abusive people."

"It's a little slow down to the plant, you see. Actually, I'm kind of on a holiday because it's so slow," Arnold said. "See, they finish with their Christmas stuff in September and . . . I don't like to let on to my wife because she'd right away think, Uh uh, he's getting the sack because of his age. It's not true, of course, but it doesn't pay to get the women all in a dither."

"And those two crazy musicians," Marvin said. "They have

no respect for other people. Last night I had a splitting head-ache, and they were blowing trumpets and banging drums until all hours. In a crowded city you have to have some respect for others. I sit and try to listen to something nice on my hi-fi, and they start blasting that trash so your ears could burst."

Arnold nodded politely. "At least the weather is still fine. Hate to be spending my days in the park in drizzle or snow."

"One can contemplate a little here," Marvin said. "One isn't abused and annoyed."

"Almost like the country," Arnold said.

They sat without talking for a while. The trees were a dark tracery against the clear morning sky, and above the modest traffic on Central Park West, the birds that stayed for winter could be heard in wing flutters nearby or an occasional piping from a thicket. The ground had that heartbreaking color of lost green and brown, and some taller winter grass was pink where the cinder path turned out of sight. Now and then the wind swung the tops of the trees and carried the distant sounds, from the zoo across the park, of the beasts that were now interned in the heated buildings. Arnold's face was rosy and was sunk into his upturned collar, which was somewhat threadbare where it met his ears; his eyes were half closed. Marvin sat erect in his velvet-collared coat, an exquisite profile against the subtle colors of the winter-bound landscape.

"I tried to speak to them reasonably," Marvin said, his eyes fixed on something too small to see. "I merely asked them to respect their neighbors. That Sidone is just a maniac, but it was Katz who was deliberately cruel. The unnecessary things, the vulgar things he said. I don't know why people have to go out of their way to humiliate . . ."

"It's sure funny," Arnold said, really commenting upon his own odd form of love.

"Hardly funny," Marvin said. "Kind of terrible, I'd say."

"Well yes, terrible too I suppose, but . . . I don't know whether I would have wanted it any different if I had it to do all over."

"I don't know," Marvin said. He looked at his watch and stood up. "Goodness, I must run along. So long, Mr. Jacoby," he said, crunching away on the path.

"Call me Arnold," Arnold answered absently, taking his hand out of his pocket to wave. Then he sank down deeper into his coat and studied a finch he hadn't seen the like of since boyhood. The wind tapped at the soft brim of his hat, and he thought of his Betty moving in beauty in the dim warmth of the apartment. The day seemed long ahead of him, and he refused to think about what he would do when the weather got too cold for him to sit there or what he would do when the money ran out. The sun rained twig shadows on the little huddled pile of him.

"That fusty little bitch Marvin Schoenbrun," Katz said in a green voice. "We're too noisy and coarse! Sidone, are you noisy and coarse?"

Sidone, costumed for the outdoors, on his way to the union office in Alpine hat and ever-present sunglasses, his skinny body human in a black Loden coat, spread his fingers in shock. "Coarse? Noisy? Why, what a perfectly bitchy thing to say, lover. I am the very *soul* of refinement. We both are. There isn't a rough edge to us. We shit vaseline. I mean we're so smooth. What a freshy that Marvin is!"

Katz laughed like an engine without oil. "Did I tell him off or did I?"

"Oh, you were so cru-el, sweetness. You accused him of being a *homo-sex-uall* Now he won't come down to see us any more." He brayed happily.

Sidone left him with only the reverberations of his laughter for company, and Katz zigzagged from littered table to stained chair to defaced wall, miming his own tiny-arced smile. He knew he had to keep moving, and the force of his panic made it difficult to adjust to the precision of dressing himself. Four times he tried to tie his tie, his wide cheery face a blur in the bad mirror. He ended up pulling the tie through his collar and off as though it were a piece of gut that held his insides together.

"That gay little jerk," he said aloud. "He had it coming to him. What does he expect? What am *I* supposed to do for him? Haven't I got enough?" He had been indoctrinated with his own unworthiness by his father, a man who had loved his son but who had lived in fear of love and its vulnerability. Katz tried a bow tie, shaking in an effort to clear his throat of the phlegm of self-hatred. In the mirror, which was worn half out of its reflective backing, he saw, behind his curly head, the face of the cancer-killed Katz Senior, speaking silently from his sour mouth, saying, "I love you Stanley," but having it come out in what seemed a safer language, so all the young trumpeter could hear was "You're stupid, Stanley, you're stupid and hopeless and you'll never get anywhere. Blow your horn, drink and whore with those nuts, those *musicians*. I'll bail you out of an alcoholic ward, I'll pay for mercury treatments for the syph. I'm your father and I'm used to what you are." And then it was that sour face extending on the horizontal from one side of the mirror frame, sunken into a pillow, and its wide structure (Stanley was in its image) stripped of the insulating flesh. And it was the last chance for both of them to redeem that tormenting bond. The sucked-in lips tried to shape those words that had always been such a horror to him, to speak ultimately what was the truth before blackness obscured even the worst of sins. And he said it, he *did* say, "I love you so much, my son, I adore you beyond the risk of love's mutilation, I love love love you." But all that the mortal ears of Katz could hear was the whispered, "You bum, Stanley, you poor stupid bumm-mm . . ."

"Ah, crap!" Katz cried, throwing the tie down and taking a little clip-on maroon bow tie that he wore with his musician's tuxedo. "Screw that little faggot Schoenbrun!"

He went into the other room and got his trumpet. A handkerchief brought it to a zenith of brightness, and he raised it to his lips.

Wah wahwah wah. The air broken through, he took a brief, swift ride, roller-coastering over the scales and then landing on a cushioning pool of melody. His fingers punted the vessel of sound gracefully along the shore of silence, in and out of tiny coves. And he was looking up and ahead for some tremendous cataract that would give him the golden rush of triumph big enough to translate a dead man's language, to convert it to the truth he knew was there. His eyes lidded, he dreamed alertly, one hand cupping the bell of the instrument in a pulsating muting. *Wah wahwah wah wahwah wahh . . .*

Doors slammed in the hallway as the other tenants went out to work. He had as long as he needed, a night worker trespassing on the day. He blew through his trumpeter's flattened lips, effacing Schoenbrun, blowing away the dead king of a hardware man who might have been pleading for some kind of vindication too; he eliminated the specter of his own frame of failure. Katz then, in the morning of the city, was adorning himself with his only covering, playing foolish, cheap little songs with all his heart and all his talent, and for a little while it was more than enough, much more than enough.

But a man's breathing is a tricky thing, and the flow of saliva, like that of blood, can undo you. He coughed and cut his soul on an evil note.

"Friggen faggot coming down here . . ." He put his trumpet in the velvet-lined case, a white, murderous look on his face. The clicks of the locks were like the sounds of nails in a coffin. He put on his belted flannel coat, his sunglasses and Hawkshaw hat. There was no staying there, and by concentrating on the union hall, he kept thoughts broken into small digestible words.

Jim Sprague came into the hallway at the same moment, his coat buttoned wrong and lipstick cockeyed on a corner of his mouth.

"Hello there, Sidone," he said with a bluff, manly smile.

"Whatta ya say," Katz answered, not bothering to correct him; fifty per cent of the time he came out Katz—it was more than enough.

"Going to the subway?" Jim Sprague asked.

Katz couldn't deny it. They rode down in the groaning elevator with nothing to look at but the "Did Not Pass Inspection" notice and the rusted drawings of genitalia.

"Our noise bother *you?*" Katz asked grimly.

"What do you mean?" Sprague shifted uncomfortably in the misbuttoned coat, his expression one of distaste for himself; he thought his body had somehow gotten out of line.

"Our practicing, you know—the trumpet, Sidone's drums." He had no real hope of vindication from this fogbound man.

"Oh, *he's* the trumpeter," Sprague said, throwing his head back in a silent guffaw at his mistake. "I thought Katz was the drummer."

"*I'm* Katz, Sidone is . . ." He waved the whole thing away, his eyes half closed in exasperation . . . no, not exasperation; he would have been happy with just that. An unhealthy sheen of sweat skinned him to the cold breeze, his skittery smile was curved around fury and anguish. "That damned Schoenbrun, you know, the fairy with the pretty face—he came up this morning and complained about our *vulgar* music."

Jim Sprague looked at Katz's face, intent on sound and look to the exclusion of confusing words. His own face mirrored the puzzling torture on Katz's, and without definition he stored something he felt, something he would attempt to tell Jane about later but which would come out only as he had received it—as feeling. And she would become as hopelessly entangled in that as she was in everything else, though it would also wed them again.

Indeed, when Jane Sprague hung up after talking to him, she felt apprehensive and sad. She got up and wondered why she couldn't see her feet any more. Oh, she *knew* she was pregnant and had Jim's baby growing like a polliwog inside, and of course she knew that their making love had brought it about. But there was a huge WHY lowered like a veil over her brain. Like everyone else, she and Jim had had sad childhoods but not terrible ones. They had sneaked out of infancy and adolescence with only their intellects impaired, and they consoled each other over and over for that with mindless tenderness. The thing was, they had never owned anything of great value, had never had to fear the consequences of precious possessions. Now, as a result of their habitual consolations—an act that always left Jane a little frightened, as though such delight couldn't belong to her— she was swollen with something too good to be true or recognizable.

She walked through the apartment humming the tone of her husband's voice on the telephone. He had asked again what he was supposed to buy for her on his lunch hour, had spoken vaguely about the mishaps he had encountered with an upper plate he was working on in the dental laboratory, had asked how she felt. And yet, as always, he had transmitted some feeling he could not articulate, and she was left with this new brand of uneasiness.

Finally she went downstairs to get the mail, just to ease herself. At the mailboxes, she met Sarah Lublin and felt comforted.

"Your face is changing," Sarah said with a smile. "That means a boy."

Jane smiled and touched her face, somehow able to accept that without the confusion she experienced from the rational. "Well, *you* have children," she said. "How does it feel? No, I mean to be a mother . . . a *mother?*" She had to tilt her head a little at that fantastic word; she, Jane Colwell of the harassed and puzzling girlhood. All she saw of herself was a short girl with a stained brown dress, smiling politely on the fringes of other people's laughter. "I mean," she went on, taking the letters from the brass mailbox and looking at her name framed behind cellophane on the envelopes, "you have the boy and the girl."

"Oh, with children you worry and are always running to them. They never let things be, they bother their father. And yet, they keep him, my husband, they keep him . . . interested. He could be a cold stone, I think, but he listens for what they are doing, he touches them. I think he would be very bad off if he could not touch them and listen to hear what they are into. He has had very bad times and he would perhaps never think about anything else except for them. Yes, with children you get out of yourself and you allow

94

yourself to accept the future. Of course they tire you, and you never run out of things to worry about, but still . . ." She stared apprehensively at the envelope she had just taken from her mailbox, her expression indicating that she was reading a language she hadn't seen for some time. "Oh my," she said in a quietly appalled voice. "It is from my husband's uncle. I just know what he says." Sarah looked up at Jane, ascertained that this vague and absent girl would not be able to repeat what she was told in the relieving mood of confidence, and went on to shake out the sudden dust of anxiety that the scrawled writing on the envelope had dropped on her.

"This uncle of Aaron's, he was in The Hell too. His family is gone, and he has been living in Baltimore with some friends. Aaron sends him money. Always he asks to come and live here with us, but of course my husband would not have it. He grows angry each time, and each time the uncle's letter becomes more strong, more *needy*. I know this man. He is cunning, he has learned to take from others. I never dare take either side in my husband's arguments with himself. It is apparent that either way, to take him or not to take him, is painful for Aaron. Still, somehow I know it would be difficult, most difficult, if he comes." She shook the letter with a little flapping sound. "I don't look forward," she said. "This letter."

"I don't know," Jane said, looking at her hands clasped on her belly. "Things are so funny, children, letters. I wonder if they really mean me when they write my name on the envelopes. And a name . . . Does that really . . . What are your children's names again? I forget."

"And the apartment is small," Sarah said, with the envelope against her lips, splitting her breath. "It would be peculiar for the children. He's an old man, perhaps not so clean. The apartment . . . Oh, and I wish that they would take care of that sink, with its dripping, and the elevator. I speak to the agent and he listens politely, but you know how these people are. Aie, I tell you . . ."

"And Jim," Jane said, leaving it at that, so the two of them stood in the morning sunlight of the entry, the gold color of the bank of mailboxes gilding their faces; they were like floaters in the lake of words to which they couldn't find beginning or end. Until, imbued with something of each other, they went back to their own apartments, sadly dreamy and adrift.

Aaron Lublin almost bumped into Sherman Hauser, who had just emerged from the candy store where he had bought cigarettes and now stood for a few minutes, bemused by the covers of the girly magazines. Had it been possible for them to avoid each other, they would have done so, not because there was hostility between them, but because there wasn't, because there was nothing. To Sherman, the short Polish Jew was as much background as the colored shipping clerks in the grocery jobbing firm where he worked, human, he supposed, but hardly on the same route of the maze as he was. And to Aaron, the nattily dressed man with the presumptuous Homburg was only part of the cold and alien stone of the city to which he was exiled.

"Morning," Sherman said, bending his lips slightly.

"Rather cold," Aaron said. He fell more or less into step with the longer-legged man.

"Winter practically, gonna have worse."

"Of course the children do not mind it. They like the snow, and it is nice to have the park so near." They entered what was becoming a stream of people headed for the subway.

"Oh yeah, my Bobby," Sherman said, his bony face becoming pulverized by that tenderness which had no transitory state and so came out like a sudden rawness. The dim, morning eroticism faded from his mind; the black howl of his recent exchange with Carol became, in retrospect, no more than a normal marital spat; besides, there was the ease of true common ground here. "He loves to play with your boy and girl. My wife tells me they play nice together."

"My girl is maternally inclined; she likes to be the little mother. Her own brother does not accept this gracefully, but your son apparently does."

"Ah, he's a son of a gun, that Bobby," Sherman wailed in a tone of grotesque frailty.

Aaron just glanced sideward with masked repugnance. "Yess-s," he said, gradually allowing the thickening stream of people to separate them, so that by the time they descended the subway steps they were out of sight of each other.

Basellecci went into the accounting office and dropped his envelope on the girl's desk. "For Mr. Kaplowe," he said. "My own personal tax information is there, as well as some things from the school. He will know." Around him, typewriters and adding machines made an exaggerated parody of summer-insect sounds.

"Fine, Mr. Basellecci," the girl said.

Basellecci responded with a strained, rather gray smile and turned back toward the door. He passed a cubicle where a man sat playing a silent tune on a small calculator, his sleeves rolled up to reveal blue, tattooed numbers on one forearm. Aaron looked up and met Basellecci's eyes, mistakenly thought he recognized their common past, and then disdained even the doubt by going back to work without facial reaction of any kind. Basellecci felt the clench of pain in his lower abdomen and attributed it to the rocklike face of the accountant. His pained smile turned to a scowl, and he went out angrily.

A few minutes later he was in the doctor's office explaining both his symptoms and his own diagnosis.

"I am very certain," he said to the patiently amused doctor, "that it is all a result of my emotions because of the environment of my toilet chamber. My lower parts," he said delicately, "clench like a fist with anger and anxiety. When, after many days and some laxatives, I do achieve a painful movement, it is hardly relief; the pain persists." The doctor gave him a brief examination, which included the indignity of a rectal exploration. Bent over in that humiliating position, Basellecci vented his hatred on the accursed wall, on his whole apartment and building, and finally on Norman Moonbloom. In that posture, he felt squeezed of all his youthful dreams of dignity and joy, and, like many people separated from the place of their youth, blamed even the land and the city that had betrayed him to age and failure.

"*Madonna mia!*" he cried at last as the cruel finger touched some deep tender place. "Such a thing to happen to a man!"

As he drew up his pants and his dignity with a white, bitter face, the doctor, a young Italian with a tiredly compassionate expression that was reduced by chronic amusement, sat back in his swivel chair, the tips of his fingers together as though to complete a circuit of thought.

"I would like to have you take some tests, Mr. Basellecci. There are indications of some kind of obstruction."

"After the holidays perhaps," Basellecci said, waving an exasperated hand. "In the meantime, could you perhaps give me some medication for present relief?"

"Yes, I'll give you a couple of prescriptions, one of which

is a tranquilizer," the doctor said, writing on his pad. He looked up with an absently frightening expression. "But I don't want you to neglect this. I want you to have those tests."

"Yes, yes," Basellecci agreed, disdainful of the threat, which, after all, was only of some future humiliation.

And in the afternoon, going back up the stairs of the reeking, dark hallway of his home, he was startled by the hooded, inhuman-looking eyes of the young Chinese as they passed on the first landing.

Wung took the hostile glance as his due, without anger, without the recourse of defiance. Going outside, he was too relieved to be deserting the scene of his insane dreams. Something was draining from him during his orgiastic nights; he had a dim recollection of bland, powerfully loving Chinese faces, and he was murdering them constantly. As he walked down Mott Street, he wondered for the millionth time how he had gotten behind his face, did not dare think that he had been born there and that he was severing himself from what he was; the tie was already frayed by abuse, and when it parted—void!

At the bus stop he kept his eyes and his consciousness on the full figure of Sheryl Beeler until, sensitive to glances like his, she met his eyes and gave him the delightful pain he took for pleasure.

Kram came down the same steps a few minutes later and slipped on some small piece of garbage. Falling, he imagined helpless crippling and cried out in a rare spasm of fear, and then landed surprisingly on his feet. He walked outside shakily, his forehead damp; he felt an immense self-disgust, as though he were a half-crushed insect.

Some half a mile uptown, Leni Cass paid her bill and went out of the luncheonette to the bus stop, trying to exorcise her feeling of shame and unworthiness. She had just been to a studio for a reading and had seen by the casting director's expression that she had failed. And yet she hadn't been able to resist smiling sexily at him and flaunting her body as she walked. In that abyss of humility, she had known that he could have gotten her to sleep with him by a single word, so desperate had she been to mark him in some way. On the whole ride crosstown, she trembled and felt sick, dreading the sight of her son, Richard. She sat erect, a rather severe expression on her face, reclaiming at least an outward semblance of dignity. She had images of herself splayed out nakedly under the bodies of the many men she had made love with. A vileness filled her so she could hardly breathe. Furtively she began crying in the warm quiet of the almost empty bus.

And in the hallway of the apartment house, she was pushed back under even that surface of dignity when she found herself smiling seductively at Wade Johnson, who terrified her with a slight bow, his rage suddenly localized in his groin.

"Good day, Miss Cass, ma'am," he said. There was vibrant threat in his voice.

And unable to return to a milder mood in time, Wade Johnson greeted Milly Leopold in a like manner before going into his apartment.

And Milly Leopold carried that intimidating excitement into her own rooms, where J. T. glimpsed its flush, saw it as a goad, and tried to escape her by coughing with insane fury, so that the blueness of his face spread out through the air and stifled Milly with grief.

On the floor below, Ilse Moeller slammed her window shut against the sound, remembering a similar cough coming from a slatted freight car in a Dresden station. She hurried out of her apartment, later than usual because she had to go on an errand up to Connecticut, to her employer's house.

She rode in an almost empty local, picked up the papers at her boss's home in Stamford, and then rode back to the city on a train from Boston. A man came through selling candy, his sales spiel interspersed with jokes and preposterous philosophic sallies. Ilse sat brooding at the rusty landscape rushing by the grimy train windows; the smoke of a Port Chester factory chimney chilled her with reminiscence, and she huddled into herself, nagged by the silly dialogue of the Jewish-looking candy butcher.

"Hersheys, Nestlés, peanut brittle, awrange drink, tequila, and dream-inducing mushrooms," Sugarman called. "Chewing gum, peanuts, Almond Joys, Mounds, aphrodisiacs, *and* sundry items." Last night, for the first time in his life, he had been unable to perform sexually with his lady of the evening, and he was near the bottom of his well of inexplicable mourning. Not that the woman had mattered, not that Sugarman had ever planned on perpetuating himself or had ever been concerned with manifestations of his manhood, because he saw himself as a neuterized figure, an implement of this, his humble ritual. "Let the good sweet juices of melted chocolate sweeten the tentacles of your soul. This is fresh chocolate made with the milk of rare Arabian mares taken at the full of the moon. There is chocolate and there is chocolate. Who'll buy? Awrange drink, ice cold, specially toasted peanuts. This offer is for a limited time only." Yet somehow that small genital failure, perhaps only a result of weariness and lack of enthusiasm for his partner, had somehow managed to tighten a lid of futility on him and to fill him with a more acute depression than any he remembered. He began to wonder about his relationship to life, to doubt that it existed at all.

And thus hollowed, he went home. In the hallway he met Del Rio, burdened with pail and scrub brush, on his way in to clean the bathroom.

"Del Rio," he said.

"Hello, Sugarman," Del Rio answered affably. Sugarman was the only one in the house who did not offend him by filthy habits.

Sugarman went sighing up the stairs, and Del Rio set to work on the bathroom tub and floor, snarling at the occasional cockroaches and silver fish that darted out of his reach with more than human cunning. And when he was done, he went out into the hallway to find Paxton waiting to get into the bathroom and Louie coming down the stairs with his little toilet-article bag.

"I'm not your goddamn maid," he shouted at the two of them. "Why do I have to clean that place every other day? I never see you two slobs make a move to clean it. You splash water on the floor and attract the roaches; you don't flush the toilets half the time."

"Perhaps we are not so repelled by the functions of our own bodies," Paxton said, walking past Del Rio with his effeminate gait.

"Don't sass me, you little black queen. I know dirt is *your* natural element," Del Rio snarled furiously.

Paxton stopped just inches from the powerfully built fighter, his dark, knobby face angled into a malevolent squint. "Now, Del Rio," he said softly, the breath hissing around his words as though he had sprung a leak because of extreme pressure. "Hear me, doll. In sex I may have my circuits crossed, and there is no denying the evidence of my pigmentation. But listen to this, you punchy bastard, I *know* what I am, and from my heritage I have an agility with the razor that does not extend merely to shaving." He stood like a pygmy lion tamer within the breath of the savagely breathing man long enough to establish his lack of fear, and then, with a sardonic smile, entered the bathroom and slammed the door.

"And you too, dimwit," Del Rio cried to Louie on the stairs, prevented by law and fear from making a physical attack. But even Louie got his revenge, just by teetering sickly on the steps, his eyes rolling samples of his weird, inner pain.

Del Rio threw his clothes on and stormed down the stairs, blackened by his own cruelty, which was a sign to him of the disorder always threatening his spirit. As he passed Karloff's door, he swung hard and crashed the side of his fist on the old man's door.

Inside, Karloff stood up in desperate rage, and the house vibrated around him like a settling penny, until there was stillness of a sort and he sat back down, staring with his terrible eyes at the beaten door.

EIGHT

NORMAN SAT ON Eva Baily's tapestried chair unable to get used to the strange clarity in his head. His nose, his ears, his eyes, all shot sensation into him at alarming speed.

"Yes, I've been sick," he answered, fondling the plastic cover of the receipt book.

"Well, there's always something," she said, anxious to get into her own preoccupation. "I don't seem to have the *time* to get sick, not that kind of sick anyways. I *worry* myself sick with that boy, but I can't get to lie down and convalesce." She smiled wanly in appreciation of her own succinctness, but did not pause long enough for Norman to interrupt. "The things a boy can get involved in! Not that he's bad, understand. High-strung is more what it is. You take a placid, dull sort and it's not so likely he'll get into trouble. But some-one like my Lester . . . I think of him like a son. He's lived with us since he was four and his mother, our sister Clara, died of polio. The father went in an auto accident the year before. It all seemed to have happened together. First my husband. You may have wondered why my name is Baily, same as my sister Minna. Well, he was a distant cousin. But anyhow, all those things happening together, it was almost like Lester being born to me. Now, of course, he's gone and gotten . . . *involved* with some girl. He thinks he's a man, but as soon as there's trouble he runs to us. Well, that's as it should be. Plenty of time for him to get independent. Of course, there's ugliness in certain things, people get hurt. Don't think I don't feel sorry for the girl, but still, *that* kind of a girl . . ."

Norman nodded, dodging the hail of words. And yet many of them struck him. He saw the long, shallow shadow beside each of her wrinkles, the flat, sightless look of her brown eyes, which were opaque with what she *wanted* to see. And the intimacy that was forced on him was an irritant to which he was no longer immune.

"Just what kind of trouble *is* he in?" he asked, knowing, but needing to get something back from her.

"Oh . . . it really isn't any . . . that is, a young man . . ." She giggled nervously, realizing the full extent of her indiscretion. "I'm just saying that a young fellow shouldn't get . . . I mean, it's lucky he has, that we have . . ."

"Has he gotten some girl pregnant?" He was surprised at himself, at the way things whistled into and out of him.

"Oh my, what a thing, of course . . . It's really a personal problem . . . Here I am, just going on . . . You probably have things to do. The rent, you're waiting for the rent." Her squaw wrinkles bunched up, intersected each other, making innumerable tic-tac-toe games.

"Yes, the rent."

"It's just that people sometimes feel they have to talk about things and they don't dare talk to themselves." She made it a plea.

"Yes, well, I'll be back next week."

"You understand."

"Oh yes, sure, I understand," he said harshly, wondering what he wanted from her. He got up, leaving the receipt. "And this is only the first call."

"I beg pardon?" Her courtesy was sleazy, threadbare.

"I have dozens of other apartments to call on," he said. "I don't look forward."

"I'm sorry," she said, humiliated.

But he wasn't able to cut her completely off. "It's just that I've been sick—my nerves are still not right."

"You should rest. Rest is the only way."

"Okay, Mrs. Baily. I'll see you next time."

"I'm sorry if I . . ."

"That's all right. Next week."

He had to hurry to the next apartment as though the empty hallway were enfiladed by a rifle equipped with a silencer.

Betty Jacoby let him in, went to the living-room table where her pocketbook lay, and then seemed to explode in a burst of acid-white light. She and Norman looked up, stupefied, at the window shade, still spinning, rolled up at the top of the window. She was old and crippled, and her skeletal fingers, knobbed with arthritis, quavered beside a mouth that radiated wrinkles and looked like a great, stitched scar.

"Oh my, that gave me a start," she said. She turned to Norman and put a hand up to her hair for some feminine protection. "I'm sorry, I'm afraid I look a fright. I haven't had a chance to do *any*thing. Heavens, I wouldn't want Arnold to walk in on me like this."

Norman tried to fit himself over the shape of that. It was impossible and wrong. He went toward her with his hand out, and she backed away, smilingly frightened.

"No, no, the shade," he said. "I'll just fix the shade for you."

"Oh, please *do!*" she cried. She watched him pull a chair to the window and silently ask her permission to stand on it, which she gave with a quick, single dart of her head. When she spoke, it was with a mixture of wistfulness and terror, and he felt it behind him as he stood spread-eagled against the glass and the daylight. "It's not that I have anything to hide from you, of course. But then, people, *people* who must live with one another for great lengths of time, must have things just so. Arnold and I have worked things down to . . . to this. People who must live intimately must be oh so delicate about what they surround themselves with."

Norman took the roller off the hooks and stepped down. "Do you have a fork?" he asked. "I think that's how to do it."

She almost backed into the kitchen. "A fork," she announced, coming back and handing it to him.

He didn't look at her face again until he had rewound the spring, replaced the roller, and drawn down the shade. "One tine is a little bent," he said.

"Don't let them tell you about the ease of old age," she said, the guile restored to her by the dimness. "They say that old people aren't concerned about appearances. Oh, no, that's not true at all. We, Arnold and I, keep more things from each other than ever. It's hard to make you see. If he walked in like you did . . ." Her breath shuddered audibly, and Norman was forced to look around for the monstrous source of horror; he saw only the shabby darkness of the apartment, like some abandoned stage-set that was lent mystery only by its antiquity.

"But was there something *I* was supposed to do?" he asked, feeling a sensation of brutishness. "It wasn't you who had the trouble with your stove?"

"No, no, I'll tell you when there's something for you to do," she answered with a chuckle.

She paid him, and he left; and, in the hallway, that was all he could account for. But he felt like a man unused to exercise who has been forced into an unpleasant scuffle. He was breathing hard, and his heart made itself known in his temples. The hallway looked strange and filled him with uneasiness; from the way his body strained against imbalance, its floor might have been tilted. For a moment he looked at the rough, dust-pocketed stucco on the walls, wondering if this were dream and the prismatic reminiscences of his illness were the real life he lived. A faintly familiar smile warmed his mouth as he thought of an ancient course in logic, a lecture about the evidence of The Now. "What is dream?" he said to himself with exaggerated theatricality, but then lost his smile as he felt the walls press their texture on him with breath-taking clarity. Nothing had ever *been* so real! He could see himself in the large, shapeless suit, the comical bootlegger's hat, a slight bundle of a man with a clean, new, discount-store shirt and a tie so somber that it lay like an apology over his chest. He could see his frail mouth and his bruised-looking eyes planted on a thin man's face that caught the faint reflection from the top of a ball-point pen in the breast pocket. He could see even the Red Cross button from another year, caught in the clumsy lapel —one of the tags he used to identify himself.

For just an instant he felt a flash of horror, a sensation as visceral as that felt by a child who glimpses the great, complex gut of adults for the first time; he had a real hint of how thin and light his long childhood had been, and wondered how in the world he would support the weight he suspected. The hollow coughing from a distant apartment, the child's ranting cry from another, alarmed him by their intimation of great size.

A bulb flicked on in that presupper hour of November. Great flexings took place on all sides. He slapped his receipt book and rushed to the next door.

Carol Hauser let him in, one hand up to her structured hair. Under her pink, quilted robe she wore black nylon stockings and red-leather shoes with needle-thin heels.

"We're going out," she said, stilt-walking over to the table where the lamp-shade river flowed endlessly. "To Radio City and then Lindy's. I'm in the middle of dressing."

He wondered what he could say to that and looked at the child for a cue. The little boy hovered near his mother, sniffing her strong scent and waving his hands. His face had the scared-thrilled expression of a rider on a roller coaster.

"Once a month we go out like this; the rest of the time it's just cards with friends. I like to go out," she said, turning an unusually soft smile on Norman. "I like to see Sherman in his best suit, his shoes all shined, his face pink from shaving. And I like to feel bright and dressed up and to say good night to Bobby when the sitter comes, and see how impressed he is at my fancy duds. That's one thing about this country, Mr. Moonbloom. When a person gets dressed up, there's no telling which are the rich and which are the poor. I mean, my husband and I may fight a lot, like other people, but when we go out like this, to a night club or a show, we're like on a date. All this boring routine and everything is like it never happened. Sherman is a good dancer too. He looks good in clothes too. Right Bobby? Doesn't Daddy look nice when he's all dressed up?" She took the child's hand and began doing a little dance with him; his small feet tripped all over each other trying to follow her cha-cha steps.

Norman watched their feet as he waited for his money, and somehow the child's seemed crippled and lost.

"Ohh, I'm sorry," Carol said, stopping and reaching once more for her pocketbook. "I'm in a silly mood."

"Why can't I go too?" Bobby asked. "I'm big."

"When you get grown up, darling, then you'll go too. And Daddy and Mommy will be grandparents." She turned to Norman with the money. "My husband is graying at the temples. It's very becoming. I'm thinking of having my hair frosted." She turned back to Bobby. "And Mommy and Daddy will stay home with *your* children, and *you'll* go out to swell places."

"But *now*," Norman said. "He's worrying about now. What guarantees can you give him?"

"What do you mean?"

"I don't know," Norman said, looking at the fake fire in the fireplace. "I just look around here and I wonder what he thinks is real, what he believes."

"I don't know what you're talking about," Carol said, a hard edge returning to her voice as she sensed some kind of disparagement. "Bobby knows what's what, don't you, Bobby?"

"Yes, I want to go *now*, not when I'm a daddy. I'm not ever gonna be a daddy, never never never. I want to go with you *this* night, *now!*"

"I think you've gotten him all upset with your nutty talk, Mr. Moonbloom. We have enough trouble when we want to go out. He gets all overstimulated and then he sleeps badly. Sherman and I come home late, wanting to . . . have a little privacy, and he's moaning in his sleep and we're always afraid he'll get up."

"I'm sorry," Norman said, looking at the thick cosmetic mask, which made her eyes exceptionally harried and restless. "I hope you have a good time," he said, somehow frightened by the sight of the child, who stood waving his plump little body as though he were in the midst of a high wind, as though he were whirling so quickly that his gyrations were imperceptible. Norman had an impulse to reach out and touch the boy, to be sure he was there. He raised his hand, and Carol drew Bobby close to her.

"He's all right, Bobby understands," she said defiantly.

"Well, good night," Norman said, using the lifted hand for that. Then he went out of there, punched in his vertebrae by whatever it was that abided behind him in the room with the lamp-river and the bulb-fire.

And just that much more battered, he pressed the Lublins'

bell button, focusing on the noise he heard ahead of him in preference to the silence of the household he had just left behind.

Sarah opened the door but continued talking to someone in her apartment, and for a moment Norman considered leaving before she knew who it was.

"Please, please," she called back over her shoulder to the room from which could be heard Aaron's angry voice. "Someone is here, stop for a while." And she drew Norman in by the arm as she spoke to Aaron, the gesture so intimate and demanding that Norman had an impulse to dig his feet in stubbornly and resist. "The door is open, calm down, everyone doesn't have to hear." Aaron's voice could not be heard then, but the considerable silence made his anger still apparent. Sarah turned to Norman without surprise, though she couldn't have seen his face till then, and continued leading him in. "I'm sorry," she said shyly, her hand out to encompass the room full of Aaron and an old man. The two children stood in a doorway, edging furtively in from their exile to their bedroom.

Aaron didn't acknowledge him, but continued to stare ferociously at the old man, who sat on a straight-backed chair, his hands folded on his lap and a blithe smile on his rubbery mouth; he looked like a tough, defiant adolescent, grown old under some chastisement he scorned.

"Sit down, Mr. Moonbloom," she said nervously. And when the old man turned his disparaging face toward Norman, she held one hand out to each of them like a referee calling two fighters to the center of the ring, balancing between a desire to have them shake hands and a concern about keeping them from premature combat. "*Fehteh*, this is the rent agent, Moonbloom. Here, Mr. Moonbloom, is Aaron's uncle. Mr. Hirsch."

"How do you do," Norman said, inwardly straining backward against the liquid rings of rage in the room.

"I do . . . Esk him how I do," Hirsch replied with a mocking wave toward his nephew.

"Stop it!" Aaron cried. "You're pushing me too far, Uncle. Don't keep pretending I'm a Gestapo agent. I've kept you all these years, I would still support you. You cannot make me out a brute because I do not want you to crowd in here with us."

"I live with strangers. You are my blood," the old man said, reading his lines without feeling, merely filling in the parts between Aaron's speeches.

"Besides the fact that we are crowded, that it would be disturbing for the children and for us, the owners would not like such overcrowding. Is there not a rule on this, Moonbloom?"

But Norman had always been audience and was not used to these experimental dramas in which the audience was asked to participate. He smiled with embarrassment and gave a few short huffs; he patted his breast, reassured himself that the receipt book was there, licked his lips. "Well-l," he said, staring at the wall molding.

"I would take up little room; I am sanitary and quiet," Hirsch said.

"You never *tried* to live with others," Aaron shouted. "You have spent years perfecting your suffering. Oh, they have written me, those people you were staying with. They told me how they introduced you to people, how they invited older men and women to the house, made card games, took you to the Community Center, where they had a club for older people. And always you were rude and insulting, laughed at the others. Now you feel you are ready, you have refined your martyrdom enough to condemn *me*." Aaron's gray face shone with a sick anger that was so terrible because most of it was directed at himself. He waved his finger, spoke from a twisted mouth; the hatred in his black, shiny eyes was frightening, and Norman, an outsider by vocation, hoped to be forgotten.

Surreptitiously, he slipped the receipt book out and began filling in the familiar lines while Sarah shushed and jerked her head warningly toward Norman.

"So all right, don't get all *fahtumult*," Hirsch said with heavy-lidded blandness, his dessicated body barely defined under his age-greened suit. "What do you have to go crazy? So I'm only your father's brother, only the last relative you have. You don't *have* to have me here; there's no law. I'm *grateful* that you send me a few cents I shouldn't starve in my little corner among the strangers in Baltimore. I know, I know, it's a jungle, I don't expect. Behind me is Hell, ahead of me . . . Eh, at least I'm peaceful, nobody hits me, I can die in my own good time. So okay, I'll go back to *Baltimore*, I'll ride all night on the bus—it's cheaper than the train and, after all, it's my nephew's money—I should be a hog, I should ride a jet? No, no, it's all right, I'll *shlep* my little valise back through the streets—thank God it's not heavy, I have so little—it hardly hurts my angina. I'll ride in the bus with my head knocking—heh heh, I get a little tiny bit carsick, nothing serious—and in the morning I'm back in Baltimore, knocking on their door, saying, 'I made a slight mistake, it didn't work out with my nephew, let me go up to my little cot to rest.' And if they look surprised, I'll say, 'No, don't blame him, *I* don't blame him, he has his own *tsoris*.'"

"Moonbloom!" Aaron shouted suddenly.

Norman snapped his head around with the impact.

"Isn't it multiple occupancy?" Aaron demanded harshly. "Can I?"

"They wouldn't even hear a extra set of footsteps," Hirsch said to Norman. "I wear slippers in the house, I weigh only a hundred twenty. Besides, I get in bed after supper and only get up for the bathroom."

The children stood with gaping mouths, suddenly impressed by the familiar figure of the agent. Five pairs of eyes bored into him, and, transfixed, Norman fluttered his hands and shifted his feet. No one had ever made demands on him, he had never been capable of making enemies. He searched in the dusty recesses of his mind for precedents, and came up with only picture post cards of hushed, solitary hours that were all the same though they stood before a variety of backgrounds. He had never asked anything of himself—what then was there for others to find? How vivid and large were their faces! His fingers groped aimlessly for the light, soft, immensely strong coverlet his grandmother had wrapped around him one night when she had cried and given him strawberry ice cream. He smiled and winked and shrugged, but they just waited.

"I'm only the agent," he said. Not a breeze of sound touched their faces. "I suppose I really . . . I mean the owner . . ." The old man looked ready to laugh; he had seen the cash and the fictitious amount written on the receipt, and the way his nephew's wife had crumpled the receipt up by habit. Norman turned his supplicating palm to Aaron, but could not really be sure what answer *he* would have preferred. Norman took a deep breath and looked down at his hands solemnly, composing himself for an act of power.

"I don't see why not," he said. "I'm sure it would be all right."

Stillness, and then a long, shuddery sigh from Aaron. Sarah gave a tiny gasp, and the boy started to pull his sister's hair in the doorway. Norman looked up to see Hirsch studying the window with a benign expression.

"It is terrible that you should come in on a family affair," Sarah said. "We are not in the habit of . . ."

"Enough," Aaron said wearily. "Leave the man alone now, let him go."

"I'm sorry to intrude myself," Norman said severely. "You asked me something and I answered."

Alerted by old instinct, Aaron covered his rudeness. He stood up with a slight, false smile that was worn thin by much use. "Of course, I did not mean to imply . . . That is, I appreciate your allowing . . ."

"I don't want to intrude," Norman said. "I just . . ."

"I understand," Aaron bleated. "You are very kind to . . ."

"No, no, it's nothing," Norman said, feeling he would like to jump through the window, but frozen there by the horrid amenities.

"These things are very complicated," Aaron said.

"I understand."

"No, no, it is *my* place to . . ."

"Of course."

Suddenly Hirsch's dry old voice smacked mockingly at both of them. "ThankyouMoonbloomnicemeetingyou."

They stared at him, saw mutually the incredible blight he was, and then turned from each other. Sarah led Norman through the wrecked air to the door. Behind him he could hear the children jumping up and down in the bedroom. He went out the door without looking at Sarah, without responding to her soft, timid "Good-by."

Neither Schoenbrun, Katz and Sidone, nor the Spragues were home. He went out of the building trying to figure out how he would plan his calls to adjust to that break in his routine. For a while, in the darkening street, he was able to be only mildly irritated by the simple problem, but then, as other things began to crumble in him, that slight disordering of his usual pattern suddenly seemed to undo him.

He stopped next to a street lamp and put his hand to his head. "I don't know, I don't know," he said in a shocked voice to the evening.

NINE

STILL HOLDING FEEBLY to the idea that the day before had only been a result of his physically weakened condition, he had taken two sleeping pills last night. Now he walked up the Mott Street stairs with the Seconal drowsiness that bore a surface resemblance to his old calm. Indeed, in the few seconds while he waited for Basellecci to answer the door, he almost convinced himself that the day would be like the flat screenings of old. Yesterday was buffered by the barbiturate, wrapped and muffled like an unpleasant dream. He prepared his bland smile.

But the Italian teacher's face was shot through with gray, and Norman had a premonition that today would be worse.

"Come in," Basellecci said curtly. "I am just pouring the coffee."

Norman sat down with his back to the open door of the toilet chamber. "I'm getting so I look forward to your coffee," he said.

"That is very well," Basellecci answered grimly. "But I may not be well enough to serve you soon. I have been to the doctor, you know. This is no longer a joking matter."

"The wall?" Norman asked with a sigh.

"The wall."

"I've been meaning . . ."

"Yes, yes, sure, you've been meaning. The doctor says I

have an obstruction inside the rectal. This is no longer psychosemantic, it is not figmet of my imagination."

"The coffee is, as usual, delicious," Norman said appealingly.

"It is practically all I live on lately, all I can keep down."

"Are you that ill?" Norman asked, appalled.

"What do you think I have been exclaiming of with such vi-o-lence? There, *there* is my oppressor!" Basellecci cried, pointing to the toilet, his face working so strenuously that Norman would not have found anything inappropriate in his words if he had said "*J'accuse!*" The flesh beside his nostrils was white, his mouth scored by vertical lines of arid pain. "I have given great appeals to you, I have considered you to be of human persuasion. But you, with your polite little smile, have nodded at me as were I a shallow-leveled moron, have humored me and said, 'I will see what can be done, Mr. Basellecci, I will look into it.' I charge you, I charge you with the fate of my bowels!"

The need to smother his hysterical impulse to laugh made Norman almost as angry as his tenant. He pushed the coffee cup away from him and stood up.

"I've been sick myself, Mr. Basellecci. You don't know what things I have on my mind. There are a million things to do in this and the other buildings I take care of. I haven't meant to humor you. Only I must put things off in order to organize what has to be done. You only see *your* problems, naturally. But I have a couple of dozen other tenants. I have limited funds, and it's a problem for me to try and figure out *how* to repair things. I'm only one man."

Norman's indignation seemed to act as an antidote to Basellecci's anger. Deeper than his pain, Basellecci was essentially a man of reason; indeed, reason had cast him into his blandly lonely life. He held up his hands placatingly.

"Yes, of course, I become carried off. One forgets that things exist outside of yourself. You live alone and you become susceptible to obsessions. I admit, things get out of disproportion, magnified. There is a selfishness involved, thinking only of yourself. I lie in bed in the other room and I think about that wall. I become enraged. I start to think about the priest in Italy who persecuted me when I was a child, who held me up to scorn because I argued with his word. I think about the ruffians who molested me because I wished to study and be gentlemanly, about the coarse girls who questioned my manhood because I was fastidious, about the unclean little politicians who made me crawl for a passport because I had no friends or money. I am reminded of the ignorant clerks who make fun of my English and my unknowing of the baseball players. And it is brought to me of how difficultly it is to dwell within dignity, to construct something of gracefulness and beautifulness. And I begin and end with that . . . that *wall*. It is the gateway to the ugliness for me, and it follows me even to the farthestmost limitation of the city, notwithstanding how distant." He spread his arms wide, as though to glide on the current of his words, and his face traced the frailest draft of humor and self-denigration. "So you see . . ."

"Yes, I see," Norman said with some stress; for the first time it occurred to him that sooner or later he would *have* to deal with that wall. "No, no, I don't feel like any coffee," he said to Basellecci's silent offer of the banished cup. And then, when the Italian teacher shrugged with an almost smug expression of martyrdom, Norman qualified harshly. "No, it's not that I'm angry; it's just that my system is still out of kilter from my sickness. Coffee gives me heartburn."

Basellecci nodded, deadpan. "And so . . ." He gestured

at the toilet chamber without turning toward it, his eyes half closed. "You perhaps really will . . ."

"Yes," Norman said from between his teeth. "Yes yes yes *yes!*"

"Ahh," Basellecci replied, his ailing smile more than Norman could bear.

"I mean, man, this one broad is really taking me far," Jerry Wung said, watching Norman's face. "She likes to have a nigger and a Chink work on her at once, me on the bottom and him on top. And that's not all; last night she called me up and we like did it *over the phone!* What it is, she begins to talk . . ."

"Why are you telling me all this? Am I supposed to applaud, or what?" Norman said, his voice coldly even.

"Well no, it's just like a discussion of sex, you know." Wung was smiling, but seemed to be running out of oxygen, for he breathed with his mouth wide open. "Are you shocked, is that what it is?"

"No, I don't care one way or the other," Norman said, faithful to the act of writing out the receipt.

"Isn't it sick?" Wung could have found relief even in condemnation. "I mean, wow, if my family ever could have seen the way I live! They were real greenhorn Chinks, quiet, calm. They never yelled at the kids. It was like you just couldn't do anything wrong no matter how you tried. Like they had some kind of invisible spell. They even died quiet. Man, it killed me how they died. I felt like sticking them with pins to make them yell, to make them scream dirty words and thrash around. I mean, I hated them, the way they just lay there and looked at me out of those kooky eyes. Sound strange for me to say that? I know, I know. I look in the mirror at myself and it shakes me up. I don't know what

120

my old man and old lady were, what went on in them. I got out on the streets here and I didn't talk their language. They used to just touch me like, that's all. My brothers and sisters used to dig it, but it was just spooky to me. Most Chinese kids are well adjusted like, you know? I used to feel like the ugly duckling, like I had the wrong face and the wrong address. I don't see my brothers and sisters. It's mutual. Hey, I just wonder if the old lady and the old man could have stayed calm under those queer old faces if they knew what I'm doing now. I mean it just wasn't *human* the way they died and looked at me, so contented, so sure. You see, they weren't real, those cats weren't real. I dream about them at night, and it's like nightmare. I grab some broad's boobs and get real rough, and it's like I'd like to wake them old Chinks up. I went to an analyst last year, when I was working more regular, told him about the dreams and my screwy sex life. Ah, but it was a waste of money. I drew a bum head-shrinker. He got so interested that he forgot to take notes—a regular voyeur." Wung slashed his mouth with a violent smile and went ranging around the room. "Not that I don't enjoy myself; I don't want you to think that. I mean, I wouldn't have it any other way. I got this new bitch now, and she's got something *really* novel. . . ."

Norman got up and walked to the door; in that moment he grasped a new emotion and, fearing to look at it, pocketed it unseen and reached for the doorknob.

"Hey, Moonbloom," Wung called beseechingly. "You're a good Joe. Lemme fix you up one night, hah? I mean, we could have a ball. It would be better with you along, it would help a lot. How 'bout it, hah?" He hung in the air over his body, haunting himself, his face full of appeal.

"I don't, can't . . . We'll talk about it some other . . ." Before nausea overtook him, he slammed the door. Then he stood in the dark hallway wondering why a simple "No" should have been impossible to summon right then.

"I still have to pour a potful of water into the toilet to make it flush," Sheryl Beeler said. "It's a little disgusting, you know?"

Norman nodded as a round stone plopped into his lower body with a disturbingly lascivious effect. "There's a million things," he said, watching old man Beeler walk slowly out of the room, the white-fringed back of his head reflecting a queer joke.

"You married?" Sheryl asked, dropping down on the couch so that her heavy breasts bounced. She lit a cigarette and then blew the smoke in a fan-shaped cloud toward him.

"Noo-o," he answered, trying to make it wry; it came out like a wail. "Confirmed bachelor."

"I bet you've got a whole stable of girls though." She ran her hand down the silken sleeve of her kimono, raising the hairs on Norman's body, among other things.

She was too ridiculously obvious. Who was she buttering up and for what? He saw himself too clearly for even clever flattery. And yet his desires were new and graceless, and they made him mentally clumsy. He chuckled pathetically and said, "Aw, no, you have the wrong . . ."

"The money," Sheryl said, jumping to her feet. She went to a table and slid some bills out from under a doily. When she handed the rent to Norman, she pressed his hand.

"How about a date?" he barked at the pressure.

Sheryl giggled and bumped cutely against him. "My, my, you're a fast worker. You quiet ones."

Her weight pushed him against the door, and he gave a short, phlegmy chortle. "No, I only . . ."

"We'll talk about it, huh," she said, squeezing him out through the half-closed door. "Maybe next time."

In the hallway he squeaked and stared at the air with horrified amusement. "Good God," he whispered. "I'm like a child." And then, still dazed by his spasm of idiocy, he began to straighten the bills to put them into his wallet. Something rational rose up through him, and he counted the small bills. Five dollars short. He started to turn to the door, his knuckles raised to knock. And then knowledge sprouted in a sick smile on his mouth. He lowered his hand and used it to put the money in his wallet, his face that of a long-suffering parent.

Kram limped away from him.

"I slipped on the steps," he said, shielding with his warped body the drawer from which he took the money. "It's a crime, that hallway, no light at all. I could have broken my neck if . . ." His coldly tranquil eyes showed a spark of disorder, and the remembrance of that repellent moment was converted to anger at the unimportant hallway. "I have a good mind to sue you. You wouldn't like a judge having this place described to him, would you?"

"I'm sorry you hurt yourself," Norman said, afflicted by the unusual sight of a splotch of paint on the normally immaculate drawing table; it was like a grievous wound in that room.

"Don't be sorry," Kram said icily. "Just put some lights in that hallway, or I'll sue, that's all."

Suddenly Norman chuckled, his hand waving apology as he did so; he wanted to say, "Wait, wait, I'm not really laughing at you."

But Kram, normally immune to laughter, was not himself either. "Do you think it's funny? Are you daring me to make trouble?" he snarled.

"No, no," Norman said, realizing it was not that funny

anyhow. "I was just remembering how, a few weeks ago, I asked you if you had any complaints and you said you didn't and I remarked how you seemed to be the only one who didn't."

"And that strikes you as funny? What an odd sense of humor you have," Kram replied, merely irritated now.

"One of my other tenants said that I was essentially humorless." Norman looked out of the window in the general direction of Sugarman. "But when I think about it, it occurs to me that no one is really humorless. Only some people's jokes are so private. . . ."

Kram looked at him suspiciously, distrusting an opponent who acted like a dreamer. "You have to look out that you don't offend people with your private jokes. Not that jokes bother me, understand. I mean if *I* didn't start out with *some* kind of sense of humor . . . Well, you know what I mean."

Norman turned to him, and for a moment everything that was between people and that made intercourse bearable fell away from him. He saw the deep bruise in the man's spirit; with remarkable vision he glimpsed the hunchback in all sizes, from the damaged embryo to now. And in that brief clarity, anything less than naked honesty seemed impossible. In a blurred voice, he said, "You mean because of your body."

Kram only opened his mouth slightly, but his eyes crumpled with light. And within the confines of that narrow patch of nakedness, Norman could see the twin prongs of revulsion and offering. They stood in the morning sunlight—one straight and frail with something like total innocence shading his face, as though the oversized hat had left its shadow after he had removed it; and the other new also to such a light, groping for what he had learned to despise in his fight to survive, exposed down to the distorted skeleton, and afraid as he had never been before. And all of it took less than a minute, so they both learned that time was unmeasurable, except in fantasy. The building stank around them, seemed to settle slightly, as though it were planted in unimaginable muck. Perhaps a howl went up between them; they would not remember afterward.

"I can't afford to get hurt," Kram said in a hoarse voice. "I have no one to . . . There has always been only me. If I couldn't go out to get those photographs, if anything happened to my hands . . ." He strained upright, and his face stretched with an expressionless agony. "It's not death *I* worry about," he said.

And Norman, out of the short glare now, was too repelled by what he had said and what he had been given back. "I'll do something about the hallway. I'll have lights put in," he said in a threatening voice. "It'll be as light as day in the hall, brighter even. There'll be a problem with the lights blinding you."

"There's no need for you to . . ."

"No, that's all right," Norman said, observing his own frenzy with bewilderment. "I'll do it, I'll do it."

And he left Kram chewing on the air, lost in his own perfectly clean apartment, the nudes for some gent's magazine waiting for his final touch and reflecting the shine of the light from a window that opened only on an air shaft.

Wade Johnson and son were throwing a football the length of their living room. Norman ducked as Wade Junior's wobbly pass came at his head, and then grimaced slightly for his timidity as Wade snatched it out of the air.

"Whatta ya say, Norman," Wade said without looking at him. "No, no, Wadey boy, grip it tight and not so near the end. Okay now, let's see a jump pass." He underhanded it to the boy, who took a serious grip on the ball, fended off an imaginary tackler, and then jumped and threw. The ball hit Norman in the center of the mouth.

"I'm sorry to be in your way," Norman said bitterly, swallowing the salt of his split lip and feeling the blood run down in a thin stream over his chin.

The boy looked dreamily sad and muttered a shy apology as he scuffed the floor with his foot. But Wade laughed and said, "My God, he bleeds! Norman, I feel closer to you now."

"Just give me the rent," Norman said, holding a handkerchief to his lip and feeling an odd grief for himself. "I don't want to see any football games, I don't want to hear any poetry. The money—then I'll go."

"Poor Moonbloom, you aren't going anywhere. Wade Junior and I are going—you'll abide. Hey, Norman, I haven't been to school for three days, called in sick. Soon they'll can me, and the boy and I will be heading west. Probably pull out owing you a few weeks' rent—just for appearances. Yeah, we're gonna go by way of Wisconsin, where we'll see his mother's grave. Wade's always been curious about what kind of view she's got. Then to Colorado . . ."

"Listen, you idiot, you'll pay your rent or I'll have you thrown out. You don't amuse me and you probably don't even amuse your son. You're a phony, a poseur, and the only thing you could act convincingly would be what you are—a bum!" But it was only a flash fire, lit by the shock of physical injury, and almost immediately after he had said it he waved disgustedly; his disgust was as much for his own outburst as for Wade's nonsense.

"Heyy-y, *Norman*," Wade said in amazement. "What's come over you? I declare, I detected a tiny glimmer of passion in you just then. Could it be that the man from the lower depths is coming out into the light? No more underground, no more remote control. Look at him, look at him, Wadey, he's stirring, his blood is bothering him. See those intelligent eyes, almost human. Oh, if he could only speak, imagine the things he could tell us!"

"You're really clever, Wade. Too bad you're afraid to demonstrate it anyplace but in here with the captive audience of your kid."

"Ah, very good, you little bastard. I've never seen you put up your fists before. I feel it's all my doing, I'm a regular Pygmalion. Or could it be a Frankenstein? I can see you getting completely out of hand."

"Oh, for Christ's sake," Norman said wearily, still able to touch ground with his toes. "Give me the money."

"No, no, don't regress now. *Make* me give it to you," Wade said, standing over Norman with his weight-lifter's body. "Consolidate the little advance you've made today."

"I swear, if I *were* a little bigger, I'd like to . . ." He smiled angrily, impatiently.

And suddenly, like a child, Wade wearied of him. He dropped the money on the chair next to Norman's and picked up the football. "Heads up, Wadey," he shouted.

Norman wrote out the receipt, pocketed the money, and went to the door. For a minute or two he looked back at the man and the boy and the blur of the ball between them. The slatted shadows of the Venetian blinds imprisoned the two figures in separate cages and laid long bars over the backs of the books in the shelves. Back and forth the ball went, spinning something not quite invisible between them while the man murmured encouragement and the boy grunted with effort. And then, in the same rhythm as his encouragement, Wade began to murmur something else, and Norman closed the door on it in bafflement, still hearing it in the hallway.

> "Little lady mouse,
> Rosy in a ray of blue,
> *Dame souris trotte:*
> (Little Lady Mouse)
> *Debout, parresseux!*
> (Up now, all of you!)
> (Verlaine)"

Norman moaned, seeing Wade elude him like a sorcerer. It occurred to him for the first time that he might be inadequate for this job too. If a man of five foot seven and a hundred and thirty-eight pounds could lumber, he lumbered up the stairs to Leni Cass's door.

"Enter, Moonbloom," she said too gaily. "I was just mixing myself a bourbon, and bourbon and I hate to drink alone."

"No, I don't want anything," he said more curtly than he intended, following her inside.

It seemed to upset her, and she gave a brittle laugh that whitened her face slightly. "Well, then, I'll drink alone," she said. She took a big swallow from a glass with harlequin diamonds on it and watched him silently write out the receipt, her big eyes somewhat frightened.

"Uh, Norman, about the rent . . ."

He looked up so suddenly that she almost jumped.

"It just happens that things got a little loused up this week, and I'm—how is it said?—financially embarrassed."

He stared at her, unable to articulate to her what she was really piling on him. And his look was as cold as possible because he was stunned by the speed with which the subtle conspiracy was being consummated.

She couldn't have known that, of course, and so was just shaken by an expression she had never expected from him. "Don't you have any comment on that?" she asked shakily.

"You're saying that you can't pay the rent?"

"Well, I've had a little trouble lining things up, and ex-hubby's check is . . ."

"What do you want me to do?" he asked in a flat voice.

"You're not acting like you. This is embarrassing for me, but of all times for you to turn stranger. I never asked you before. . . ."

"I wish you had—before."

"Well, what should I do? What are you going to . . ."

"All right," Norman said, getting up. "What *can* I do?" She followed him to the door, trying to thank him, but he had no patience left for graciousness. "Don't thank me, I'm not happy about it."

"Oh," she said in a small voice behind him, unable to afford anger or self-respect. He heard her close the door quietly with an excess of humility and abasement, and that angered him further.

"How about that stove burner?" Milly Leopold asked, her Mother Goose face slightly soured by resentment. "It's been a long time. It's like you don't feel you *have* to, so you don't. Well, I suppose I can't force you. You know quite well that J. T. and me can't just move out or anything. I just put it up to your conscience is all." She turned to the chair where J. T. sunned himself in a small amber beam of afternoon light. J. T. coughed profoundly, the sound not brought out, but resounding broadly from within like a threatening volcano.

"I've been sick myself," Norman barked. "I'm putting things

in order, trying to get caught up. I said I would take care of it. You'll just have to wait your turn."

"Oh, we'll wait," she said sarcastically.

"I don't know what you think I'm running here," Norman said. "It's ridiculous. All the buildings are falling apart. I'm just the agent, you know. You all seem to expect me to get down on my knees and start plumbing and hammering. What did the last agent do for you? Don't tell me all these things just started to go wrong when I took the job. I bet the last agent did nothing. I bet *he* wasn't hounded like this. What is there about *me* that makes you all think I'm going to be able to renovate everything from top to bottom?"

For a few seconds she appeared intimidated by his unusual outburst, amazed too. But then an element of slyness crept over her face; she had discovered a promising weakness in him, and she cast her eyes downward and spoke forlornly to her right toe. "No, no, that's true; the other agents never did anything for us. Nobody ever has. People like us . . . Well, we just don't have recourse. Oh, you're right, we're just lucky to have a dry place to live, J. T. is lucky to have a chair and a bed to . . ."

Norman stared at her with a quiver of anger. From the chair the Vesuvian rumble began. The late light struck the colored-glass shade of the old lamp and cast pale lozenges of red and blue on the ivory-lace covering on the table. All around was such a dustiness, a mustiness, a sense of antique intimacy, that he almost imagined a smell of old people's underwear; he could visualize the two of them naked under the yellow light of a bare bulb with their ruining bodies slowly, sluggishly seeking a furtive ease, the painter's chest crunching from the exertion, her mouth making a silently horrified "Oh my."

"You don't have to talk like that," he said weakly. "I *said* I would . . ."

"And the warped window in the bedroom," she said, exacting more and more as his grip loosened. "And the missing tiles in the bathroom, and the falling plaster over the fridge."

"Yes, okay," he agreed, writing on the inside cover of the receipt book. "Warped window, tiles, plaster."

"Because all those things upset J. T., and when he gets upset he coughs to beat the band, and I just *know* you wouldn't want that on your conscience." She moved closer to him as she spoke, and he backed away, still writing, suddenly afraid to look up at her. "I'm sure that you're not like the other agents," she said. "I can see by your face."

At first, Ilse Moeller noticed nothing different about his face. She moved about the room in a green-knit dress, waiting for him to write out the receipt, touching personal things with her peculiarly heavy hands, smiling unattractively. "Here he is again," she said in her tart voice. "On his mission, so dedicated, so businesslike." Why had she come to *this* city, she wondered for the thousandth time. *They* were all around her, by the millions here, with their sly, melancholy faces, sleepy looking, bored, hiding accusation behind eyes thousands of years old in the art of secrecy. There *were* other cities, where Jews were in a tiny minority, where you could go for weeks, months even, without seeing one. An inner spasm went through her in Norman's presence; she recognized it as revulsion and it made sense to her. "A miniature Rothschild, eh, Moonbloom? What was it you said you were—a bookkeeper before? It is a natural talent, adding and subtracting. It makes you strong."

"What are you talking about?" he asked coldly. "Are you

trying to be humorous?" He looked at her with dull eyes, holding the receipt out to her without moving, demanding that she take it from him.

"You seem to be not in a good mood, Moonbloom. Do I rub you in the wrong manner?" She sounded almost hopeful, gazing with morbid interest at his small, unsmiling face.

"I don't get your joke," he said harshly. "Perhaps you'd better try your humor on someone else."

Ah, she thought, noting with satisfaction the little threads of blood on the inner walls of her body, he *is* human, he does feel something oppressive in me. Her smile was like that of a victim of Bell's palsy, her mouth creeping up one side of her face so extremely that it seemed her flesh might split.

"See, now it comes out," she said gaily. "You denied it before, but it is revealed. You do dislike me after all."

There was something noxious about her face. She was an exceptionally clean person; you could tell she scrubbed her face almost raw, because her skin had an abraded look; her clothes were always spotless, and Norman had never seemed to notice any smell in the room. It had given the apartment a curious quality of emptiness. Now, for some reason, he sensed a terrible odor, which escaped him in an olfactory way but which reached directly to his brain and filled him with revulsion.

"I don't understand you," he said carefully. "You seem eager for me to dislike you."

"Oh no, that is a strange thing to . . . I, of course, am only . . . teasing." She seemed unnerved by his very simple deduction and covered her breasts with crossed arms, shaking her head in mild reproof. "You seem to have a very poor sense of . . ."

"Humor," he supplied. "Yes, that seems to be the consensus." He stared for another few seconds at her, then jerked his

132

head sideways impatiently and went to the door. "We seem to talk at odds."

She had no response to that, but only stood covering her torso and staring at him with glittering eyes, fascinated by something just beneath his hairline.

He nodded and left her, somehow scalded by the after-vision of the green of her dress.

TEN

KARLOFF'S PERPETUAL ANGER seemed somewhat frayed, and he led Norman into the room, walking on stiff, tottery legs. With his great hunched size, his movement had the frightful majesty of a wounded elephant. Norman held his breath until the old man sank with a grunt onto the chair.

"*Ehr gehocked offen mine tier, deh fashtunkenah momser,*" he growled, running his eyes suspiciously up and down Norman's body.

"Who, Mr. Karloff, who beat on your door?"

"Ahh," the old man said, nodding, his down-pulled mouth fighting upward toward a faint smile. "Who, who? *Ich vays, dun vurry. Uber ich nit geshluphen.* Hah, I em not easy. I vait, I let him come close, he should think I am through. And then—grab him by throat. take him along ahlso!" His eyes peered out savagely, slyly, like those of a beast waiting in a thicket for the man who has wounded him.

"Was one of the other tenants bothering you, banging on your door?"

Karloff tossed his hand derisively. "Dem," he snorted. "Dey are notting. Not dem."

"Who, then?" Norman asked, gazing at the decaying mask.

"Who, yes, *who?*" Karloff suddenly grinned, causing an explosion in the network of lines on his dark face.

Dismayed, Norman made a face. Karloff thought it was Death who had knocked on his door. Caught in the whorls

134

of senility, he planned to seize that which would seize him. What shape did the intruder have for the old man? Norman looked at the massive gnarled strength in the ancient hands, the veins hard and black under the loose, liver-colored skin, and he shuddered for the human being Karloff might mistake for his one enemy. God help Del Rio or Paxton if they trespassed! He himself kept the table between them as he wrote out the receipt and took the damp bills.

Then he looked around at the room, which seemed to be melting into a solution of filth. Whole families of roaches trooped across the walls. Here and there were clottings of now unidentifiable food remains, and, with a final swoop of disgust, Norman saw a swarming mass of tiny ants in the cubed conformation of the sugar they were devouring.

"Mr. Karloff," he said in a firm voice, "I don't think I would have the heart to put you out of here, although that would be the sensible thing. This place is the most revolting mess I have ever seen. The whole building will be condemned. Perhaps you are not capable any more, but . . ."

Karloff brayed mockingly, his purplish mouth opened wide.

"But I've just made up my mind about something. I am going to have this place cleaned, maybe painted. I'm going to tear down those curtains and burn them with your bedding."

Karloff began laughing, almost silently, his eyes narrowed so they appeared to be just two more lines in the crowded road map of his face; his large hand slowly beat the time to his amusement.

"I'm not kidding!" Norman said loudly, feeling anger pumped into him with each slap of the old hand.

"*Oy vay*," the old man rasped, rocking, beside himself in his almost soundless laughter. "Listen to him, duh *graysa mench . . . oy, oy . . .* ah reguhla . . . eee-e . . . ah re-

135

guhla Tartsen fuhn deh apes!" And now his laughter broke thickly, lumpily out of him; it rolled around the room and poured over Norman, who became wild with an emotion he thought was rage.

"You'll see, you'll see, Karloff," he cried, standing near the door and sweeping the room with his hand. "I'll scrub this place to the bare wood. I'll burn the rubbish and disinfect the floors and walls. I'll take every piece of food out of here and see that you only have enough to eat. I'll paint the walls white, I'll scrub right around your chair, and you'll be the only dirty thing in here. This place will be so shiny it'll blind you. I'm getting sick and tired of all this." He seemed to be floating on a swift rush of something, and he flailed without sense or reference. "On Mott Street I'll put in fluorescents in the hallways as bright as arc lights. I'll rip out Basellecci's wall, I'll fix stove burners and faucets and elevators and wiring. I'm sick and tired of all this ridiculous . . ."

And suddenly he was staring at the old man's puzzled face and he was stunned by his own echoing insanity. He tried shaking his head, attempted a smile of sorts; his head kept ringing dementedly. "It's just that I . . . I mean, there has to be some order. I'm going to . . . to clean up. I have to. . . ." Karloff shrugged helplessly, and Norman looked at the floor. "I mean it," he said. Then he spun around and went out of the reeking room, Karloff temporarily immobilized behind him.

"Do you know," Sugarman said to Norman with the expression of a preacher revealing hell-fire, "that last night my manhood slipped away from me. I could not summon the rod of my virile office, and instead was landlord to a dead and harmless worm who lay upon my belly like the crude

136

likeness on a mummy case. I was the victim of a coarse woman's scorn and laughter. That was less than nothing. But the demise of something valuable, which I had not yet determined the extent of—that was the mortal blow. The logarithms of life are written in exceedingly small numerals; what chance have you at. answers when the pointer has softened to the consistency of melting rubber? Can I find my way without the needle to the compass? I have visited the shores of melancholia often in my errant life, indeed it is home port for me. But always there was my rod, my staff to comfort me. One thing made me a positive creature. I could enter things, could plug into mysterious sources of power. In the times of dire emptiness I could hope, yes, even perhaps subliminally dream of perpetuating Sugarman, of extending his raucous cry over the track-bound carcass of this America. I might be buried like a dormant root, but my fruit would spring up through the cinders of the roadbeds and the prone ladder of the ties. I had always had that vague trump card of life. But last night I played it and it was revealed to be a blank, an unprinted piece of paper. She laughed, that Lysol-smelling tart, laughed and farted hysterically. So, this is what I present to you today, Moonbloom. I pay you in the same small change, but there is no warmth in the payment; you might just as well pick pennies from a dead man's eyes."

Through the disorder of his own recently tumbled nerves, Norman looked at the morose, yet stubbornly vigorous, face of the candy butcher, and he felt a trio of impulses: irritation was tepid and came in the thickest stream, but there was the cold trickle of pity, and, right in the pit of his belly, the hot fount of irresistible laughter. He snorted, hissed, finally brayed.

"Oh, Christ . . . Sugarman . . . what the devil . . . oh

for . . ." He held on to the table and shook, surprised at a physical relief. Through watery eyes he beheld his tenant's miserable and outraged face. He was mortified at the excess of his own voice. The room rang, and it was strange to him, because he had never laughed like that before; his fascination with the phenomenon perpetuated it. Sugarman sat like an affronted rock. If only he would smile, or display positive anger. But he just sat there, parodying himself, mournful, self-pitying, wretched, yet richly abundant.

Finally Norman flopped onto a chair and wiped his eyes with a handkerchief, shaking his head to rid himself of the hysteria.

"I entertain you?" Sugarman said in a cold, delicate voice. "You have the humor of those who made lamp shades from human skin. I speak to you of infinite loss, of the tragedy of the irrevocable, of the end of something—end, *end!* Is there a more frightful word? And you, you dry pod of a bookkeeper, you crustacean with ball-point claws—you laugh, just laugh. You are worse than I."

"I don't know what you want from me," Norman said. "You spill yourself to me. I don't ask for these intimacies. I'm the agent, I collect the rents. This whole setup is a madhouse. Did you give these great speeches to the agent who had the job before me? What deludes all of you people into thinking that I'm interested?" He sat very still now, suddenly feeling something in his grasp, his eyes intent on the florid face before him, noting the small, burst blood vessels that gave Sugarman's face a spurious outdoor look.

"All us people," Sugarman repeated, stumbling over Norman's unexpected rejoinder. "Because . . . because you have a look, your eyes are starved. Don't you ever look in the mirror? There is something masochistically inviting in the center of your raccoon eyes. Like the little square of confection

138

in *Alice in Wonderland*, there is written all over you 'Eat Me.' I know that with me I rant and rave in moving trains, deaf to my own voice and blind to the laughing faces. Only in here, in solitude, my voice rises to sound, and I wait for anyone to listen. And then you come along in your dark suit and vest and your pin in your lapel and your Al Capone hat, and you are like a queer microphone into which my pent-up words can pour. To what purpose? God knows. Perhaps we all wish to be inscribed upon something. Maybe it has to do with perpetuating our silly little consciousnesses. If we are wrong, it is the fault of your face—it is a fraud. Change your face, Moonbloom, or else listen and do something for us."

"What do you want me to do for *you*?" Norman asked in bewilderment. "All right, I'll do, I've promised to do things. What is your complaint? Do you want wall-to-wall carpeting, a stall shower, air conditioning? Is something broken? Name it, don't be shy. No one else is. Make a demand on me. A refrigerator, a paint job, what?"

"No, no, Moonbloom, it is not so easy. Man does not live on fringe benefits alone. What I want from you . . ." He stared musingly at the floor.

And Norman, the dread rising in him at the thought of some unimaginable request, scooped the money from the table and poured it into his pocket as he rushed to the door.

"Wait, wait, what are you running away from?" Sugarman called after him.

Norman waved in panic, and his answer was cut in two by the closing of the door.

"That's why I'm running . . ." *Slam*. ". . . because I don't know."

He said nothing to Paxton, who, fortunately, was too busy working to do more than indicate the money in a litter on the table. Norman counted out the rent, left the receipt, and went upstairs to Louie.

"I was suppose to go to that movie," Louie said, "but I come down with a bug. Had a little fever. I'm drinking a lot of juices and all. I didn't miss any work though. Went in with a hundred point three. They promoted me a little. I answer the phones now and only do a little delivering. Kind of keep a eye on things. That's because of Ralph. Ralph's okay; it's Sal is the wise guy. If it wasn't for Ralph I woulda . . ."

"I don't know what you're talking about," Norman said tersely. His cruelty was turned on himself though, as he took away with him the dimly hurt face of the man, standing in the simmering air of his room, his tiny television screen flickering its ignored performance, something bland cooking on the stove. The windows rattled slightly in the cold evening; Louie stood like the victim of a thrown custard pie, gaping, injured, forever lost to the joke.

"I ony was sayin' . . ." The rest of his plaint was lost to the closing of the door and distance; yet that fragment drew itself out as fine as the tapered sound of wind drawn through the finest of cracks and crevices. It was like a thin spray of lacquer and served to fix the small simian face of Louie on Norman's brain as he rushed out into the December darkness of cold wind and stone and stars.

"I am no longer Norman Moonbloom," he said aloud in the great privacy of the city night. And then, seeing the floral brilliance of windows and distant sign lights, he was suddenly confronted with a more terrible possibility, which made him bite the windy blackness and gasp, "Or I never was."

ELEVEN

GAYLORD CALLED HIM at seven o'clock in the morning to tell him that there had been a small fire in the Lublins' apartment. For the first time in his adult life, he rushed out into a business day without a tie and without shaving, only to find upon his arrival that such disturbing impulsiveness (like all impulsiveness, in his opinion) had not been necessary.

About two square feet of the wall beside the stove was charred, and the wastebasket that stood there was blistered to a colorless gray. The little girl stood behind her mother with wide, frightened eyes, biting silently on her guilt, while Sarah Lublin lied unhappily.

"Of course the stove is defective," she said. "I attempted to light the burner and a sheet of fire went up, caught on the drape and . . . started to burn. I called the superintendent when I heard him with the ash cans, and together we put it out." She studied Norman's face. "It is a menace. It should be repaired."

"A *sheet* of fire," Norman echoed expressionlessly.

"Shee-et," Gaylord muttered disgustedly behind him.

They all stood in the kitchen—Aaron, the old uncle, the little boy, each eying the black smear of the wall with a different contemplative expression, like people studying an unusual natural phenomenon. Only Gaylord looked bored; he knew better, but didn't have it in him to side with landlords. He leaned on the cabinet that separated the kitchen from the dinette, blowing softly over his thumbnail. Norman squinted at the burned wall, searching for an attitude. He had responsibility, no matter who he was now. What else was there to hold on to? He was cut off from the place and time that had at least given him a spuriously familiar shape, and if he relinquished duty, he would be totally lost here in this sunlit kitchen, among the strangely discreet torments of these pale foreign people. He assayed the alternatives.

"We do not wish to make trouble," Aaron said confidently; he was professional and poised with strangers, only gave in to screaming fear and rage among his own. "If you would just check the stove and make some adjustment for the paint, I will be glad to paint the kitchen myself."

Norman darted his eyes to him, swiftly moved them to the uncle, who might have been the weak link. But Hirsch, an enemy of sorts to his nephew, was conditioned to larger, outside enemies.

"It's a fire hazard," Hirsch said blandly. "Your whole building could burn."

Sarah's lips were tight, and the morning sunlight grouped her solidly with her family; they had endured worse interrogations. Their skins were sickly white, and yet strong, absorbent. How was it that he had never encountered people like these tenants?

His eye fell on the little girl. "Do you play with matches?" he asked suddenly, feeling the exhilaration of righteous cruelty.

The girl looked up at her mother in supplication, the tears starting from her eyes. Sarah pushed her out of the room, and Norman heard her running toward a bedroom. Hirsch just shrugged, smiled, and followed after her, too old to be concerned about anything less than ultimate defeat. Aaron tried to spread his body over Sarah and the boy, but Sarah, with sudden determination, shoved him and said, "Go see to Ruthie." She must have given him a significant glance, because he went, his back somehow defeated looking.

"Please," she said to Norman and Gaylord. Gaylord waved both hands at her and left too. "It is difficult here, with the old man. We have tension. We are nervous people, you understand."

Norman nodded firmly. "Your little girl did it, didn't she?"

"She didn't know," Sarah whispered harshly. "She wished to boil water for tea—to surprise me."

"The stove wasn't defective. I could see by the wastebasket that it started in there. She dropped a match in there."

"Yes, yes, but please."

"I don't know what you're so upset about," he said. "I'm not going to do anything to you. The damage is slight."

"You will have it painted?"

"Me? I'm sorry, you'll have to take care of that yourself."

"We are so short of money. . . ."

"Well, then, leave it as it is until you have some extra money."

"I can't," she cried desperately.

"Why not?"

"I cannot explain it to you."

"Look, I don't understand any of this. All I know is that the bills are piling up. I've promised to do a lot of things. I'm going to. I'm going to fix your sink; I don't know how but I am. Now you expect me to paint your kitchen too. Some things are impossible. There's a limit. If you only knew the finances of this setup. It's a nightmare. I have to draw the line. What is so terrible about your leaving the wall like that for a while?"

Sarah's look embarrassed him, made him feel he was being measured, and he worried perversely that he might be found

143

wanting. In the other rooms he could hear the soft, mouselike sounds of the family being quiet. The old, lumpy putty on the window glistened and made the room seem like a cave.

"*I cannot stand the signs of the fire,*" she said slowly, placing each word in him like a dart. Her eyes were like mirrors, and he saw a tiny Norman Moonbloom in each of them. He smelled the burned odor, but it seemed to come from her. Something made him put his hand up to his tie, but his fingers recoiled at its absence. She looked wild, and he was afraid.

"All right," he said hoarsely. "It's already beyond reason. Why not?"

"Thank you," she said with the expression of a whore.

"Sure, sure, sure," he snarled.

She smiled.

"Our Lester," Minna said, "has gotten into trouble, but he knows where to turn. We'll take care of everything. And when it's all cleared up, I want to have you come to dinner. You seem like a nice young man, both feet on the ground. I think you'd be a good influence on Lester."

From the other side, Eva returned coyly, "I'll bet a lonely young bachelor like you could appreciate a home-cooked meal."

"Everything is going to be *all right,*" Minna said, starting a new serve.

"Oh, he *needs* us, all right." Eva, like her sister, did not recognize the manic quality of their conversation. A doctor had agreed to abort the girl, and Lester was sulking safely in his room. The green years of the nephew's childhood would never end for them, and they remembered how he had looked in sailor suits and promised themselves they would feast on the photograph albums that night. Age and loss became distant and unreal, someone else's blood was only as sad as that which was shed on the other side of the world; one clucked pityingly but lived on in personal love.

"Now you just tell us your favorite menu, Mr. Moonbloom, and we'll set a date," Minna cried on the edge of laughter.

"And I make pies," Eva threatened, rolling her leather-enclosed eyes.

Norman looked from one to the other of them like a spectator at a tennis match but with the painful sensation of being the ball.

"I mean it pays for a boy to have a family," Minna said.

"Loved ones," Eva qualified.

"People to lean on," Minna shrieked, speeding up the volley.

Norman reeled.

"Don't want him to know," Betty Jacoby murmured from the dimness as she lay on the couch, sick and hopelessly old.

"Mustn't let on to the little woman," Arnold said to him, caught killing time in the lobby of the apartment. "Just a brief slack period at the place. I can always get a job; it's not that. Don't want her to think I couldn't go right out and get a job. You understand." He winked slyly, his cheery, round face somehow obscene and weird to Norman, who could only nod in the viscosity in which they were submerging him.

"Katz is out auditioning," Sidone said, his fish eyes protruding behind the sunglasses. "The leader told him that if he made it, he would let him arrange and all. It's a big deal, but Katz is counting on it too much. That whacked-up bastard is already apologizing to me for his success. I don't build up, so I don't fall down. Trouble is, he doesn't want to be a bum. That's murder when you really are. That poor bastard. Maybe you'll help me pick up the pieces, Moonbloom?"

Pasty and trembling, he stepped into the Hauser apartment, where he was assaulted by Carol's screaming rage and then hit by an ash tray she had aimed at her husband.

"Aghh," she gargled in fear and disgust. Sherman, and the child too, froze in shock as Norman put his hand up to another wound. His forehead was bleeding, his eyes were blurry. He sat down, completely at a loss.

The lamp shade turned slowly, animating the river; the fake fire consumed something beyond comprehension. Ripples widened from a drowning that had not yet taken place. The child began to cry, and Carol ran from the room.

"Let me get you a Band-Aid," Sherman said dully. "That bitch, she was aiming at me." He trudged heavily out of the room; when he came back, the child went into the other room and began throwing blocks savagely; each block's impact detonated a nerve in Sherman's cheek.

"I'm sorry," Sherman said in an undertone. "It'll be all right, it just broke the skin."

"That's all," Norman intoned; he had the sensation of sitting in a rocket with the flames of propulsion already roaring beneath him. Slowly he raised his eyes to the ceiling, anticipating the impact of the plaster against his head. Sherman's large white fingers tangled before his eyes; he felt the pressure of the Band-Aid against his brow. The rocket pulsed, ready to lift him. "Hurry up," he said, as still as stone.

"Well it *was* an accident," Sherman said, breathing Sen-Sen at him. "The whole goddamn thing was an accident, from beginning to end." His cheek continued to transmit the rhythm of his son's furious mischief in the bedroom, so that

146

the *clockety clock thud* seemed a destruction taking place in the bones of his face. "I went with her for two years, and she teased and teased until I thought I'd flip. Then once, just once, she made a big production when her mother was away, gave me the big thrill finally. For Christ's sake, she probably had it plotted on temperature charts. That one time, and she was knocked up. We got married, we had Bobby. All an accident, see. But oh, that Bobby, he's a beauty anyhow, he's a miracle. How can I wish it never happened? Can you really wish you'd never been born?"

And Norman, his head hardly hurting, realized that the greater shock had happened to Sherman, and that fact caused him new pain. He could hear Carol Hauser crying furiously in the other room and he noticed that as Sherman became aware of the sound of her crying, a curious, lustful expression came over his face. He leaned away from Norman, crumpling the Band-Aid paper in his hand, his eyes turned toward the sound of her weeping.

"Oh that bitch," Sherman breathed passionately. "Do you see how she is? Isn't she a hot sketch, that broad? Isn't she something?" His voice burned with his own grotesque form of love, and when he stood up he appeared to be an actor playing Romeo who has completely lost himself in the part.

Norman went out as Sherman entered his wife's room and closed the door. The child stopped rioting. Everything was still except for the hot, terrible whispering from behind the closed door and the rotating lamp shade and the heatless fire.

Ashen and crumpled, Norman went directly home, wondering whether or not he was at the bottom of his fearful descent. In his bed, he lay with the pillow wrapped around his now throbbing head, and he drew a thin thread of comfort from the realization that he probably wouldn't survive anything worse.

TWELVE

THE NEXT MORNING he was forced to seize upon one piece of reality. His head cleared at the sound of Irwin's voice on the phone, and hand over hand he crept back to a ledge of his former life.

"I must say you took me at my word, Norm. I haven't heard from you in a month. That would be fine except for the fact that I also haven't gotten any *mail* from you either."

"Yes, I know, Irwin," he said, surprised that he still sounded the same. "Things have gotten a little mixed up. All those repairs and . . . well I was sick for a week."

"You're not letting things get out of hand, are you?" All this was, was a hole in Irwin's fourth-best suit, but he hadn't gotten to where he was without paying attention to details. "There's nothing you're keeping from me? You know I trust you, Norman."

"Of course, Irwin." He wondered if he were still recognizable with the scab on his lip, the too large Band-Aid on his forehead. Never in his former life had he displayed the marks of violence; it had been like a symbol of his complete disbelief in it. His comfortable association with small talk was gone, and in its place was a growing discomfort with words of all kinds. He who had never been sure that sin existed now wondered whether he was involved in it. Would the mirrors of his old house far away reflect him now?

"Are you still there, Norman?"

"I'm not sure."

"Norman?"

"Oh, yes, I was thinking about something else."

"Well don't. Think about this. Is everything as it should be there? What is it with the money?"

"As I was saying, Irwin, I'm just in the process of straightening things out. Going to put one of my old studies to a little good use, heh, heh. Do a little complicated accounting and see where I am. You don't have to worry about a thing on this end, Irwin. Just a matter of sort of inventorying, Irwin. You know how jumbled up these things can get, Irwin. I'm back in the groove after my recent illness, Irwin. Have everything in apple-pie order by the first, if not sooner, Irwin. You know, Irwin, I . . ."

"Stop with the Irwins!"

Norman looked sickly at the mouthpiece, suddenly feeling like crying for the little heap of himself. "Well . . . what should I call you?"

"Look, this is ridiculous. I'm going to wait until the first. I still have confidence in you. But if I don't get some satisfaction by the first of the year . . . Well, I'll have to really re-examine your status, Norman. After all, this is a business rannana, rannana. We don't rannana rannana rannana . . ."

For a moment, Norman had the comforting feeling that he was some two months younger, that all this hadn't become a horror. He watched the headless bodies passing along the sidewalk; he noticed that the last m in Moonbloom was chipping and might soon become an n. Of course the angle of sunlight measured a different hour now, as the days reached the winter ebb. Here was his ball-point pen, the familiar receipt book. But then a mouse ran across the floor— *a little lady mouse*—and he was instantly crushed by the immense web that had grown up around him.

149

"Irwin, I will!" he cried fiercely into the phone.

Irwin was blown into momentary silence.

"I'm going to take care of the whole goddamned thing! You won't have a thing to complain about. If it kills me, I'll put things in such order that you'll be amazed. Now let me hang up because I'm going to begin."

"All right, sure . . . okay, Norm." Irwin's breath became delicate with shock. There was a long stillness in the phone, and Norman realized that Irwin was waiting for *him* to hang up first.

Slowly, with the tremor of power in his hand, he did so. Then he drew some sheets of paper before him, ejected the nib of the ball-point, and began searching the watermark in the paper for the place to begin. Norman, scarred, changing, looked into the depths for a beginning and caught a glimpse of it, heard the sound of it, a sort of awful yet uproarious laughter.

He began writing:

70th St.:

Repair elevator
Wiring for house (Schoenbrun's air conditioner)
Clean walls (paint?)
Paint elevator (to cover dirty pictures)
Repair loose tiles in lobby floor
Replace bulbs in lobby
Repair dripping sink in Lublins' kitchen
Paint out the marks of fire in above
Plumbing (rusty water)

Mott St.:

Basellecci's wall ***
Repair Beelers' toilet
Install fluorescent fixtures in hallway (Kram)

2nd Ave.:

Things beyond my control?
Plus the wiring
Broken stove (Leopold)
Warped window (Leopold)
Missing tiles in bathroom (Leopold)
Falling plaster (Leopold)

13th St.:

Roof leaks
Toilets
Stair banister
Furnace
Lights
Windows
Cockroaches
Floors
Clean ⎱ Karloff
Paint ⎰

Now all he had to do was go out on his rounds once more, check to see if he had covered everything, ruthlessly determine priorities, and then find out the cost of everything—*everything!*

The paper covered with his small, pretty writing reassured him. Everything lined up like ordered troops. He could visualize his own delicately drawn numerals heading each column like officers keeping the ranks disciplined, looked forward to the time when he would be able to add them and, with finality, write the sums. Forgetting his marked face for the moment, he reaffirmed an old belief in codification. The watery winter sunlight could do nothing to his brave list. He smiled and awarded himself a Sunday holiday.

Next week he would dig in. Muscles appeared in his body.

His native town would recognize him. He would take an early train north, and come back Sunday night, refreshed. De Lesseps had nothing on him; rather late in life, he realized he could build a *dozen* Suez Canals.

The pain in his brow lay slyly dormant.

THIRTEEN

IT WAS A LITTLE too warm for his overcoat as Norman walked through the streets of his native town under the fine drizzle. Indeed, there was nothing to suggest the season in the atmosphere of remembered Sunday quiet; it could have been summer or spring fogged by his memory of the place. The few figures were distant, the shops remote in familiarity. Yet he was oddly relaxed by the monochrome look of the sedate old buildings. He could hear his own footsteps. The rain-softened edges of roofs, the blur of elm branches against the smoky ivory of sky, the dull shine of the iron railing around the green, and the heavy lift and fall of the flocked pigeons, all had the stillness, the inviolate calm of pictures in an old photo album; all was sweet and touching, but delicate enough to shape his frail memories in a form too light to elicit pain.

He was glad he had come, he thought, anticipating that the day here would show him himself as he really was. It would allow him to hold himself off from the chaos of the recent months, to see his job as no more than a job.

A car went by with a swish and a whine of tires; he smiled in sudden memory of an uncle's old Essex, whose wooden steering wheel he had manipulated in a solitary game of speed after the wheels had been taken off the car and it had rested at the back of his uncle's yard. Full of cheerful sentiment, he peered into the Sabbath-closed coffee shop he had once frequented, and he was moved by the empty cake stands on the counter and the dull sparkle of the grill.

Now he crossed and walked along the western perimeter of the green, eying the college buildings and the rusty moss along their foundations. A bus hissed by with lighted windows, and he was warmed by sadness. His face was soothed by the gentle mist.

Soon he reached the beginnings of his own neighborhood, and he remarked the quiet homeliness of the Victorian houses. How small it all was! And then he was in front of his own house, with no feeling of drama, looking at the gray clapboard stained by rain. The familiar windows, that door. My God, he half expected to see Norman Moonbloom come walking out, calling over his shoulder to someone dear inside. For some time he stood there, bemused, comfortably haunted, pressing the house and the ground and the sky upon his heart, only to find with some dismay that, when he closed his eyes, all of it had left no mark he could discern.

And then a fat man in a raincoat came out of the house. He stared at Norman blankly. Norman smiled and walked on.

"It's like walking through the past," he said to himself, enjoying the role of ghost. He passed the junior high school he had attended and of course remembered it as much bigger. Here he had passed from room to room among other children, weighted with books, unsolicited, circumspect, earnest, smiling on the fringes of pushing boys and girls, often thinking he was part of everything that went on, sometimes feeling otherwise.

The street widened to contain long blocks of esplanade masted with elms and looking like great green barges sailing into the park at the far end. He passed tall old houses with oval windows in their doors or stained-glass fanlights or shingled towers. He remembered romping here. Romping?

154

No, dreaming, or at least sleepwalking. Suddenly he stopped in the pearly mist as something regrettable struck him; *he* was not the ghost here, not now—this place and his former life here were ghostlike. No matter how intensely he desired to return to the peace and quiet of the way he had lived most of his life, he was irrevocably cut off. He looked around at the still and shining town in the rain, and his yearning choked him as he realized that the ghastly life of his recent months was all he had. The terrible images of the tenants rose up and strode over the toy landscape, crushing his serene past. And the town did not cry out to *him* for help, but somehow lumped him with those awful alien figures. What a mistake this had been! If he had not come back, he might have been able to maintain a dream of his old home, might have used his memory of it to sustain him. How he hated all of them, those grasping, importuning tenants, with their filthy illusions, their sickly disguises!

With a feeling of grief, he waved down the first bus he saw and rode back through the town. From the lighted bus the streets were grayer, dimmer. The occasional people were like shades, the buildings like tombs. His own house was a blur of nothing; downtown, with his favorite luncheonette, was an unlighted slide that revealed contours without life.

It was a relief to board the train, where the sound of people's voices and the feeling of movement returned him at least to his body. For a while he watched the landscape sliding by in the early twilight, not thinking about anything ahead or behind. He rode the air without anger or pain or hunger, a sort of mote being sucked toward a great nucleus of noise and size, unanimated, almost peaceful, until the candy butcher came ranting through the car, pouring his lyrical madness over the plush and damp wool and flesh.

"Awrange drinks, cheese sandwiches, peanut-butter Nabs,

ambrosia, nectar, *pâté de foie gras,* Hershey bars. This car does *not* have a diner. Buy now, I accept Diner's cards and Carte Blanche. Mounds, Nestlés, ham sandwiches made with ham from the very finest of Estonian suckling pigs . . ." Sugarman's eyes lit up like a blue gas flame. "Ah, Moonbloom, you thought to run away? No dice, little agent; you are hooked, addicted. The withdrawal pains are worse than everything. Meanwhile, how about a spot of refreshment?"

Norman groaned and steeled himself for what could not be avoided, and the train whistle howled derisively as it sped him back to the city.

FOURTEEN

IF ANYTHING, HIS visit home made things worse; as with pressure on a wound, cessation invigorates pain. The Thursday following was snow-flurried and blustery. Blown along as he was, it seemed more than ever that his schedule was shattered, so that at the end of the day he had the feeling that he had shuttled back and forth between the buildings, seeing one tenant on Mott Street, and one on Second Avenue, and so back to Mott Street or Thirteenth Street or Seventieth Street, crisscrossing his own tracks, weaving some chaotic web of intention.

Basellecci merely looked at him, but the follicles of hair on his head were thin eruptions of pain and something waxy coated his brow and his nose. He handed Norman the money silently, his mild brown eyes thickened, beyond protest. The mouth that doted on the subtleties of pronunciation, and that had never been able to shape his cry for dignity, now had a pursed expression, as though a fine, strong thread were drawing it shut, stilling the appeal he had never been able to make convincing to other people. He stared without anger, without charging Norman, only, more terribly, presenting himself in the revolting manner of those deformed people who have not the discretion to hide their deformities; he just stood in the existing light, the toilet chamber an umber unexplainable background for him.

Norman attempted to speak, but his words for Basellecci

had been used up and he mouthed dry air. He gestured toward the toilet, nodded, and went on.

Wung was reptilian, his flesh going green, his long, drop-shaped eyes frantic, as though sensing his descent to a place where he couldn't breathe.

Beeler sat before a new television set, his blue, enigmatic eyes going from an interview program to Norman and then back again, all quite rapidly. "A *Chanukah* present from my doll baby," he said in his ragged voice. "I can't get over my little Sheryl, going out and getting a expensive set like that. Can you imagine, that little curly-locks? I shouldn't count my blessings? Immaculate, that child. Her mother started her out like that; it goes into the heart eventual. Driven snow. I'm not religious, but a man needs a altar, a clean place. You'll admit this is no castle, but with her, it's a oasis, a senctuerry. Lemme tell you, confidential, while she's in the other room, I done some pretty dirty things outside—with women, screwing around, you know. Fect is—I should be forgiven—even while my wife was alive. I admit, no excuses. But lemme say this: I never, never brung a woman here, even while Sheryl was away. I respect the virginal spirit of that child too much. Here I get my spirit nourishment and I know that much—you don't shit where you eat. What else a guy like me got, hah? God? Who knows? I seen too much of people to believe. Money? Nothing—buttons. Guy like me never owns nothing. I had a brain, I went to pharmacy school, worked for years in other people's drugstores. Didn't I see the filth, the crookedness? Didn't I do myself, selling phenobarbital to hopheads, putting on a fancy label with a Latin name and selling to knocked-up high-school kids—castor oil. So tell me, would this be a life without you have someplace and someone which is clean and innocent and sweet?" He gazed at Norman. The fringe of silver hair around the bald scalp made him look like an aged monk, and yet the stitched seams in his cheeks and around his eyes and mouth were hard and wise: it was as though he were two people, or, rather, one disguised man. But there was no knowing which was the disguise and which was Beeler; perhaps he himself had no way or desire to know. "Look at her," Beeler commanded, waving at the old studio photograph where Sheryl, cast forever as Shirley Temple, smiled sweetly out of time. "Is that a doll baby, is that a doll baby or not?"

And Norman, just in from the outside, breathed timidly, too heavily assessed for horror, too smashed by the weird irony of Beeler's heedless dream to assert even his own name.

And then Sheryl came out in the dragon robe, her face and body almost shaped in Beeler's image for Norman too. She kissed her father's shiny pate in passing, her large, coarsely pretty face avid, amused, yet savage. With her full red mouth on the old druggist's head, she could have been sucking something from him or injecting an odd hallucinatory venom into him. Beeler's face smiled so deeply that you could see without question that his head *had* been punctured, one way or another.

"Daddy, honey," she said in her smoker's voice, running her hand along his shoulder as she went toward Norman. Beeler tarnished in the cloudy light.

"See, I've got it all ready for you," she said slyly, pushing the money into Norman's hand. Her tweezed eyebrows shone with cold cream, and the lubricated look of her smooth, large-pored skin added unrelated heat to Norman's ailment. "Save you effort—you look tired, sweety." She walked him to the door, opened it, and fitted it between the heavy swell of her breasts, so that the dragon there looked apoplectic. "I been thinking about your offer, you know. How about a week from Saturday? I got a shower, one of the girls in the office. You could come up around ten thirty, bring a little booze. We could dance to the radio and like that. Hmmm?"

"It's a date," Norman said in a normal voice, doing something with his face he hoped was smiling. "I'll see you then."

"I'll look forward," she said, keeping her eyes on him as she closed the door so that he couldn't look down at the money in his hand. "And by the way, don't forget about our john."

Resignedly, he counted the money and was not surprised that it was now ten dollars short. A drop in the bucket of his blood. How many murders can you be hanged for, anyhow? he thought. It seemed he was at the bottom of his fall and was only writhing around at the same level. Either he would rise up from his abyss or the mercy of a great stone would bury him there; it seemed not to matter either way.

Leni Cass paid him with a check, and he didn't even remind her that checks were no good to him, were worth no more than his receipts. Shame made her speak to another, better Norman over his shoulder, and her immense, lovely eyes had yellowish matter in the inner corners, as though for too long she had been seeing herself in humiliating postures and was now infected by the ugliness of her real role. Norman promised her something, which bewildered her; he himself had no idea what it was.

Karloff shoved him with surprising strength when Norman told him that the following week he was coming there with water and soap and paint, and was planning purification by fire. The ancient's eyes were glittering with a blue-and-yellow complex; walking away from Norman after his assault, he moved on petrified limbs and sat down with a movement that hinted he might never get up.

"Go, go, *vas kenst du tuhn tsu mir?*" he asked rhetorically, in a voice like a clatter of stones. He smiled with vicious scorn and held his two great hands apart. "A hundred years ago I vas spilled all over vit boiling vater, from every inch duh body. Duh old vomans say, 'He cannot liff, *erh shtaben.*' Dey put me around all over vit mud. I vas cover, around duh *aigen*, duh mout . . . mine *klayna petzel* looked it vas a butt fuhn a tsigar like in a ash tray. Over a year I lay in dis mud fuhn duh oit—I vas like dead, cover vit oit, duh flies bumpin' my face, duh sounds fuhn duh peoples, duh other children, duh horses, duh cows, duh birds, duh boats, duh *gahntsa velt,* and I'm laying like in mine grave. But all duh time, all . . . duh . . . time, I'm *breathing,* I'm tasting, I'm hearing, I'm *knowing!*" He made silence something that could be heard. The length of his consciousness was like that of a long, long steel string, and his striking of it made the deepest, most resonant note Norman had ever heard. No daylight came into that room, and Karloff was made of the brass light of a naked bulb; he was filthy with age, like something dug out of damp ground, the crevices filled with a green cuprous mold, his eyes reflecting things that were no longer there. "You vill clean, vat—vat vill you do?" he said with great and inhuman pity.

And the thought of Karloff's approaching death suddenly filled Norman with dread: he imagined some immense thing crashing to the ground and reducing everything in sight to piteous rubble. A hundred years of knowing! Of knowing what? What an ant's life had Norman Moonbloom led! The

161

aged presence compressed him. He hoped to be distilled there in the reeking room with the ancient monstrosity peering at him, daring him to tamper with life and death.

"Anyhow, I will do it," Norman said with great courage.

Karloff just sat there, *knowing*.

"Ah, *you*," Ilse moaned with a flagellant's smile. "Rent, rent, rent. I shall never be done paying you, shall I?"

"You're not paying me," Norman said in a recorded voice. "I'm only the agent. You owe me nothing."

"Ah, aha, ahaha . . ." She began to giggle, and her laughter was nerve-racking because her face expressed only hatred; her skin resembled the inside of a pelt and was reversed only at the cost of great pain. "You . . . *you* say I owe you nothing, yes, sure. You people, how your mouths say one thing and mean another." Norman stepped back involuntarily, but she continued to smile, and her hands' fluttered down the length of her body, displaying herself. "What can you get from me? If I have taken the most terrible things in the greatest quantity, taken with my eyes and my ears . . . Oh, all you can get is the rent, that is all."

"Some time you'll speak plain and tell me what you're trying to say. I don't understand what you throw at me every time I come here." He said it to her blotchy red face, said it sincerely, believing it. And yet somehow he had the feeling that if he turned his eyes just a little, all of what she meant would be quite clear.

And this was the sensation he felt all that day, running in and out of the buildings, losing his route, visiting each of the buildings many times, always so fresh from the outdoors that the crystals of fine snow were glistening on the mammoth crown and brim of his hat. Each of them existed on the edge of unbearable chasms, places that overlooked great and monstrous views. It was as though one tiny adjustment of his vision would bring it all to him, and he feared the unguessable touch that could bring it about. Dimly, he was aware of trying to check his list of things to be done; he attempted to peer past the faces for those defects he had missed.

His expression made the tenants suspect subterfuge; he seemed suddenly quite strange as he avoided their eyes, his small face crowned with the absurd hat and its tiny brilliants of snow. The tension became mutual. They spoke less than usual to him. Some of them suspected he carried some kind of hope with him, but even those were apprehensive about how he would give it to them.

Marvin Schoenbrun thought the agent was going crazy, and he was repelled because a crazy man was worse even than a sane one to him. The Lublins were settling into another chamber of Hell and for the time being imagined Norman's abstraction would make him merely irrelevant. Sugarman looked at him pityingly and began, subconsciously, to compose an ode. Minna and Eva Baily didn't renew their dinner invitation. Del Rio didn't notice one way or another, because he was going mad himself.

"I've got me a date tonight," he said in a steely voice. "I've been too nervous. The trainer says I should blow off some steam. It's been a long time since I've bothered with girls, but I've got to blow off steam, blow off steam. . . ." He stood, socking the words into his palm, the cords standing out in his neck. The room was so clean it looked cold; but Del Rio burned.

So Norman, at the end of his rope and connected to it at his neck, went out into the dark of millions of cold wet touches, tasting snow and reeling under the invisible fallings.

FIFTEEN

But the following day still only moved him sideways in his pit. He went into the Seventieth Street lobby, catching a quick glimpse of a graying Mussulman in a huge pallid hat in the mirror. Going up in the elevator, he tried to pick the color of paint he should use to efface the rusted pornography. Only semiconsciously, at first, did he sense an approaching noise. Voices—more particularly, one voice. Screaming. But there were other voices too, and the screaming was segmented into short, dry regularities, too precisely spaced to be quite convincing. Norman shuddered as the elevator reached the top floor, and he almost pushed the button to go back down again. Was it only curiosity that made him open the door and step into the sound?

"What's happened?" he asked Eva Baily, who stood with Betty Jacoby and Sidone at the door to the Hausers' apartment. The screaming came from inside, harsh, obligatory, and inhuman. Eva was crying and shaking her head. There were more voices inside, and between the screams Norman thought he recognized Sarah Lublin's voice and even the drowsy monotone of Jane Sprague. He smelled the scent of clinics. "What is it? Is someone hurt? An accident?" he asked. Sidone pointed inside and shook his head, bewildered looking without his sunglasses, his long, oily hair chaotic from bed. A man in a white jacket came out and went to the elevator, calling back to someone, "I'll go down and get it."

The screams made welts on Norman's insides. He became angry at his ignorance and seized Sidone's arm, noticing briefly his own surprise at the arm's thinness. "For God's sake," he pleaded.

"The kid," Sidone said. "It's the kid."

Still holding Sidone's arm, Norman looked toward the half-opened door, suddenly aware of the rapid increase of his old sensation of stretching. All he could see was the little entry and a sliver of the living room. The movement he recognized as the lamp-shade river. Someone crossed the thin rectangle too quickly to be recognized. Another figure, in a white jacket and white pants, stood with its back to Norman, blocking off the lamp.

"Did you give the father something?" someone said.

"Both of them," another strange voice answered.

"Bobby, Bahh-beee," an unrecognizable voice wailed.

"There, there," Sarah Lublin said from somewhere out of sight.

The screaming went on uninterruptedly, the intervals between measured precisely.

"The child strangled . . . something he swallowed," Betty Jacoby said from beside him.

"Ohhh, yess," Norman breathed, letting go of Sidone's arm. He stood joined to them in the hallway, making a foursome— not of grief, but, oddly, of commemoration. The moment was significant; it deserved formality. There came the sound of something crashing, a confused murmuring, and then Jane Sprague's voice saying, "No, no, it's my fault, I'll clean it up. I'm sorry."

The elevator door opened again, and the man in the white jacket returned, carrying a collapsed stretcher. He went inside, turned to look back questioningly at them, and, when they made no move to enter, closed the door in their faces.

With the door closed, the screams became more hollow and resonant, the other voices muffled and mysterious.

"But how?" Norman asked, looking from one to another of them.

Eva shrugged.

Betty said, "Nobody knows."

"Dead?" Norman whispered.

Eva looked at him with an expression of some revulsion.

In the hallway, in the entire building, the silence compressed the din inside the apartment, made it sound immensely important. Norman sweated rivers and groped with his eyes for the injuries to the hallway. Part of him knew that the gigantic city pulsed and moved in its intricate life quite oblivious to the one smothered cell, and yet to him death had appeared for the very first time. The deaths of his family were merely burst daydreams in retrospect. He had lived most of his life in a deep-shadowed glen and had come out into an open ravine where towers of rock rose up all around him, where things falling made great destruction. The screaming was metronomic, the four of them just small pillars in the hard hallway. He discovered several huge cracks in the stucco wall, a missing bulb, a cavity where a tile had been. Betty Jacoby grunted and leaned against the wall. Sidone said, "What are we doing . . . I mean there's no point to . . ." And then lapsed into silence.

The elevator door opened again, and two men wheeled some kind of machine to the door and opened it. One of the white-clad men appeared and said, "No, forget it; there's no use." The two men wheeled the apparatus back to the elevator and went down. When the elevator came up again, a white-haired man with skin like a worn rug hurried past them and went inside. There was a crescendo of crying which quickly settled down. A policeman came up the stairs and went into the apartment.

Betty Jacoby shook her head and said, "I must lie down. Call me if . . ." Then she went down the hall, holding on to the wall. Sidone said, "Well, Katz is inside," as though that explained his staying.

Finally there came a long, high scream that broke something in Norman, a sound of struggle, and then no more screaming. The door opened, and someone said, "No, no, no, no, no, no, no." Two white-clad men carried the stretcher out; the blanketed form was too small to take seriously. Norman hurried ahead of the stretcher-bearers and opened the elevator door. He got in behind them and pressed L. The motor whined and dropped them slowly. He stood, half consciously shielding the dirty drawings from the stretcher. One of the men adjusted a corner of the blanket. The whining of the elevator had a peaceful sound, but the lump of the hidden child entered Norman's stomach or heart or soul. As they bumped to a stop, he unthinkingly tore off the "Did Not Pass Inspection" sign and opened the door for the stretcher-bearers. They passed out of the elevator and through the lobby; Norman looked after them from inside the elevator until they were out of sight. When he heard the ambulance motor start, he closed the door and went back up.

The policeman and another man came out; through the opened door, Norman saw the small table and noticed that the lamp-shade river was gone. That was what had broken, he thought.

The funeral was oddly disappointing. Norman, expecting unbearable demonstration, was presented only with lifelessness. The child, in a white open coffin, gave him the nasty

167

floating feeling of a nightmare. The parents were dry. Carol's hair was drawn back in an institutional bun and showed the dark roots. Her face was boggy and gray-white, and the only resemblance to what she had looked like was in the shape of her mouth and her nose. The brightly painted woman had been the decoration on a mummy case; now the case was opened to reveal the livid remains. A life of divorcement from real feeling had wasted her. She stood over the coffin for some time, her handkerchief against her mouth, as though only her mouth could cry. Sherman stood beside her, much more well groomed. Together they were mute and hideous, not like mourners, but like creatures numbed into animal pain by flaming clothes. Their eyes were gelatinous, and what was left of their faces only expressed the intense bewilderment of people who are told they have been robbed of all their belongings but who are uncertain exactly what they had owned.

Norman looked along the row of mourners, all of whom were tenants. He realized that they knew no more about what they felt than he did, and he contrasted that with the time of his grandmother's funeral, when he had felt excluded from the shared feelings. A minister recited Biblical words; an old man cried quietly. Katz, two seats down, stared his eyes out at the now closed coffin, trying to open it by the force of his will. He licked his squashed, trumpeter's mouth; a tear ran down his plump cheek like the slimy track of a snail. He seemed to be muttering something, his lips working. His fingers made rigid arches on his thighs. Beyond him, Sarah and Aaron Lublin sat without expression, much more used to the scene (Hirsch freed them for the occasion by sitting with their children). Right next to him, Norman smelled the toilet water on Marvin Schoenbrun and saw his clean, perfect fingers in repose on his flanneled leg. Around them all the beige walls of the chapel rose up to a white ceiling. Little scrolled fixtures held candle-shaped bulbs, and the entire room had a nonsectarian quality that gave the ceremony an official feeling, like something performed by and for civil servants. At the end of the row he glimpsed Betty Jacoby, dressed in black and with a heavy veil over her face; Arnold was framed against her dress, slumped in his seat and gazing petulantly at the ceiling. An "Amen" made the audience shift in their seats. The minister invited those who so desired to come to the cemetery. A huddle of strangers, family of the bereaved, formed a clot and moved through a side door to the sound of an animal grunting—Sherman or Carol. Norman couldn't tell which.

Barely able to see, he rushed out, aiming himself toward his office with body and soul.

SIXTEEN

ALL WEEK HE spent his evenings in the office, figuring his position in terms of dollars and cents; it seemed the only way to chart his personal latitude and longitude. Suddenly lost in a forest of lives, he yearned for a tabulator, longed for it as a mariner, adrift in a night without stars, might long for a sextant. By Saturday night, however, he had made a makeshift instrument from a week of plumber and electrician estimates.

He sat in bad light, picking bits of a bad supper from his teeth with a toothpick and staring at the black shine of the night-backed window. "Moonbloom" had become "Moonbloon" and a leg of the remaining n was chipping away, would soon become—what? "Moonbloor"? Above, his brother's name was, stolidly, permanently, still "MOONBLOOM." He sensed people passing, occasionally saw the mirror-like window briefly transparent in the light of a passing car. Mostly, though, there was just the image of himself, cadaverous in the overhead light, a sort of grotesque portrait of an executive, based by the desk. The building creaked, and he remembered that people lived over his office too. And what were they like? Could they all be as horrible and dangerous as his own tenants? For a moment he shivered at the thought of the infinitely long list of complaints of all the millions. Good God, he thought, what would the advancement that Irwin had once promised entail for him? Longer lists, more complicated charts of tormenting complexity? It occurred to him that he really didn't want the "opportunity" Irwin had promised (or threatened?). Why, then, was he laboring so mightily to do something? Because he now seemed to have no choice, because he was not like that mariner setting out from a port, but, rather, one adrift in an empty ocean, his movement no longer dictated by ambition, but by a need to survive. Somehow he had been cast into the inferno of people; at this point it didn't matter whose hand had done the casting.

Pipes ran, a hissing came from the radiator, a buckling sound from the hair-colored linoleum. He scanned the spread-out papers covered with figures and notations and telephone numbers. On a clean sheet he accumulated what seemed to be the facts.

The total cost for what he considered to be the minimal repairs came to five thousand three hundred and eighty-seven dollars and twenty-two cents; the owed rent, counting what Sheryl Beeler had cheated him out of, came to a hundred and seventy-three fifty. Irwin expected, on or about the first of the year, a total of seven weeks' rental, roughly thirty-five hundred, out of which he would deposit some five hundred for maintenance. This meant that Norman would be in the red for approximately . . .

He began to laugh, caught himself, and shivered the mirth to a stop. He picked up the pen and tried all over again, conscious that he was floating in a stream of lunacy, yet unable to stop paddling. And was he including what needed to be repaired in the tenants? Suppose he made a list of those things too, tried to find the cost of those breaks and chippings? Three hundred dollars for the Hausers for new hearts; six hundred and fifty for Kram's new body; eight hundred and twenty dollars and sixty-six cents for refurbishing Basellecci's dignity; a thousand for a new dignity for Leni Cass; nine hundred for a retread of Ilse's soul; five thousand for a brand-new one for Katz (souls must come high) . . . He began to laugh again, but stopped, chilled, when it turned to screaming. He looked around wildly, ready for collapse. Then he remembered that he had a date with Sheryl Beeler for that evening, and numbed with amazement, he was able to collect himself, even to the towering fedora, and he got up, put his coat on with mechanical motions, and went to his rendezvous.

He knocked softly at the door and was almost bowled over by its sudden opening. Sheryl stood before him in low-cut splendor, as bright as a poster in a red dress and gleaming lipstick and a silvered jewelry sword pointing toward her awesome décolletage.

"Well *hi*, sweety, I just this minute got in. Come on in and make yourself at home." She smelled powerfully of some unnaturally sweet flower, and Norman, partly dazed, partly incredulous, came blinking out of the dark hallway. "Lemme just slip into something more comfy," she said.

Norman couldn't believe that she had actually *said* that, and he slumped onto the couch and stared at the depression in Beeler's empty chair. He heard the water running in the bathroom, the feeble sound of the faulty toilet flushing, and, from another room, the sound of snoring, very loud and emphatic. He wondered whether, at this late date, he might lose his virginity; the thought didn't excite him, because there seemed to be nothing that was real about his presence there.

Sheryl came back in the dragon kimono and swished by him to the television set. Hypnotized, he looked past her broad, silken back to watch the small square burst open into

172

a scene of a smily band leader waving his hand. The sound came like a spilling of hot fudge on hollow metal pans. "Music to dance to," Sheryl said, holding her arms out in invitation.

Beyond fear, Norman went to her, grasped the warm resiliency of her torso, and began earnestly to do the two-step. For a few minutes he was able to concentrate on the unfamiliar fact of his *dancing*. He looked down past his arm to the imitation Persian rug, guiding himself in the pattern that made an invisible checkerboard of the floor. One, two, slide, then sideways, one, two, slide. The music oozed over him as he navigated the boxes. Dancing, and this step so appropriate for him, *his* dance of life. Beeler snored, the toilet tank drained feebly. One, two, slide, one, two, slide. They passed the lamp, and Sheryl deftly switched it off without breaking the rigid form of his dance. One, two, slide. He could barely see the floor, which was now lit only by the cold flicker of the television screen. One, two, slide, one, two, slide. There was a warm trembling against his body as Sheryl laughed silently. One, two, slide, he emphasized, the roots of his hair planted in sweat, so that his head felt like a rice paddy. One, two, slide. Her large breasts made big blunt concavities in him. One, two, slide, one, two, slide. Belly, thighs, the jut of her buttocks just below his hand like a cliff edge. One, two, slide. He was making square holes in the floor and expected momentarily to fall through one of them. One, two, slide, one, two . . . Something was reaching out of him for the warmth. He danced bent over, his body held away at the middle, his head resting in the hollow of her neck. She began to giggle softly and move after his escaping groin. He bent over more and more, and her giggle grew more violent, Beeler's snoring grew louder, the candy violins of the orchestra rose in sappy crescendo. Suddenly his back reached an extremity of discomfort, and reflexively he snapped erect, plunging like a rivet into Sheryl's kimonoed loins.

"Ohhh-hh," he gasped fearfully.

"Ahhh-hh," she responded cheerfully.

"I didn't mean . . ."

Sheryl, lovely in the blue-white television light, chucked him under the chin and said, "Let's sit on the couch, hon." She took his hand and led him there, grinning at his stiff, aching walk.

They sat down, and she leaned away from him, studying his face with amusement. The dragon seemed to wink in the wavering light, and Norman addressed his apology to it. "I hope you don't think . . . that is, I don't know what happened to me, I mean, I *know*, but I don't know why. No, of course, I know why, but I really wasn't thinking of . . . I haven't danced in years, and it just, the blood seemed to rush into . . . What I mean is, sometimes when a man gets close to a . . . girl, there's a nervous response that forces the blood into his . . ."

"Why, honey, all that happened was you got a hard on."

Norman smiled feebly, hearing the crackle of fire consuming him. From his stomach to his knees a cooking process rolled his organs around, and the steam reddened his face. "Sheryl," he said weakly.

Sheryl came close, her face blurring. He felt her lips fasten hotly on his. With a moan he tried to climb her, his hands clutching air. "Easy, easy, hon," she said with soft laughter. "Here, there, ahh, yeah, sweety, yeah . . ."

His gratitude knew no bounds when her warm, naked breasts fell into his hands. "I love you, I love you," he groaned. He was tossed like a chip by the sensation of skin against skin. "Sheryl, Sheryl, Sheryl," he cried through his teeth. "I love . . ."

"The toilet," she whispered from below, holding him up in the air like a child. He nodded wildly. "And a rent cut?" He tossed his head, trying to shake it loose from his body, and her demands did nothing to reduce his feelings. Distended, breaking, he agreed to carte blanche. For a long moment he observed and passed through many things. Sheryl's face expressed profound affection and bliss; he knew an instant's mortification as he noticed the band leader's face sweetly smiling at them; he worried about her father, whose snoring began to caricature itself; and, finally, he felt himself on an eminence he had never achieved before and he looked out with wonder upon the vast valley of the world, dizzied by the height, astounded by the immensity of the view. Sheryl raised him higher, her arms extended full length, her face full of savage and delighted mischief. And then she plunged him down, hara-kari fashion, immolating herself with a great sigh. There was a splat of impact, Norman rolled his eyes back into his head, held on to unimaginable pleasure for a short while, rearing and bucking to the tune of the string section playing *Bei Mir Bist Du Schoen*," and then exploded frighteningly.

He never noticed when Sheryl removed his body from her but only lay for some time muttering into the dusty cushions, "I love, love, love. . . ." Strengthless, his skin charged with sensitivity, he felt the warm flickers of the television light over his buttocks. The bathroom sounded busy with water and movement. He heard footsteps on the ceiling. Something profound had changed in him, and he sought to recognize it. Like a dusty bug, the image of a small man in a large hat walked across his brain, and he felt deep pity for the figure. He felt no peace, though, but, rather, a great shapeless ambition that saddened him. For a while he lay there, wondering what he really could do with the impossible situation. Something began to occur to him, and he cupped it, patiently gave it time to mature.

But there was no more snoring! He sat up quickly and drew his pants on, stepped into his shoes barefooted, and slipped on his shirt. When he was all dressed, he shoved his underpants into one pocket, his socks into another.

"Okay?" Sheryl asked, coming back into the room.

"I can't begin . . ."

"Gimme a kiss and then go home, huh?" she said, sleepily. "I'm just bushed."

He kissed her tenderly and wasn't in the least disillusioned when she said at the door, "Now don't forget what you promised."

"I'll never forget," Norman said with a strange lilting note in his voice.

And then he went out, heading for his office with the wind cold on his sockless ankles, feeling reckless with its tricky insinuation up his trouser legs to his loins free of underwear. And the thing that had occurred to him as he lay exhausted on Sheryl's couch, now, in the clear dark, formed unmistakably. He would do all the work himself, he decided, his face seeming to sparkle, as at the idea of a holy war. But, what was more important, he would do it with laughter, for it occurred to him that joy resembled mourning and was, if anything, just as powerful and profound.

He was not upset, or surprised either, to recognize the presence of pain in him as the tenants filed through his mind, stepping brutally on the tender places in his heart. He thought of the dead child, the trampled dignity of Basellecci, the constant hell of the Lublins, the erupting of Del Rio, the desperate defiance of Karloff, and all the rest of them in their agonies; and where he had the choice of crying, he chose irrevocably its opposite. He laughed loudly in a tone Norman

176

Moonbloom would never have dared. And then, for the first time in his life, he sang aloud without shame.

A sophisticated policeman just studied him wearily as he sang out of tune, *"Bei mir bist du schoen,* again I'll explain . . ."

SEVENTEEN

IN HIS APARTMENT he took sensual pleasure in writing a new itemized list, setting down words of things he could anticipate using, things he himself could touch and smell. His own expert, he estimated grandly, and knew the delight of his own generosity for the very first time.

"Paint," he wrote, "fifty gallons—white, ten gallons—various colors. Brushes—two of each size. Turpentine—ten gallons. Linseed oil—twelve gallons. Plaster—two hundred pounds . . ."

And couldn't he just smell the sharp tang of the new paint, the wet, cereal-like odor of the plaster? The sound of the city was a great, cavelike murmuring, filled with the wing beats of motors, the little, distant bleats of horns and cries. The pain settled down in his body and made itself at home. He wondered how they sold wire.

His refrigerator made a steady, glassy vibration; the streets outside took long asthmatic breaths, never exhaling. He wrote: "Trowels or plastering knives or whatever they call them. Stuff for the tiles. Pipe (ask Bodien). Other tools (check with Gaylord)."

The wind shook his windows, from another apartment he heard a Christmas carol on the radio. He was, at that moment, teetering on the unreal, and when he was unbalanced he didn't really know which way he fell. He hardly noticed the sound of someone coming up the steps, but knocked over his chair at the crashing of a hand against his door.

"Who?" he cried. He swallowed. "Who is it?"

"Moonbloom, Moonbloom," a voice wailed. "You gotta . . ."

Norman went to the door, trying to balance on the thin sense of joy; he was frightened, though, and wondered about the talent for laughing under threat of death.

"Who is it?" he demanded, opening the door a crack, with the chain still on. The reek of alcohol made him grimace, and dimly he made out a mad face that was somewhat familiar. "Del Rio?"

"Please, come on, Moonbloom, help me," Del Rio said in a harsh undertone that made him sound gutted.

Norman let him in. Del Rio walked into the light blinking, contorting his mouth. Norman gasped at his filth; there were his features, his Greek athlete's body, but his jacket sleeve was ripped at the shoulder seam, and the jacket was crumpled, filthy. Worst of all were his padded, fighter's eyes; they peered out from under the scarred folds with an expression Norman remembered seeing in the eyes of a rudely awakened sleepwalker. Del Rio was awake now, and it was unbearable to him to have his dream authenticated.

"What happened to you? What are you doing here?" Norman sat, then stood quickly, unsure of Del Rio's place.

"Look, look," Del Rio said, holding one hand out to Norman; unintentionally, his face expressed threat. "You know how I am, you know. What did I want? Was it terrible? I wish for things . . . me, to be clean, clean. You saw how I kept myself, how I lived."

Norman sat down with some permanence now, staring open-mouthed at two parallel scratches on Del Rio's neck. The black hair was wild as a burred mane and could have been carrying some frightful rubbish in its tangles. He sat in his formerly peaceful room and wondered anew at the presentations he was being offered with increasing frequency.

"See, because I know about how they live in dirt, I know damn well." Del Rio began walking back and forth, tossing his hands about, jerking his head awkwardly, as though all the fine mobility of his muscles had deserted him. "We lived six in a room, in a filthy, filthy room. My grandmother stank from disease. We saw my mother and father screwing, and when he was only nine and my sister was ten, my brother did it to my sister. And they smelled, on both sides of me they smelled. On a summer night, like he was my father's shadow, there'd be Ramón going up and down on my sister while the old man was on my mother. And the old woman and me were the only ones without anything to do, and sometimes we'd look at each other in the dark, and I'd see her eyes gleaming. Like she was laughing. And voices and radios all around, in the other rooms, and the smell of garbage, and of *them*. I got to be thirteen and I start going to the gym, I start keeping myself cleaner than anyone who ever lived. I slept in the gym when I could. I took showers twice a day. It made me happy to live like that. I didn't mind being out without a coat in the winter, and my body got strong and my mind got strong. When I had to sleep there, at home, I put myself like in a trance, rigid—I made myself go to sleep. After a while Ramón went away someplace, I never saw him any more. But my sister would still be there, and I'd lay stiff as a board, not looking at her, not hearing her. She used to whisper to me . . . I went in this trance. I improved my mind. You saw, I study acting, I trained, I kept myself . . ." And suddenly he was crying, his fists in his eyes. "You saw . . . them bastards with their roaches and their shit. How I cleaned that place, how I . . ."

"What happened?" Norman asked, feeling a queer elation from his own aching body. Laughter swam beneath his great expanse of pity, blurred but visible, like a huge fish seen through ice. He was being treated to some awesome privilege, he felt, and he knew better than to answer it with despair.

"I went out with this girl. We drank liquor. . . . I don't know what happened. We got to my room. I got excited, crazy. I tore off her clothes. I don't know what I was . . . She got all hot too. . . . It was all mixed up. She began to whisper to me. . . . And I'm a virgin. I don't know, I don't know. . . . I began to beat her up. I left her. Maybe she's dead. I'm all, all . . ."

Norman began to laugh with sad eyes, uncontrollably. Del Rio looked up at him, dazed, disbelieving, then believing, understanding that now there was no up or down any more. He sat with his head down, accepting Norman's laughter, totally unable to feel indignation or hurt. Not so Norman, who felt an exquisite pain from his laughter. Standing over the seated fighter, he knew that much of his laughter came from a sensation of pure funniness—that he and Del Rio should have been deflowered on the same night was a thing of fabulous humor. True, what had prepared them for the ridiculously tardy initiation was as different as could be—the one being a lifetime of desperate and epic courage, the other, his own, a long sleep. But the tragic quality of Del Rio's experience seemed only to lend a depth, a resonance to Norman's laughter. Weeping and laughter both expressed the irresistible, and pain and joy interchanged between them. How had he chosen laughter? he wondered, shaking with it and dabbing at his eye with one knuckle while with the other hand he made a mute offering to the wrecked man, who couldn't see his hand. He could only guess at some instinct for survival, or some hereditary tendency to pray in a dance of joy.

When he stopped laughing, the wounds of his laughter began to bleed. Weakly he sat down beside Del Rio and put his hand on the muscular arm. "I wasn't making fun, Del Rio. I can't really explain; it would sound too silly to you. Of course this is all terrible. You've had an awful life—you won't believe how much I feel it. What can I do for you? Shall we go to your room and see how the girl is? Come on, I'm sure you didn't kill her, I'm sure you couldn't have."

"You don't know. I feel like . . . like hell. All the rotten things. Didn't I try? What could I have done? Is a guy supposed to have a life like that? What kind of shit is all this? Tell me that, will you? Is it just a big shit pile, with everybody rotten and smelly? And me too, me too . . ." He looked at his big hands with loathing; it was too steep a descent for a man who had despised others as he had. Where was he without that carefully carved superiority? Bloodied, soiled, incubated in ugliness, he had imagined strength could deliver him. In his anguish he sighed with relief. "Now what? Tell me that. What am I supposed to do now?"

"I don't know what . . . what kind of . . . 'shit' this is, Del Rio," Norman answered, staring hard at the pale, oil-colored skin. "It's all new to me. I never was involved in things like this. I couldn't describe to you how *I* lived. Look at how I look, can you see? I saw myself in a mirror today and I thought it was someone else. I bet I'm down to one fifteen. My body hurts me, I'm tired, almost sick it seems. And yet, yet I feel like I could do great things now. What? I don't know. It's all so foolish, the way I feel. A year ago, less than that even, I would have worried about the way I'm feeling, the way I want to . . . do something, the way I feel like laughing even though I get very sad and upset. Sometimes I tell myself that I'm heading for a breakdown, but mostly, these last few weeks, I have the sensation that life is just opening up for me. I'm considering hope, although I realize I might end up in a terrible state. Why did I laugh? Oh, just one thing in particular, a coincidence—there's no sense going into it." He allowed a minute for his raving to have some remote chance of getting to Del Rio. Then he tapped him vigorously on the arm. "Come on, let's see where you stand. I feel like I can do things for you. Let's go to your room. Then we'll see."

Del Rio, who had never asked for help before, now looked upon it distastefully. "What can *you* do?" he said scornfully, stirring in the chair, still dangerous both to himself and to others. "I'm sorry I came here. You're a nut, you know that? I ought to let you have it too. Now that I'm started, I ought to let everyone have it." He stood up and made fists at his sides, breathing heavily through his mouth, his eyes glazed against the total darkness revealed to him.

And looking at him, Norman grew frightened. Right then it was not so much physical injury he feared as the ghastly things that powered Del Rio. The tendons in Del Rio's neck stood out, his eyes narrowed, he began to rock slightly. Norman became fascinated by the barely moving fists, which looked like great cured-leather clubs. He tried to prepare himself for the sensation of splintered bone and cartilage. Del Rio hunched himself, hissed slightly. Norman yearned for his murky plans. Del Rio stepped forward, and Norman closed his eyes.

The moments became interminable. Within his head, Norman began to disengage his vague hopes. He heard the floor creak in front of him, heard the tremendous yet quiet voice of the city, with its feel of such gigantic weight that you lived in expectation of the earth's giving way beneath it. He opened his eyes to see Del Rio weeping again, his hands harmless. Norman smiled.

"Ah, you *are* hopeless," he said with both mockery and tenderness. "Let's go now. You'll just have to leave it up to me."

Del Rio agreed by silence, and they went out together to ascertain his crime.

Norman came home very late and he was chuckling, filled with the strange and melancholy mirth that had first visited him early that evening. Now it was three o'clock in the morning. He fumbled secretively with the keys, unlocked the door, and tiptoed into the apartment like a drunk hiding his glee from a sleeping wife. For a few minutes he stood facing the glum light of the window, shaking his head with a queer smile. He remembered the sight of the enraged girl, with her two black eyes, the policemen standing nervously in Del Rio's room, tensed for violence and unbalanced by the fighter's mute submission. And his own farewell to Del Rio before the police had taken him out to their car: "It was like pus from a wound, Del Rio—better out than in. I'll save a room for you, and you'll be surprised how clean the place will be." And of course he had had to shout above the screaming of the furious girl, so that he couldn't be sure that Del Rio had heard all of it. The policemen had seemed to consider taking Norman along when they heard what he said and saw how he said it. But then they had gone, and the house had become so quiet that he could hear Paxton's typewriter from the floor above, and even dimly, from two floors up, Louie's tiny television set playing some silly music that was distilled to a haunting quality by its distance. And he remembered thinking, "Look at me, see what I'm in. I never *dreamed* there was this."

Without turning the lights on, he walked into the bedroom and, in the dim light from the window, he studied the small skull of a man floating in the black water of the glass. This should have all happened to a bigger man, he thought, a monumental character. It will *kill* me. Then he smiled and made a creamy strip in the blackish-green image of the head. And the laughter trembled inside him, causing an increase in the pain, which in turn boiled the laughter more rapidly, which increased the pain, and so on.

That child, he thought, laughing silently before the mirror, how terrible. And the Lublins and Basellecci and . . . His laughter was not because they were all funny; it was only slightly because of anything's funniness. Rather, as he stood there, fantastically weary, it was an expression of profound modesty and wonder and shyness.

"Oh God," he said in the ashy light, "all this for *me?*"

EIGHTEEN

HE WAS AT his office by eight o'clock, fully awake after some three hours' sleep and scornful of those drugged risers who had slept deeply for eight or more hours. If his limbs felt somewhat alien and fragile, it was a small price to pay for the wonderful ringing clarity of his brain.

A child, hanging on the iron rail up on the sidewalk, stared down at him in open-mouthed curiosity. Norman waved without interrupting his furious house cleaning. He threw away papers by the armload. The dust flew; to the child, Norman was like an unusual engine warming up amid clouds of smoke. In a half-hour the place had the stripped-down aspect of a warship's bridge. Norman surveyed it with a savage smile, and the filing cabinet seemed to hunch up against the wall, intimidated. He gave a short bark of laughter and sat down by the phone.

First he called the elevator people and demanded in Irwin's voice that they repair the elevator immediately.

"We'll schedule a man for January seventh," the man said dryly. "We're booked up till then."

"I said *this* week," Norman-Irwin replied with a sharp quietness of command.

"*Hey,* buddy—you're only one small job. You don't give orders like that," the man said, nevertheless slightly uneasy under the brassy voice Norman affected. "First come, first served."

"One small job?" Norman said incredulously, feeling himself falling into the part; Del Rio would have been awed by his ability to project. "I guess you didn't hear me. I said this was Moonbloom Realty."

"Moonbloom?" the man said in genuine ignorance.

"You've heard of Uris, Zeckendorf, Levitt?"

"Yeah, I heard of them."

"Well, put them all together and you have Moonbloom. You're lucky I'm even taking the time to reason with you. Do you know that my time is worth . . . two hundred dollars an hour? Now I don't like to throw my weight around, but we rannana rannana rannana. I'd hate to rannana rannana rannana . . ."

When he hung up in the middle of the man's fervent promise to have service by the middle of the week, Norman lost his breath in laughter. He stopped only when he felt a pain in his chest; then, with a deep breath, he collected himself and dialed Irwin's number.

"I just wanted to explain why the check I'm sending you is a little smaller than you probably expected, Irwin."

There was a sputter of words from Irwin, and he waited patiently to go on.

"Four tenants moved out because the apartments they lived in became uninhabitable. I'm working on repairing them." Norman's voice had the tiredly patient sound of a father.

"This is getting utterly impossible, Norman," Irwin said, the indignation making his voice go up like xylophone notes. "I don't know what's come over you. You were always so sensible, so down to earth. I used to look at you every so often and I'd say, 'My brother is one guy you can depend on.' Are you getting deranged, or what?"

"What did I say that's got you so upset?" Norman asked, enjoying fraud as though it were an unaccustomed liquor.

"I've heard every kind of excuse from the rotten agents I've had, but yours beats them all."

"Irwin?" he said politely.

"Well, for Christ's sake, telling me the goddamn buildings are *shrinking!*"

For some reason the silence was like the sound of a voice stuck on the letter "Y."

"Norman?"

"YYYYYYYYYYYYYYYYYY . . ."

"Are you there?"

"Yes, Irwin."

"Well, what do you have to say?"

"Only that some things are beyond explanation."

"That's no answer."

"Perhaps, Irwin . . . perhaps buildings *can* shrink."

"I don't know what this is all about. All I know is that if I wasn't up to my neck with some tax people right now, I'd come over there and straighten this out, one way or another."

"Please don't worry, Irwin. Everything is going to be wonderful."

"I don't want to hear anything. Just you hear *me*—that next check better be here in two weeks. And by God, it better show me that those buildings have grown back to normal size."

"Rest assured, Irwin."

"Don't talk, don't say a thing. I can't stand to hear your voice. Just do, *do!*"

"I'll do," he promised with a diabolic smile that would have maddened Irwin completely.

"You . . ." And Irwin hung up, leaving Norman with the phone in his hand like a dumbbell he was having difficulty lifting. Finally he placed it in its cradle and caressed it dreamily for a few minutes. Then he cleared his eyes and dialed Gaylord's home number.

"H'lo," a child's voice answered.

"Is this Knight?"

"Nosir," the child replied.

"Is this Henderson six, oh five eight seven?"

"Yessir."

"Isn't this Knight then?"

There was a long pause. Finally he heard the breath in the phone again. "This here mornin'. "

"What's your name, sonny?"

"Harner."

"Harner what?"

"Harner *sir*."

"Your *last* name, Harner?"

"Knight."

Norman sighed delicately. "Is your father there?"

There came the sound of whispering. "Who speakin' please?"

"Moonbloom," Norman said impatiently.

A whisper again and then, "He not here."

"You tell him to get to this phone or I'll fire him."

The whispering, then "Oh my gooness, he just now come in," Harner said woodenly.

"Yeah?" Gaylord said, breathing stupendously into the receiver; in Norman's ear it sounded like a power saw.

"Now, Gaylord, I want you to stand by. All leaves canceled," he said, feeling the presence of jehad. He was small as Bonaparte, but knew the importance was not himself; rather, perhaps, he was Marshal Ney, animated by obedience to the spirit of his impulse. This was the great campaign —what happened afterward was Irwin's problem. Let Irwin throw all the tenants out afterward; the fulfillment was in the immediate future. Later was as irrelevant to now as the

Hereafter was to life. And he was alive, burned down fine, responsive, passionate. "This afternoon I'll meet you at Karloff's room. We are going to wash and paint and burn filth."

"What do you mean?"

"And tomorrow we paint the Lublins'."

"What, what is all that?"

"We're going to work, Gaylord," he said, almost singing. "We're going to fix *everything*."

"Oh my God," Gaylord moaned. "Oh my God almighty."

NINETEEN

THEY RENTED A pickup truck and loaded all the paint and plaster into it, together with brand-new pails and scrub brushes and mops. "I *got* pails already," Gaylord moaned, depressed by the extravagance. "No, no, we need *new*," Norman insisted. "The best." Gaylord scowled as he drove toward Thirteenth Street. "I don't know what got into you," he said. "What you trying to make out of my life. Them junky buildings, all them nutty people. What they care for paint and all? You act like you gone crazy, all of a sudden painting and cleaning. This job was only tolerable because I could take it a little easy, do things slow. Pay so lousy I work as a night elevator man three days a week to keep the wolf away. Forty-dollar-a-week man ain't suppose to kill himself like a *laborer*. What the devil you trying to do—make the *world* over?" "Uh huh," Norman said smilingly, "for me." Gaylord snarled and drove brutally, jerking to stops, turning corners so acutely that Norman crashed against the door or into him. The pails rattled in the back, cans of paint fell over —they were like a mobile earthquake going someplace to happen.

When they got out at Thirteenth Street, Norman paused a while to study the truck while Gaylord stood sullenly against the fender, his arms crossed, his eyes blankly on the squeezed building.

"I kind of feel we ought to paint something on the sides of

the truck," Norman said, his frivolity like that of an aged widower out in the world for the first time, hectic with freedom.

"Ain't our truck," Gaylord reminded him. "They'd charge you for defacing."

"Something like 'Moonbloom Renovating,' or 'Renewers Inc.' How's your lettering, Gaylord?"

"Goddamn it, Moonbloom, you got me all set up for inhuman labor now. What you think you are, a sultan or something? I draw the line someplace. You push me too far, I just walk off right now, leave you and this truck full of stuff. You can't drive neither. Don't crowd me now."

Norman smiled wistfully, shrugged, and then went to the back of the truck. "Okay," he said, "let's go."

A bum stood watching them carrying their equipment into the hallway, his veinous eyes bulging with curiosity. Gaylord moved doggedly, but Norman was full of the enthusiasm of the neophyte, taking the steps two at a time, overloading himself dangerously, gasping on the edge of laughter.

"Wha' yuh gonna do, tear down tha' buildin'?" the bum croaked.

"That's up to the building," Norman shouted back, giving the effect of a whole crew. Gaylord grunted derisively.

Norman knocked on Karloff's door.

"VAS?" Karloff roared.

"Just Moonbloom," Norman answered.

"I cannot get up; mine legs are sore. So come already."

Norman opened the door and felt a thrill of dismay at the sight of the room with its centerpiece of Karloff. The murky depth of the walls and the sense of rounded corners where the filth seemed to destroy all geometry faced him, together with the old man, as something appallingly large; his own presumption excited him almost unbearably.

192

"We've come to do the place," he said.

The mountain of a man stared at him, the ancient slopes and gullies lit by the sickly yellow of the small bulb. "If not for mine legs," he rumbled, "I vould . . ."

"It has to be done," Norman said, waving Gaylord in.

Karloff watched them bring in buckets and cans of paint. He sat there while they tore down the malodorous curtains and removed the filthy bedding, his eyes going from anger to curiosity and finally to helpless bemusement. The sound of Gaylord filling buckets in the hallway seemed to grind at the sides of his head; his eyes narrowed to the width of a thousand other wrinkles as Norman began to sweep. The dust rose chokingly, and he shook slightly with a slow, profound cough. Gradually his mouth lifted at the corners, came up enough to make the line of his sunken lips straight; for him, this was smiling. When the first water was sloshed onto the floor and the coarse *shush* of the brush began a rhythm, he began to speak. After their first curious look at him, Norman and Gaylord went back to their work, listening to him, during the whole afternoon and evening they spent there, only as they would to the words of an ancient choral background whose meaning just left flickers of understanding in them.

"I ran from home. Mine *tata gehsucht*, 'He is a animal, a peasant.' Vell, I vas strong. I vished not to sit praying, mine nose in a book. Mine body vas full vit blood. Ven duh *goyim* yelled names on me, I could not look up to God and *pray*. I smeshed duh face in fuhn dem. I leffed too much. I liked horses, I liked to drink. So I ran fuhn mine house and I vent about Roosia, and dere vas no end to dis country. Ve had dere skies so big, fruits so sveet . . . And such pipples vas dere, like is no more—men bigger as me, men vich could drink vodka a gallon, vich could sing in duh snow vitout duh coats on. And in duh city vas such different kinds pipple, not like now, vit all duh same like little dollies. No, no, faces like fuhn Hell, fuhn duh angels, fuhn duh jungle. How terrible it vas!"

The room was invaded by the sly smell of detergent, and the odor of the rich, dark filth grew weaker. Gaylord worked slowly, steadily, as though under a spell. Norman, who had removed only his jacket, worked in vest and tie, looking more like a demonstrator than a laborer, his face shinging and strained as he listened to the hoarse running of the voice, hearing it as a river of lava, molten enough to flow, yet grinding and awkward because of its chunks of cooling crust.

"Vat vas children den—vite and tin, all *aigen*, eyes, beat up, loved. Duh cities so full fuhn colors, so much blood, so much cries, such leffing, such veeping. How dey vas like animals and hoomans both. Dey could kick a man to dett and den cry for his soul. Dey could do crimes on dere children but could love dem terrible . . . terrible. . . ."

The day slipped down like water, and the other tenants—Paxton, Sugarman, Louie—could be heard ascending the steps after a brief, curious hesitation outside Karloff's room.

"And in duh voods, duh steppe, duh mountains—such big, big nights, such voomans like could burn you up altogedder. Ve screamed, ve howled, ve fought—oh, oh, I could leff such leffs. And duh horses. *Oy, ich gehut ah faird,* vit coal-bleck skin, so big like a elephunt. I rode him vit no seddle. And den I liffed in ah Cossack town—duh spetzel Yid—dey luffed me. . . ."

They scrubbed him into a tiny island, and he seemed desolate there, like the last of life on an empty ocean. And the more Norman felt the sorrow of it, the more he smiled; it was as though his expression were the mirrored image of the strange species of grief inside him. Gaylord took out the piles of rubbish. The sharp, mercilessly clean tang of paint beat like an astringent wind on the isolated figure of the old tenant.

"I vent in ah vawr vit dem, duh Cossack. Ve vent across Siberia and ve fought duh *klayna*, duh Jepenese. And ve vus killed, many fuhn us, duh men, duh horses. I vas shot duh neck troo, so I could not speak for many month. And after I vas a tailor, a baker, a cook fuhn a river boat, a pimp fuhn duh *koorva*, a coachmans fuhn a dook. I vas in jail six month for I kill a man. *Ich gehven* ah bum. Mine femily vas dead; mine brudder did not vish to know fuhn me. I come here to America, I vork, I fight, I am couple times in jail here. I marry, I have childrens, I eat, I make love to mine vife, to odder man's vife. I eat, I drink, I vork, I sleep. I grow old. Duh vorld dies more and more. I eat, I sleep, I drink. The children are dead, duh grendchildren are old. I eat, I sleep, I drink. I em alone. I eat. I drink. I get veek so I cannot valk. I eat. I sit. I . . ."

It was very late as clocks reckon, and Karloff sat in a strange white room with a large bright bulb making everything glow unnaturally. With questioning eyes he looked at the Negro sitting on the snowy bed, smoking tiredly and staring at the floor. Then he turned to the thin, burning-eyed white man, who returned his gaze with a smile of tormented joy.

Norman gestured to the bag full of groceries he had placed within Karloff's reach, and to the chamberpot on the dark circle of floor around his chair. "We'll go now," he said. "You're set up for now. I'm going to call your grandson. Someone will come for you soon."

Karloff began nodding, his head like a burnt-out planet, his eyes receded into an infinite past. "Yess," he said slowly, beginning to nod. "Yes, yes, yesss . . ."

Norman and Gaylord lugged their equipment wearily out to the truck. And when they started off, to a rattle of pails,

Norman sighed loudly, ecstatically. "How terrible—like the old man said, how terrible."

And they rocked through the city like voyagers on a queer and funny odyssey while some modest church bells chimed a tune of holiday.

TWENTY

WHAT BEGAN IN physical stimulation became, after a day of the varied and strenuous work, a sort of hallucinatory cruise of time. He went from tiredness to exhaustion, until finally, in the second day, he achieved a lightheadedness that made him feel inexhaustible. But it had its effect on his reception of time and on his ability to give his feelings their proper proportions. From one cellar or another he heard Bodien's clumsy wrangling with pipes or the ripping of the electricians. He lived in the acoustics of concrete sound, which muffled whatever music his crowded brain might have been making. The rasp of plaster knife, the swish of brush, the routing, cutting sounds of Gaylord healing walls and floors by the age-old method of enlarging the wounds—things must get worse before they can get better. His hands became caked with paint and plaster, his face streaked, his hair aged by them. If Gaylord had any doubt of his madness, it was banished by Norman's insistence on wearing the same pants, vest, and tie, and defending himself by saying dreamily, "No disguises; this is all happening to Norman Moonbloom."

And in this role he fell heir to even greater intimacies. As a laborer in the tenants' kitchens and bathrooms, he assumed a familiarity that transformed his very species to them; people will tell their maids things they might hide from their immediate family. Underfoot, silent, diligent as a dog burying his bone, he seemed eminently trustworthy, as ideal for confidences as a religious image. To some, speaking nakedly in his presence was like talking to themselves, but better, of course, because they did not have to fear the sounds of their own voices. In one way they had to despise him in order to confide. They heaped things on him and transcended disgust for their acts. One parades nakedness to provoke, but also it is an act of complete trust. Maybe he was an ear of God.

On a Tuesday noon he was fitting tiles in the Jacoby bathroom. The mortar covered that part of the floor, and he placed the sloppy shape by feel. Betty Jacoby came in, took something from the medicine cabinet, looked at her face in the mirror with expressionless anguish, and then plopped down on the cover of the toilet, staring at the oozy area surrounding Norman.

"Can one live in constant tension for a half-century, Mr. Moonbloom?" she asked, speaking to the floor.

Norman hmm'ed as his fingers slithered for the slot.

"People might wonder why we keep secrets from each other, Arnold and I. I'm sure by now it never occurs to anybody that, more than most men and women who have lived together for so long, we are protecting something quite different."

Absorbing her voice, Norman nevertheless hummed distractedly as he more or less got the tile in and fumbled with another. There was no question that he used too much of the cement, but frugality was hostile to his purpose. Perhaps he was gradually getting better at it. He was humming *"Bei Mir Bist Du Shoen."*

"Maybe people would be shocked at the facts—I half hope so—because that aspect of it is really part of it. Courtship can be a terrible thing too. I have heard that certain versions of Hell are merely too much of what you had once thought

198

so desirable. Love, too, can be carried too far, at least in certain forms. Did you ever guess about us?" she asked, just humanizing Norman enough to require his answering.

"I've only begun guessing about things lately. Now I guess about everything," he said from the floor.

"We, Arnold and I, are not married," she said, her voice echoing in the porcelain and tile chamber. Norman looked up at her in small delight, seeing her aged face with the wonder of one glimpsing a marvel of craftsmanship, as though she were a miraculous toy that spoke in a girl's voice from an old woman's mouth. The noon whistle fountained up through the middle of the city and fell back down in an immense spray of echoing silence. "I stole him from his wife and child fifty years ago. It was a terrible thing. I left my own husband. We are still selling our beauty to each other, although I was long ago satisfied with Arnold and knew that the bargain was well made. And I guess that Arnold has felt the same about me. Yet neither of us have been able to feel certain about the other. He is still trying to show his good physique to me, trying to demonstrate his manly strength. I know he is old and decrepit, but it hasn't mattered for years. I have loved him too deeply for anything to matter. And I have kept the light from me, thought I could still present the illusion of my beauty to him. It should have been obvious to both of us that all of it was foolish. But it hasn't been—probably never will. We'll each die in the near future and we will continue this terrible play-acting. He will hold in his stomach and pretend he is working; I will speak a certain way and keep the shades drawn. . . ."

"Oh my," Norman said, sketching absently with his finger in the wet cement. There was a giddiness in him, a compulsion to laugh; all that held it back was concern for the old woman's feelings. He was amazed at the long, long reverberations that passion could elicit—one could laugh at octogenarian lovers, but that laughter must contain awe and terror too. In the pale winter light that came through the frosted window, he watched his drawing finger as it tried to make the shape of a soul. She watched him too, as though she had given him a specification and expected him to come up with a diagram of the house she had dwelled in for a half a century. The box of Gelusil tablets made a rattling sound as she moved it in her knobby fingers; a booming radio in another apartment gave a feeling of rooms inhabited by housewives, their aural daydreams only occasionally interrupted by advertisements for soap and flour.

"I had the feeling that there was something strange," Norman said, his pose like that of a mooning schoolgirl. "And now that you've told me that, it's more real and more fantastic at the same time. You see, most of my life I thought that mystery was only in things that had nothing to do with me."

She laughed softly. "People carry on so about love and hatred—what is so much worse, so much more a burden, is tenderness and pity. Even grief is nothing beside those two things."

Norman sighed through the next moment of his perpetual metamorphosis and then went back to his sloppy masonry when Betty Jacoby tottered from the room.

"What are you *hocking* their heads with that crap, those Hebrew lessons?" Hirsch said to his nephew Aaron. "What will those children get out of it? Let them alone; they should be like the other American monsters. They'll chew gum, they'll swear, they'll earn money and marry and be like everyone else. You want them to be foreigners? You want them to be little *Yidlach* that everyone can see right away they don't belong? Unless maybe the boy you think will get the good racket to be *efsher* a rabbi with a good salary, a social director for the caterers?"

Norman painted the dialogue in odd symbols with his paintbrush; he was already on the second coat, but the burned wall seemed still to char through.

"Stay out of it, Uncle," Aaron said in a clenched voice. "You must not interfere. They must know they are Jews, no matter."

"Aaron, Aaron, don't get excited—he means well," Sarah said from another room.

"*Oy vays mir,* haven't you learned anything from our teachers we had over there?" the old man went on. "You want they should know they are Jews? Okay, so take them down to the tattoo parlor; the man can use you or me for a model. He will copy the style numbers perfect. They will know good then."

"They hear all this, the children," Aaron cried fiercely. "Will you keep your wretched ideas to yourself? And how about their connection with . . . God?" One could sense Aaron's inner wincing at the trap of words he had been driven into.

"Ah, yes, God," Hirsch said in his moderate nasty voice. "Our good friend God. Oh yes, that is very important, to keep good relations with Him. Sure, sure, we are his Chosen People. *Chosen for what?*" he snarled, his usually quiet voice suddenly raised just enough to chill the listener.

"The children," Sarah said in a loud, frantic whisper. "Please, Uncle." "He is a madman," Aaron groaned.

"Chosen for torture, chosen for murder, chosen for humiliation, chosen for insanity, chosen for . . ."

"Stop, stop, stop," Sarah hissed. "The man is here." She was the only one of them connected to the everyday earth.

"God," Hirsch howled, his voice seeming to take some weird

delight in hurting them. "You know what He is? He is the biggest, oldest, greatest *shvantz* in the universe!"

Norman, between stove and sink, studied the ingrained white on his hand and felt himself to be in a magnificent place, a place so huge that it oppressed his heart. Oddly enough, he felt blessed.

"You are mad," Aaron said. "You should be locked up and put in a strait jacket, behind bars."

"Ahhh-h," said Hirsch. "Yes, yes, you are right. . . ." It sounded as though he had achieved that wound for which he had labored all his life.

"No, no, Uncle, I didn't mean . . . Please, have mercy," Aaron said in a shuddering voice.

And in the silence that followed, Norman knew that the old man would stay with them. For the Lublins, Hell was never over. But the constant presence of Hell, its garish, molten glow, was a sort of back light which threw their lives into strong relief and made them tangible, reassuring for each other. Unlike Norman, they had never doubted their existence. They knew their passions and their thresholds of pain. And, strangely, the persistent accompaniment of Hell's savage and wheedling voice also gave them whatever was the opposite of Hell. The fact was, they loved.

Norman, covering the marks of the fire, caught the reflected light of their lives and changed color slightly himself. Outwardly, he turned paler.

And on an afternoon when the outside air was so clear that the buildings and the people seemed imbedded in the purest crystal, he was doing his best to repair the warped window in J. T. Leopold's bedroom. Already dangerously deep in the wood, he planed with suicidal delight, feeling his mouth water at the sight of the thick, sweet-smelling curls of shaving. J. T., wrapped snugly in several blankets because

202

of the opened window, watched him with an expression of deep disgust for the amateurism of Norman's work.

"It seems mighty odd to me," Milly Leopold said from the doorway, where she stood, coated for the outside, "that you, the agent, should be doing that kind of work."

"There are agents and there are agents," Norman said gaily, his fine-boned face coated with beige dust.

"Well, it beats me," she said. Then she took a breath for change and said, "Well, I have to run out for a few minutes. You don't mind if I take advantage of you being here? Sort of keep an eye on J. T."

"No trouble at all," Norman said. "He'll want for nothing while I'm here."

J. T. rumbled his disgust, whether for Norman's inept carpentry, which must have offended his artisan's eye, or for the idea that he had to be looked after like an infant. Whichever it was made no difference to Milly; she took it as a hand upraised against her and hurried away.

For a little while after she had gone, the air seemed lighter; the old painter had somehow relented, with her out of earshot and gone from his sight. He watched Norman planing with a rather drowsy expression, as though in the clouds of wood dust, which swam in an orange-gold cloud around the agent's small dark head, he caught dim glimpses of himself, vigorous and happy, clad in the white overalls and cap of his trade; perhaps he could even hear the voice he had had, full of anger and rebellion and lust.

"Gonna ruin that window, way you're going," he said in his deep, froggy voice. "Ought to shorten up the blade considerable."

Norman turned toward him with some surprise. "I'm like a babe in the woods with all this," he said, adjusting the blade and holding it up for J. T. to check. "How's this?"

"More," J. T. rasped. "Just let a sliver of the blade out."

"Nothing can discourage me," Norman said. "But sometimes I feel I'm trying to chop down a sequoia with a butter knife."

"Why you doing this, anyhow?" J. T. asked.

"That's an excellent question, Mr. Leopold," Norman answered, blowing on the blade of the tool. He began to plane once more, somehow disappointed at the fine, meager shavings that now oozed out. "I can only say that I seem to be approaching explosion. I'm trying to live up to the feeling."

J. T. hissed incredulously. "Kind of talk is that?"

"Doesn't make sense in words, does it? Well, let's just say that I want to fix these buildings up, that it seems important to me. There is no money to renovate—my employer only wants things to stay as they are. The property has a particular value for him as it is. He's not even aware that people live in the buildings. All of you are just tenants. If I were in his position, I would feel the same way. I myself was as happy as most people. But suddenly, one day, after I took this job, something started to happen to me, something terrible. I'm at a point where I'm a slave to impulse. Doing all these things seemed imperative." He paused a moment to study the tiny worlds of wood floating in the cold air. "Perhaps I'm trying to give a name to what is happening."

J. T. stared at him from his bundling of blankets. "The hell you need a name for it. Take me, I know what's happening to me. Don't matter whether you call it dying or living or whatever. Alls I know—*I'm* not what I was and *she* ain't what she was. Like stuff that turns in hot weather, we don't smell good to each other any more. Only thing is, she feels guilty about it and I'm just goddamned, killing mad about it. She looks at me every time I cough, scared that she'll be glad, afraid to be caught feeling relief in the second that I kick off. And I can't help trying to scare her, because her face burns me up. I used to like her face, and it seems she went and changed it out of spite. I was always stronger than her too—used to be able to lift her up with one hand and pin her to the bed looking scared and excited, knowing J. T., the I.W.W. bull, was going to give her what-for."

Norman planed, and the sill grew straight and smooth, changing its shape from its conformity with the ravages of time and weather. "I.W.W.?" Norman asked in the gritty air.

"Industrial Workers of the World," J. T. rasped proudly. "I was one of a great bunch of men. Our heroes didn't wear white shirts and ties."

Suddenly there came an astounding sound; it was like that of a man singing from beneath a lake of mud. J. T. was singing!

> "I dreamed I saw Joe Hill last night,
> Alive as you and me . . ."

But the tons of mud were too much for the lone singer. He began to cough terribly, hiding his face in the swathing of blankets. The present honked and squealed from the street below; the luminous afternoon glistened. Norman worked now with severe attention, his feelings blossoming like threads of blood in water. Dimly, muffled by the blanket he hid in, J. T. snarled, "Lousy, rotten, stinkin', putrid, scummy . . ." And on and on without end.

Gaylord discovered Karloff's death six days after they had cleaned his room, and Norman, after notifying the sulky grandson, went over to see what death could have done.

The corpse sat upright, with only the head tilted forward to indicate that Karloff no longer listened for knocks at his door. Since Norman's last visit, the old man had had time to make a small settlement of dirt on that part of the table within his reach. There was a strong urine smell, and the chamberpot lay on its side. Norman studied the dull flesh, the whole stubbornly erect figure, and he tried to picture what small shape, now fled, had been the thing that had carried the great creature through the world. Where were the shining black horses, the savage women, the huge sweet fruits, the terrible men and children that Karloff had drunk in through his eyes and his ears? There was just this decaying body, robbed of color, unrecognizable in a small room of the city. Why did he feel a connection between his efforts with the Leopolds' window and this dead flesh? The gnarled fingers were spread stiffly, seemed to be reaching for a hard, torn crust just out of reach. The white walls and ceiling glowed and made a great cubic frame for what was, after all, nothing now. And Norman looked around carefully, as though he thought to surprise the last wisp of the vanished spirit, as though he would be able to determine from it what he had in himself.

That afternoon he puttied the windows in the doors of the Thirteenth Street building, as inept as ever. He got the glass in solid enough, but used so much putty that the panes looked like portholes. Nevertheless, when he stood up from his work in the evening, he was somewhat taller.

TWENTY-ONE

THE FOLLOWING WEEK, after another enraged call from Irwin, Norman drew two thousand dollars from his own savings account and sent a certified check for the amount to his employer. Temporarily, this freed him for his crusade. He went back to the work with an energy that seemed to grow in proportion to how much he assaulted his body. Chronic tiredness engraved fine lines beneath his eyes, and turpentine could not remove the flecking of white in his dark hair. He slept excitedly and woke up out of breath. How much can a body take? he wondered with amusement. Joy wrapped him with stinging tentacles, but he would take nothing to relieve the pain. Not too far ahead he perceived a breakthrough, perhaps a break*down*—neither alternative worried him; it was sufficient that he would achieve something, whatever one called it.

By February he had done three quarters of what he had set out to do to the buildings. He had used a lake full of paint, a small mountain of cement, and enough wire to go from New York to his home town and back again.

Paxton came to his office on an icy afternoon, dramatic and gay in sunglasses, with his coat over his shoulders, thespian style. He carried a suitcase and his portable typewriter, and he plunked them down as he sat exhaustedly in Norman's one chair.

"God," he sighed, "I never thought I'd make it. I humped this black ass to the breaking point. Now I can breathe."

"You're leaving me?" Norman asked, admiring the exotic look of the Negro with his cloaked coat and sunglasses.

Paxton flashed his superb smile, and Norman had to return it with interest. Such a gift, that smile, he thought. How can he have problems?

"At last," Paxton answered. "The manna has arrived. I have finished the final draft of the *thing*. Yussel is free, sweety, free as the *luft*. From here I go to my agent, then to say bye-bye to Momma, and then—one-hundred-per-cent American Airlines to the City of Light. Like a big-assed bird, I fly, *fly*. . . ."

Norman took the keys Paxton tossed on the desk. "That's wonderful," he said. "I'll miss you, Paxton."

Paxton's smile grew sardonic, yet tender, as he studied Norman's face. His eyes widened slightly, then narrowed; he speculated upon what he saw.

"You're changing, dad. What is it with you?"

"Changing?" Norman considered. "Or *becoming*?" He went to the window and gazed at the flaking n, almost r now. "I don't know what it is, but I'm glad, I'm practically merry."

"You look like a senile Huck Finn. I see agony. What kind of merry is that?"

"Maybe," Norman said softly, "maybe it's agony to become." For a moment he tried to pick at the flaking letter himself, but stopped as soon as he realized the words were painted on the outside.

"I think I will miss you too," Paxton said rather slyly. "You are a very interesting creature, Moonbloom. Would that I had the time . . ."

"Well," Norman shrugged modestly. "So you're going to

fly away from everything. Is it so easy? Can you leave everything behind?"

"Oh no you don't," Paxton said, waving a finger at Norman. "You're not going to get me on to that. I'm moving, I've got no time. Oh, I'm no fool. What kind of idiot do you think I am? I know what I'm taking with me, don't worry about that. I'm taking the actor, but at least I'm leaving the lousy set behind. You can examine and examine—three psychiatrists have already. The thing is, I know what's happened to me and why, just as clear as day. I was a fresh black boy in Dixie, and they took it out of me the only way they could —invisible castration. Now I know, but of course I can't put back that invisible dingus, can I? So I mess around with boys just to keep my prostate active, but in my work, dad, in my work I fuck the bejesus out of the world like the biggest old bull this side of the labyrinth. And when I fly over that Atlantic Ocean, I really *do* fly, I goddamn well *soar!*"

"Yes, yes, I guess you do," Norman said wonderingly. "It's amazing the funny ways people can fly. I have some hope of it myself."

Paxton studied him further, observed how the cold sunshine through the glass dimmed the outlines of his wasted figure. "Man, I think you'll make it, I truly do," he said. Then, because he was one of those people sensitive to the subtle reverences due to certain resonant moments, he sat in silence. There was a propriety involved; simpler people waited twenty minutes after eating—Paxton would not eat and run. And Norman, staring out at the windy street with its scuddings of paper and bent-over people, appreciated the deep courtesy that could occur between people, a courtesy that many aristocrats in name, who would sooner die than belch in company, had no idea of. The Jacobys had it, Kram had it, Basellecci had it. It was not necessarily understanding what the other person said, but, rather, a great awareness that he had spoken.

Paxton struck a match, and the sound was large in the little office. He sat puffing clouds of smoke, and Norman thought about the Negro, pictured his ugly, malicious face hurrying through foreign streets, imagined him in postures of lust, in a position of repose as he lay in some dark room thousands of miles from his childhood. He smiled sadly, feeling a proprietary glow, and with his face almost touching the cold lettered glass, he awarded Paxton some of his love.

Finally Paxton sighed and stood up. "Well, baby, tempus is fugiting. Those airlines have cold, cold schedules."

"Have a good life," Norman said, shaking his hand and smiling.

"You too, Moonbloom, you too," Paxton answered.

Then he left, and Norman watched his short, slight figure move down the street, the coat over his shoulders and billowing behind him, his dark glasses making him look like a celebrity.

And in that moment, Norman discovered that losses increased him too.

That evening he was the victim of a typical Moonbloom miscalculation, something that he was surprised hadn't happened before. A week earlier, the Hausers had moved out; memories, or the lack of them, had been too much for them, and they had decided to take their emptiness someplace else. Norman had looked at the bare rooms, at the silhouettes of cleanliness where the false fireplace and the pictures and mirrors had been, and he had made up his mind that the apartment should be painted and the floors redone. With the mysticism to which he now was subject, he felt that people's sorrows must soak into the walls and floors that surrounded them, and that new tenants should have new canvas upon which to paint their lives. He had painted the rooms in his favorite color—white (not for purity, but for its inherent depth), had scraped the floors with a rented scraper (ending with a surface as duned as the Sahara), and now was just in the process of shellacking them. The smell pleased him, and he liked the process of brushing shine onto the dull wood. His movements echoed in the empty rooms, and his occasional whistle made a bugling sound; overhead he could hear Sidone's and Katz's feet. He made great virtuoso strokes, stopping now and then to squint at his handiwork. His hands became tacky with the drippings of the shellac. His strokes became, of necessity, shorter, more acutely curved. Suddenly he wondered why this was so, and he looked up.

"Oh boy," he said. He had shellacked himself into a corner of the room. He looked out over the gleaming waves of the floor, looked back at his small dull island, and then read the instructions on the can. It took twelve to fourteen hours to dry sufficiently to be walked on. "Wow," he said wistfully. Then he took up the brush and made the shape of his perch a little neater. Finally he leaned back against the wall and began to wait.

Sounds that had until then made no inroads upon his consciousness now made clear intaglio impressions. He heard the water in the pipes, the steam in the radiators, the dim traffic sounds, the almost imperceptible noise made by the walls of an old building. He heard doors closing in the hallways, heard voices tacking the never silent air, heard electricity in wires, heard wind carefully shaping the complex architecture of the city, heard the strangest beatings and flushings. He shifted within his small dwelling and wondered how he would measure the elapsed hours.

He shifted several other times before he realized that he

was hungry. In his pocket was a candy bar. He ate it and chewed the nuts under the chocolate with tiny bites. Still hungry, he thought of the great wealth of Sugarman and muttered an impersonation of him.

"Awrange drinks, cheese sandwiches, Hershey chocolate bars—male and female, *pâté de foie gras* . . ."

He began to feel drowsy and tried to doze; it would certainly pass the time. With his eyes closed, the lights gave him the impression of sunlight. He lost contact with time and could have been whiling away a boyhood afternoon. Just beyond the periphery of hearing, his grandmother's voice called a gentle admonition, an aunt offered him something, his grandfather chuckled shyly. He might have been in his quiet, quiet bedroom with a book across his knees, with serenity covering him body and soul.

But distant, sarcastic laughter opened his eyes. He saw where he was and recognized the remote laughter to be Hirsch's, the resultant shouting to come from Aaron Lublin. The rooms stoned him with hollow bits of feeling. He pictured the flowing-river lamp shade, the red-bulb fire, the lumpy, livid face of Sherman, the bright tawdry figure of Carol, the golden unreality of the child. Yearning for his laughter, he tried to remember some jokes, but found they had all melted together into one tremendous mass. He wondered what time it was.

But really, he reasoned, this is too silly. So I'll just walk on my toes to the door. I can come back tomorrow and touch up. What prevented him from doing it? Perhaps he felt that any flaw in the gleaming coat of shellac would be like a hole in the earth's crust, through which burning lava would burst forth. Whatever the reason, he realized he would stay where he was until at least twelve hours had gone by. He looked at the window and saw the black of night. How many hours until dawn?

His body became cramped and full of restlessness. He had an urge to urinate and felt a pain in his kidneys. Hunger teased him with pictures of food. Upstairs became noisy with many footfalls and dropping sounds, squeals of women, laughter. It seemed he lived in the walls. He was chilly, too, and this kept him from really sleeping. "Oh God," he sighed, and composed himself for some sort of half-sleep. The light seemed to cast a blackness that resembled darkness. He dozed, woke, dozed again, innumerable times. Sometimes he forgot where he was, sometimes he remembered. He heard the roar and swish of a sanitation truck, the rattle of garbage pails. Upstairs was quiet for a while.

A sharp cry of terror and anguish woke him; there was the crash of something falling over. He gazed at the room and felt a terrible loneliness in the white walls. Outside, the light was a warm gray, and before his eyes the electric light paled to a match flame.

Some time later he heard a man's voice screaming, and thought it might be Sidone's, because it seemed to come from directly overhead. He looked at the floor and decided that its hard gleam indicated that it was dry. He touched it with his fingers, but they were too coated with shellac to feel anything, so he tried it with his lips. It was dry. He stepped from the island onto the icy shine and painted his resting place. Then he took the can and the brush, walked out of the apartment, and went upstairs to find out what had happened.

TWENTY-TWO

"WHY DID YOU do a thing like that?" Sidone screamed at the ashen Katz, who sat with his head back on an armchair, so that the blue-red welts on his neck were displayed. "Do you know what a thing like that does to me? Are you crazy completely?"

"You're now my worst enemy," Katz said hoarsely, staring at the light fixture, from which dangled the piece of severed rope he had tried to hang himself with. "For two hours I worked at it, and when I finally managed to . . . you had to come along and . . ."

"You're inhuman and lousy, do you know that?" Sidone shouted. "You were my friend. I trusted you. I lived with you for three years, more than I could stand to live with anyone, including my mother. I said, 'Katz is my buddy, we get along. He knows how ridiculous everything is, and we can laugh together.' Then I have to come back from sleeping with that broad, all set to tell you how funny it was, and what do I find? You, gurgling and twitching on the end of a rope! Is that your idea of a joke?"

"I've been a failure all my life. I failed at being a baby, I failed at being a son, I failed at being a musician. I almost had it made as a suicide. There's no hope for me any more. My father is laughing at me from Hell." Katz was dressed in a neat blue suit and had a handkerchief in his breast pocket, and except for the fact of his speaking, he could have been a professionally prepared corpse.

Norman, coated with shellac and porous with exhaustion, stood in the morning sunlight looking from one to the other. "Now now," he said with a weak smile, not expecting them to pay any attention, although his rate of growth had accelerated and he was, on some level, nearly six feet tall now.

"Yeah, yeah, don't make excuses," Sidone snarled. "You betrayed me. You were always smiling and full of fun. But now it all comes out. All the time, on the sly, you were *moody!*"

"It was my father," Katz croaked wretchedly at the ceiling, his face all welded together with pain.

"Yah yah, don't start all that Freudian shit! You were my friend and you turned out to be a scheming Jewish fink!"

"I loved him," Katz went on. "And he loved me, he *did*. But he couldn't say it, he couldn't say it even at the very end. I used to help him in the hardware store. We hardly talked, and when we did, it was nasty. He'd yell, 'What for did you mark the saucepans sixty-nine cents? I told you seventy-nine. Hey, *musician*, you stupid bum, if you'd stop with the *bluhsin*, stop with the whores and the shnapps, maybe you'd be able to hear something. Stanley, Stanley, you retarded bum, you *shmegeggy* . . .' But I'd catch him looking at me from the darkness where he was bent down under a shelf, and he'd be staring at me like he could eat me up, like a starving man. And I'd try, I'd try to say something that would make him . . . But I never could, and he never could. He died a failure and cursed me with failure. Maybe this was my last chance to succeed. For eternity we'll sit across that big campfire of Hell and he'll say cruel things to me and it will be his torture and mine. Ooooooooo-ooooo . . ."

"Goddamn it, Katz, do you know what you're doing to my nerves? Haven't you got the least bit of consideration? Don't try to make excuses. The fact is, you were trying to pull a nasty trick on me."

"Don't you have any pity, Sidone?" Katz wailed, pulling out of the long-diving "oooo-ooo" just in time.

"I have plenty of pity, even compassion," Sidone cried indignantly. "You're the one, you're the one with no pity. You're the intolerant one."

"Me?" Katz said, astounded. He sat up and began rubbing his bruised neck. "Me?"

Sidone turned to Norman. "Tell him, tell him," he demanded.

"How can he say *I'm* the one?" Katz asked, both hands pointed toward his wounded neck and face. "Does it make any sense?"

"Don't listen to him," Sidone said angrily, as Norman turned back and forth trying to choose. "I had a horrible childhood too. Everyone had a horrible childhood. My father deserted us, my sister was mental, all my teachers hated me, I'm a latent hemophiliac. Do I try to take it out on others? No, not me. I drink whisky, I make ficky-fick with the girls to give them pleasure, I take an occasional reefer just to be social, I drum diligently for money, I tell jokes. Why can't he live wholesome too?"

"But my *father*," pleaded Katz.

Norman contemplated. He looked at the drumstick capped with a condom, he looked at the woman's stocking on the light fixture with the severed rope, at all the burned grooves in the furniture. The sun felt warm on him and he felt like collapsing and he felt very strong. The building burbled and mumbled and made ready for the day. Jim Sprague's voice called through the hallway, "What do you mean, Janey?"

216

and his wife answered tenderly, "When?" The two musicians stared at him with haggard faces.

"It's all very strange," Norman said, looking to them smaller than ever. "The point is, I'd appreciate if you fellas would kind of push the furniture into the center of the rooms."

Sidone made a face of incredulous bewilderment and leaned forward. Katz seemed to become slightly more animated by curiosity.

"You see, I'm going to paint your walls. I'm painting everybody's walls."

"Oh," Sidone said, holding his hands out, palms upward, a crooked, dazed smile on his mustached mouth. "Naturally, nothing could be more reasonable."

Katz just put his head back on the chair and began to cry quietly, his features relaxing as though for sleep.

And Norman left them, walking on the great wooden stilts that made him so tall, and as he went out into the brilliant cold morning, his fingers felt unutterably weary and cold But he was filled with excitement; there was no doubt in his mind that the summit was very near. Moonbloom, in his massive, soiled fedora, his thick, black overcoat, his blue suit with its old, old Red Cross pin in the lapel and shellac and paint stains all over it, traveled through the city, aspiring.

TWENTY-THREE

NORMAN HELPED A one-armed electrician put in massive fluorescent fixtures, working under the man's flashlight and following his directions with trembling fingers. It seemed he was so close to the finish now, and he began to worry about recognizing victory.

"Is it this?" he asked himself when the switch was thrown and the electrician came up to stand with him in the artificial daylight of the Mott Street hallway. For a few minutes he stood there with his mouth opened, ready to smile or cry or shout. There was a faint buzzing from the long, glowing tubes; the electrician gulped in the smoke of his cigarette and blew it out with a long breezy sound. Kram would no longer be in danger of falling, but nothing further happened.

He collected the rents and searched carefully for hidden omens in the tenants' faces.

"You look so down in the mouth," he said probingly to Eva Baily.

"Lester has gone off and married that creature," she said bitterly. "After all we've done." Her Indian face appeared inconsolable and ready for the clay. But as she handed him the money, a slight dawn of smile softened her lips.

"Yes?" he said curiously.

"You look thinner than ever." She put her hand on his arm, and he smelled vanilla and allspice and broth.

"I've been working very hard. You've seen the hallways?"

"They look perfectly lovely."

"It's the best I could do."

"Well, you need nourishment."

"Pardon?"

"Lester left yesterday, and I've got a huge leg."

"Well . . . I'm sorry to hear that."

"Minna and I are so broken up. We could never eat it alone." She gave a tremulous smile, and the hard despair of her eyes became shrouded in mist.

"Lamb?"

"Lamb."

"Ohh-h . . . Could I take a rain check? This next week or so I'll be up to my ears."

She bit her lip and seemed ready to cry.

"I really will come for dinner after that. I haven't had a home-cooked . . ."

"Oh, wonderful," she said, suddenly looking exactly as she always had. She touched his lapel. "Button up when you go out," she said.

"Any day now, Mr. Epstein," Jim Sprague said.

"Moonbloom," Norman corrected. "What will be any day now?" he asked, tilting his head, intent on the answer.

"The baby," Jim said. "Right, Janey?"

"What was that, Jim?" she asked, knitting an incredibly long sock.

"The baby," he said.

"What about the baby, *silly?*"

"Oh, I don't know. What do you think, Epstein?"

"Moonbloom," Norman said with a dull smile.

"Oh gee, I *am* sorry. I don't know why I keep calling you . . . What *do* I call you?" His clean young face was disproportionately perplexed.

"Epstein," Norman reminded him.

"Epstein? But you're Moonbloom?"

"I don't know," Norman sighed, looking around the room for the omen they would never be aware of.

Jane laughed, and they both turned to her.

"No, no, I was just thinking," she said. "It's hard to believe. I was such an untidy little girl. Even the nicest of the women at the orphanage used to twist their mouths when they looked at me. Just like yesterday. I just couldn't seem *not* to have candy stickiness on my hands and face, and I can remember feeling damp all over. I was always stained and untucked, and my hands were forever perspiring. I had tartar on my teeth, the school dentist said, and I told him I brushed them but it didn't seem to help. A little girl . . . so sticky and dirty . . . always a little girl. And now I'm this, and what will happen? Will the same little girl be again? What will *I* be?"

"Do you have pains again?" Jim asked, scraping his shirt with the receipt, trying to find the pocket.

"Well, why don't you ask Mr. Epstein if he wants something?" she said.

"You're feeling them again, I can tell," Jim accused. "Do you want me to time them now?"

"Oh dear," she said, looking at the long, long sock in dismay. "I wish I hadn't lost that pattern. I'll never know when to stop."

"I don't know which I want, a boy or a girl," Jim said, blind with tenderness.

"Silly," she said, laying the sock across her crowded lap.

Norman eased himself out. If there was answer there, he would never find it.

Marvin Schoenbrun's face was clear and more serene than Norman had seen it before. He let Norman in and, after giving him the rent money, gestured toward the severely simple box resting in his window.

"I thank you, Moonbloom. The air conditioner has made a simply marvelous difference."

"Have you had it on?" Norman asked.

"No, not yet. But I actually feel better already. Most sinus conditions have psychosomatic origins, you know. Just having the anxiety taken away has done wonders for my passages."

"Well," Norman said, a little awed. "As long as it's made you happy."

"Oh, 'happy,'" Marvin said with a wave of his beautiful hand. "One doesn't think about *that*. One merely celebrates little things—kindness, for example." He looked at Norman meaningfully, and his face, without the habitual sulk, was viscous, almost sickening. "There is something for everyone."

"Ohh," Norman said.

"You don't understand, you little jerk, you just don't understand about me and Quixote and Verlaine and Taras Bulba and . . ." Wade Johnson squinted suddenly. "Why, Norman, you little clod, you've gone and grown a face." He sat swaying drunkenly on the couch while Wade Junior dropped ice cubes into his glass with a beatific smile.

"I thought you were going to sneak off owing me money," Norman said with a grin. "And here you are paying me off just like a civilized human being."

"That's because Wade Junior and I want to go out of this mare's nest unsoiled by curses. Wade Junior and I are heading west in the morning, and do you know what we're going to do?"

Norman shook his head.

"Wade Junior and I are going to get up at five o'clock and we're going to get dressed and go out into the street and we're going to stand there mocking every son of a bitch who has to go to work or to school, aren't we, Wade Junior?"

Wade Junior smiled angelically and nodded.

"And do you know why? Because Wade Junior and I have decided that we are human beings and we have to be free."

"Ohh," Norman said.

"Why am I smiling?" Leni Cass said. "Well, maybe because I've gotten me a new beau."

"You seem to have great expectations."

"I feel good right now. I'm paying you what I owe you and I'm loved once more."

"How do you know your beau loves you, I mean in such a short time?"

"It doesn't matter whether he does or not, as long as I think he does," she said, pitying his ignorance with her huge, lovely eyes.

"Ohh," Norman said.

"My sister din want me to come this week, said she was having company, said I'd be in the way," Louie said in a dull, dry voice, staring without seeing. "Said I embarrass her with my talking when she's got company. Hah, she's a fine one. Tells me the kids learn not good talk from me. I never never said a bad word in front of them kids, never. People think they're so smart; they like to mock, you know. Who she think she is, Queen frun England or suttin? She's afraid sometimes because from the couple times I was in a sanatorium with nerves. What's she got to be afraid? I never did nothing to anyone else them times—just to my own self."

The television picture seemed pale, and Norman wondered whether a new picture tube would help the gnome.

"Say, I meant to ask," Norman said, "did you ever see that movie you were talking about?"

"No, no I never," Louie said, his face brightening. "I think I'll go this weekend. I'm glad I thought of it. Maybe Manucci wants to see it again. Yeah, yeah, that'll work good. Then *next* weekend I'll go by my sister's—she said she's going out then."

"You have a lousy life, Louie," Norman said.

"No, no, its gonna work out swell. This week I'll go to that picture and *next* week I'll go out by my sister." He was animated now and went over to his stove and began to fuss with some pots.

"You never had a woman, you'll never have children, you'll never have money, you'll never have respect," Norman intoned in wonder.

"You know what kind of house she got, my sister?" Louie said, his back to Norman as he stirred something, his ears brushing his narrow, hunched shoulders.

"No," Norman said dazedly, "no, I don't."

"Colonial split," Louie said proudly.

"Ohh," Norman replied.

After he got Bodien to fix the Beelers' toilet, Norman stayed behind, and when the old man began snoring in the other room, Sheryl took him on a more adventurous tour of lovemaking. He was a quivering, brainless mass when he looked down and saw Sheryl's smile harden. She darted her eyes sideways without losing the smile. First Norman realized the snoring had stopped. Gradually he worked his eyes toward the bedroom doorway. He saw the slippered feet, the baggy trousers, the small paunch. An icy sensation came over him, and he longed to wake up. Sheryl's legs were around his back, his buttocks were bare, the room was odorous. Like a firing-squad victim, he brought his eyes up to the silver face of Beeler.

"Baby Doll," Beeler said, "you seen my pills, the ones for the arteries?"

223

"In the medicine chest, Pa," Sheryl said, squeezing Norman in her powerful scissors grip.

"Thanks, Doll Baby," Beeler said tenderly, gazing right into Norman's eyes. "Don't stay up late."

"Good night, Daddy," Sheryl said.

"Driven snow," Beeler said directly to Norman, his weird blue eyes coated with reverence.

"Ohhh-hh," Norman said with great wonder.

"I've converted," Ilse said viciously. "What do you say to that?"

"*From* what *to* what?" Norman asked, beyond sense.

"I've become a Jew," she said.

"Why did you do that?"

"Because I couldn't stand all of them staring at me like that. Because I had nightmares."

"Why did you have nightmares?" he asked reasonably.

"Because I worked in a concentration camp and I did horrid things to them." She looked like a witch, her eyes blood red, her mouth pale as soap.

"Does it make you feel better?"

"I hate them, I hate them," she snarled.

"Who?"

"The Jews," she said, beginning to weep. "The goddamned Jews."

"Ohh," Norman said.

"On the train tonight, Moonbloom, I figured it out," Sugarman said from where he lay on the bed, his face like a fat saint's. "There is a Trinity of survival, and it consists of Courage, Dream, and Love."

"Well, you're a poet," Norman said, neither admitting nor denying, but only smiling at the familiarity of the candy vendor's voice, which now seemed to have accompanied him all his life.

"I'm not just being lyric," Sugarman said, raising his coarse red face from his pillow to stare chidingly at the agent.

"Of course not, you have proof." Norman smiled but said it without insolence; he was worn down too fine for such a petty attitude.

Sugarman remained on his elbows a little longer, looking at Norman with astounded eyes. "What's happened to you? You look terrible. You look like *I* should look with *my* spirit. I have a slender, wan, ascetic spirit, and my outer man deceives the onlooker. I should look like you look," he said indignantly.

"But you were saying . . ."

"No, not exactly proof," Sugarman went on, lying down again and staring at the ceiling. "But examples, examples I have in abundance. Remember, I am sensitized by the peculiar setting of my work. I see people in transit. I see them sleeping, I see them doing nothing, I see them, as it were, between living, and so I know. I saw tonight, two Chasidim making love to their books and wrapped in their ridiculous clothes, carrying their own stupid lunches with them—like men in space suits. And I saw a young Negro showgirl going to Bridgeport to sing in a crappy little club up there and wearing a certain smile that was left on from when her brother brought her sandwiches to take along and who also was a clown and made faces at her from the platform; in other words, her brother gave her food and laughter to carry her through a rough, long evening. And it sustained her through the drunken advances of two silly white boys, and probably through the whole of that night, no matter what she was forced to do. And then I saw a man who had had his jaw removed and carried a crutch, and on top of which he was a Negro; this man continued, through the whole run to Boston, to tolerate breathing—my guess is that he is still tolerating it and will continue to until some outside force, less tolerant than he, stops it. Then I think of Karloff, that old beast, I think of Del Rio, and Paxton, and Louie, and my evidence is in, my theorem is proved: Courage, Love, Illusion (or dream, if you will)—he who possesses all three, or two, or at least one of these things wins whatever there is to win; those who lack all three are the failures. So now I know, and I wonder about me. . . ."

His words reverberated through Norman and beyond, out to the whole of the city, and beyond, out to the whole of the earth, and beyond. Norman shielded his soul from the immensity of it, and in so doing saw with fluttering heart that there was only one chore left to do—he still had to repair Basellecci's wall.

"Ohh," he said.

TWENTY-FOUR

"TOMORROW MORNING I'M coming down there," Irwin said into his ear, a tiny yet powerful voice that threatened change. "We'll wrap up this whole fiasco then, Norman. I have nothing further to say."

Norman, however, was filled with the more imminent excitement and was able to shut out apprehension. "Yes, okay, Irwin," he answered impatiently. "We'll talk then." And he took just long enough to hang up for Irwin to hang up too and give him back the dial tone. Then he dialed Gaylord.

"Hello, Gaylord?"

"Nosir, this Harner."

"Put your father on."

"Uh . . . he not here? I mean, he not here."

"Put him on whether he's there or not!" Norman roared.

There was the usual studied pause, and then Gaylord puffed ostentatiously into the phone.

"Yeah . . . who's there?"

"Moonbloom."

"Oh gee, I . . . just this . . . minute . . ."

"Never mind, just listen to me. Tonight . . ."

"Oh no, nosirree, nothing doing. This been going on for months now, and I had it. No, negative, *nyet, nein,* and unh-unh."

"Gaylord, listen to me . . ."

"Nothing to listen to. You want me to work tonight and I'm not gonna, that's that."

"Just this, Gaylord, only this."

"Moonbloom, you're a sly guy, you know? You been saying that to me for months. What I been getting out of it? Nothing but tired blood. My back, which always was chronic, is now practically broke. I fall asleep on my elevator job, take people right past their floors. I been too tired to eat, too tired to enjoy my marriage bed, too tired to take Harner here on the educational excursions I used to. Go ahead, even ask the child hisself. Tell Mr. Moonbloom when the last time I taken you to the Planetarium."

There was the sound of a throat being cleared and then Harner's voice intoned, "Long time."

"For months and months I been painting and plastering and fixing like a slave. I sit back today and wonder what possess me to go along all this time like I don't have a brain in my head. I think I been hypnotized or something. You, you quiet little, meek guys—hard to recognize. Man on his guard when he see a fast-talking smoothy, but not with one like you. None of them other agents, with all their yelling and bossing, got a thing out of me. Oh, you cool, Moonbloom, but I had it. I draw the line, right here, straight as a arrow. You can fire me or whatever. *This* isn't the last time—the *last* time was the last time." Now his panting was legitimate and had a fury even he couldn't have simulated. "Them's my final words."

"Gaylord . . ."

"Nope!" It was like a plug popped into a drain.

"Bodien said that he would help if you did. It all depends on you."

"Nope."

It was such a stubborn, cruel sound. Suddenly Norman felt the ironic despair of a shipwrecked man who feels his little boat going under just as he spots land. All the strange, long months took on the quality of a disastrously frivolous binge; he had taken his meager store of energy and security and bet it on a hallucinatory dark horse, and now he would not only lose, but also never even get a chance to see the weird beast. Frustration and grief enlarged his heart and made it pound like an imprisoned hawk. He felt rage and misery and an unbearable desire to laugh himself to death. He was sweating and chilly when he spoke again in a low, intense voice.

"Don't say a word until I'm finished," he said almost sternly, keeping his eyes fixed on the lettering on the window. (The n had now receded from r and was merely a ragged i—Moonblooi?) "Tomorrow morning Irwin Moonbloom, my brother and employer, is coming down here. He can want only one thing. I am delinquent in the rents, I have improved the houses so that they will be assessed for more than they're worth. He will officially fire me—no question about it. You'll be rid of me once and for all."

Something in his voice kept Gaylord quiet, and only the faintest whisper of his breath indicated he was still on the other end of the line.

"I was a very sensible and efficient person, all my life. I never did anything unreasonable. I never was unduly involved with even the most sensible people I knew. I never would have done all these things, never. It's possible that I've become unhinged, deranged. It's very possible. But the way I am now, my former life seems to be the crazy one. That's how far gone I am. It's all those people, Gaylord, all those people. For the first time, people entered me. I don't know what I mean, so don't ask me. Some of them are disgusting, some are pathetic. Most of them I don't even like, I can't stand them. But they *entered* me, and I don't know how to get them out. It has nothing to do with reason. There's no earthly reason why I decided I had to paint all their rooms and fix all their rooms and sinks. But once I started, there was sure no way to stop. I mean, once you're falling you don't change direction. There is only one job left to do. Maybe because it's the last it seems like the most important. I've got to fix Basellecci's wall. I don't think it will do him the least bit of good; I think he's got cancer. I don't think I did any of the others any good either. But I've got to finish and see what it has all done for me. That's all. I'll try to do it myself, but it will be awfully hard, probably impossible. I need Bodien and I need you. After this job I'll be gone. I'll even send you money from wherever I go—but of course there's no reason for you to believe that I will. Please, Gaylord?"

There was a long silence. It stretched thinner and thinner, and finally broke.

"You're real cool, you know? You're real, real cool," Gaylord said viciously.

"Gaylord?" he wailed.

"This is the absolutely, impervious last last time—on my mother's spirit in Heaven."

"Ohh Gaylord, Gaylord . . ."

"Never mind, never mind," Gaylord snarled. "I see you there after supper, and then no more!"

"Gayyylord," he sighed in gratitude and amazement.

TWENTY-FIVE

AT TWO THIRTY in the afternoon he went to his apartment to eat and rest a little for the night's work. He force-fed himself with oatmeal and steak, almost gagged on a pint of milk, and then lay down on his bed to watch a stormy patch of sky through the window. The roiling, subtle violence of the gray-on-gray heavens made him feel that he was moving along on a flood-tossed piece of flotsam. His windows shook. The outlines of the buildings became suddenly soft; large wet flakes of snow kissed the glass and died. The contours of roof and ventilator and chimney grew dimmer as the snow increased; by contrast, everything within the room became much sharper and more vivid. The forgotten picture of his grandparents caught his eye, his old brush set stood out like museum pieces, and the photograph of himself in knickers impressed him with a vivid sense of pity. He grieved painlessly for a vanished life and wondered what had come to replace it.

"So late in the season," he said aloud in gentle admonishment to the dense world of snow outside. And then he slept.

When he woke it was dark, and he had no idea of where he was in time or space. First the old anticipation of pain came over him. But it had no power to orient him now, for the pain had arrived some time ago. He drew upon early memories as a man will grope for a rope ladder, but found the rungs of that ladder to be made of spider web, or of something too soft with age to bear his weight. And when he might have fallen back into sleep or some more irrevocable void, he suddenly recalled moments of his more recent history and found this ladder to be strong and real and capable of lifting him.

Minna and Eva joined in a line of vision that was drawn through Lester's head. Arnold and Betty Jacoby were set like lustrous stones in the dim apartment, their odd, apprehensive love almost pungent. Katz's face, with its little electric arcs of agonized smile. Kram, frozen in the cleanliness with his warped body. Louie's wheeling, falling eyes. The golden, drowsy Bobby, like a pearl in the muck of his parents' presence. Karloff, horrible, iridescent, and huge in his futile battle with death. The Spragues groping brainlessly yet surely toward life. Beeler's monstrous fiction, which made his face like those on ancient coins. The crazy, tormented Chinese who kept prodding his dead parents for information about who he was. Ilse, the female Barabbas. J. T., the fallen warrior. Wade, the poet out of his time. Del Rio warring against a filth of soul. Sugarman, the melancholy minstrel. Leni seeking love under the stones of humiliation. Marvin Schoenbrun trying to armor himself with grace. Paxton, with a woman's lust but a man's desire. Basellecci . . .

"My God," he cried, sitting up and groping for the light. "What time . . ." He rushed into the other room and looked at the clock; it was six thirty, and Gaylord and Bodien were to meet him on Mott Street at seven. He threw on his clothes and ran out without locking his door, buttoning as he went. He bruised his thigh on a rail post, banged his fingers on a corner of wall; these wounds only made him smile. Didn't he have worse ones on his brow and mouth and inside?

But when he stepped outside he was dismayed. The great lumped shapes of abandoned cars and buses were like the crude huts of a lost civilization. The old buildings looked blacker than ever in their outlines of snow. Now the wind had stopped, and the snow fell silently, ceaselessly, and with such density that it seemed the earth rose up into it.

"Hah," he cried; the sound was stifled. "Ahaha." He was astounded at the muffled quality of it. "Ararara . . ." It was flattened against his stinging face. "Rannana," he called. Then he waited. "Aardvark!" Like a canny madman, he searched the dissolving street. "Norman Moonbloom!" Nothing changed. Now he could make out a seething whisper all around him, a hissing in the cold dim air. His feet grew cold, and he looked down to see the snow three quarters up to his knees. He began to plod toward the subway, bent forward against nothing palpable.

After the bright loneliness of the subway ride, Mott Street was a twist of dark and swollen cold: he labored through a tortuous ravine in a lonely country. He gasped for breath, his ears hurt, his eyes were clotted with snow. All the door-ways looked the same. He went up several stoops that looked like the one he was searching for, brushing at snow-covered numbers and then reading them like Braille. For a moment he had the strange feeling that he was the only person left in the city, or that he was in the wrong city, or . . . He sighed in relief as the unbelievable brilliance of the recently installed fluorescents suddenly spilled out upon him through the swarming flakes.

Going up the steps to the door he could see no other foot-prints, and he wondered whether Gaylord and Bodien could have, or would have, bothered to fight the storm. What would he do? he asked himself, looking at his empty hands. Could he pray Basellecci's wall into transfiguration?

After one last study of the dark snowy street, he went inside and up the brightly lit stairway. Jerry Wung's apartment was silent. From Kram's door came the hiss of his airbrush. Beeler's television boomed complacently. At last he was on the fourth floor, and he knocked on Basellecci's door.

Slow footsteps approached. The door opened, and Basellecci looked at him.

TWENTY-SIX

"WELL, I'VE COME to do it," Norman said.

"What?" Basellecci asked, holding on to the door for support. His face was barely more than a skull, seemingly held to familiarity only by the glasses and the hairline. His skin was loose and hung below his jaw in a tissuey fold. Worst of all, his eyes seemed to accept the fact that nothing at all was owing to him. "Do what?" the two words together made him sigh wearily.

"The wall," Norman said, stepping inside.

Basellecci wrinkled up his face, and his eyes tried to recall when *that* had troubled him last. "Oh, that," he said. "Yes, he plumber is here. He . . . said he was . . . here to do . something."

Bodien got up and waved a cup of coffee at Norman. "I'm here," he said, smiling like a horse. "Ready to go."

"How come you left no footprints?" Norman asked him, with his eyes upon the ailing Italian.

"Neither fire, flood, nor . . . I been here an hour. The snow musta covered them."

"You brought your tools, the plaster and all?"

Bodien gestured grandly at the metal box and the bag of plaster sitting in the small cement trough.

"Ahh," Norman said. "Well then, we only have to wait for Gaylord."

"The colored guy?" Bodien asked.

"He should be along any time now."

"Sure. Have a cup of coffee while you wait. This fella makes great coffee."

"May I?" Norman asked Basellecci as he sat down across from Bodien.

Basellecci stared at him dazedly and then nodded. He poured coffee with a trembling hand and sat down between them, looking from one to the other with eyes much too large for his face.

Norman took a sip and nodded smilingly at Bodien. "Mmm-m," he said.

Bodien shrugged modestly.

Basellecci appeared to be swimming upward through his pain. He chewed his lips, he squinted, he turned to look at the seething black at the window, at them, at the dark mouth of the toilet chamber. A part of him that had been anesthetized to his fate now broke free and assaulted him. He was in the presence of madness, and wondered whether to fear it or welcome it.

"Why are you here?" he asked Norman.

"To fix the wall," Norman answered, sipping the fragrant coffee.

"What in the world for?" Basellecci asked.

"It's been bothering you for a long time."

"No, no, it doesn't matter now. I see it was all so silly now."

"Why do you say that?"

"You will look at me and know. I am suffering from cancer. The business with the toilet, with the wall, was all a dream."

"A dream of what?" Norman asked with a merciless smile.

"Of what? Who knows what men dream of? I have been modest in dreams. I had dreamed perhaps of dignity. . . ."

"Of dignity," Norman echoed musingly, his eyes flaring up like prodded coals. He looked around as though to acquaint himself with a place where he might have some great success. "I wish I knew what I dreamed of. How about you, Bodien, what do you dream of?"

"Sexy girls," Bodien answered shyly.

Basellecci looked at both of them as though they were figments of dream. "On such a night, a blizzard, you come here to fix that wall? Are you insane? Is this a joke? I am a dying man. Don't bother. Drink your coffee and let me die in . . . Let me alone."

"The wall is important," Norman said solemnly.

Basellecci gaped. The night sped around them in thick, falling silence. Basellecci was appalled by the resurrection of a part of himself he had already buried. "Do you know how long it has been since I dreamed *anything?*" he cried, his emaciated fingers clambering all over each other. "Don't you understand? I am almost sixty years from where I began. The world has diminished to the space my body occupies. From here I can see that none of it mattered. I feel only impatience now. The humiliations, the loneliness, all are less than nothing. The wall, the wall, stop trying to make it of significance. I don't care. I am just decaying flesh. I was never more. I was . . ."

Norman said, "I think I hear Gaylord coming now."

Basellecci closed his eyes and posed for his death mask.

They heard a pair of feet clumping up the stairs, stamping on the floor outside the door.

"Gaylord?" Norman called.

"Who you think?" Gaylord answered sullenly, stepping inside. His black head was frosted with snowflakes, which twinkled in the light like tiny chips of glass, and he brought the sweet smell of cold in with him.

"Well now," Bodien said. "What's the deal?"

"That wall," Norman said, going to the small chamber and

turning on the light. Bodien and Gaylord groaned. "We have to fix it."

Bodien went over to it and touched it. He made a face. "It's terrible," he said.

"What do you think it is?" Norman asked.

"What do I think it is?" Bodien repeated. "I think that there's something wrong in there."

"Sshhee-et," Gaylord muttered disgustedly.

"Do you think it's some pipes or something?" Norman asked.

"Do I think it's some pipes . . ."

"Or something," Gaylord supplied mockingly.

Bodien looked at him disapprovingly for a moment before turning a professional expression back to the wall. "Now it just *could* be some kind of pipe trouble," he said.

"Well isn't it lucky we got a plumber along, then," Gaylord said sarcastically. "Just in case it *is*."

"Do I have to be insulted by him?" Bodien asked Norman.

"No, please Gaylord. We're all in this together."

"You said a mouthful *that* time," Gaylord agreed, looking at his wet trousers.

"Well how . . . where do we begin?" Norman said.

"This is ridiculous," Basellecci croaked from behind them.

"Maybe it's got something to do with that wood box up on top the toilet?" Gaylord ventured.

"I *could* go down and turn off the main for a starter," Bodien suggested.

"Maybe, just maybe it's got something to do with the heating," Gaylord said contemplatively, warming to the challenge.

"Or the wiring?" Norman added. "Is this one-ten?"

Gaylord looked at him, and Norman shrugged.

"Could come from the roof," Bodien said, looking upward.

Norman tilted his head, considering that. One by one they sat down and took on serious expressions. Basellecci began to look faintly interested: a certain suspense had slipped beneath his sheath of despair.

"Or the floor," Gaylord said, bringing their eyes down.

"How about . . ."

They looked expectantly at Norman, but he shook his head. "No, it couldn't be that."

Basellecci stepped outside his pain and began studying their faces with great intensity. The snow piled up on the window ledge, and little drafts crept in around their ankles. Gaylord and Norman and Bodien stared at the wall, grimaced, squinted, contemplated. Basellecci felt a vague premonition of warmth, imagined something was being done. He pushed himself up with some effort and said respectfully, "I'll make a fresh pot of coffee. Perhaps a little Strega will not be amiss?"

"Yeah, do that, Mr. Basellecci," Norman said seriously, without taking his main attention away from the silent conference.

Bodien scratched thoughtfully at his mangy skin; Gaylord played his lips like a guitar; Norman fondled the scar on his forehead.

"How about the roof?" Gaylord said.

"Bodien already said that," Norman answered.

The smell of fresh coffee leavened their thoughts, and the silence grew richer. Basellecci grunted as he moved against his murderous pain. A cat squawked dimly from the air shaft. The building hummed like a great hibernating beast.

"Anybody said about the wiring?" Bodien said excitedly.

"Moonbloom said that," Gaylord answered testily.

"Oh," Bodien said.

Basellecci sighed in shared disappointment.

They drank the coffee with Strega, then the Strega with coffee, and finally just Strega. When they ran out of Strega, they had another pot of coffee with anisette, anisette with coffee, and finally plain anisette. Their contemplations grew more fertile, more subtle and complex. They wore responsibility with greater expressiveness. Bodien sat forward, his fingers dug into his scalp, his eyes burning with possibilities. Gaylord reclined on one forearm, studying the ceiling with the gaze of an astronomer. Norman sat with his hands on the table, poised, ready for levitation, staring intensely at the horrid, narrow tableau of the toilet chamber.

"How about magnetism?" Gaylord asked.

"Termites?" Bodien said.

"Air pressure?" Norman whispered.

"Underground spring?" Gaylord said, intent on the ceiling.

"Something growing in there?" Bodien said.

Basellecci found a half-empty bottle of Chianti, and no one noticed its vinegary taste as they sipped it from the coffee cups. Silence came from outside, a different silence; the snow had stopped. Basellecci, quite drunk in his weakened condition, lurched around the kitchen looking for other bottles, an odd animation on his skeletal face.

"Radioativikity?" Bodien muttered.

"Shounwavesh," Gaylord rasped, "from shouns."

"Organismm-ms," Norman hissed, "from organs."

"Human . . ." Basellecci hiccuped and looked around apologetically.

"Molsh," Bodien said ponderously. "One mole or a lot of molsh."

"Or ternsh," Gaylord added.

Suddenly Norman stood up, his face wild with decision. Gaylord almost fell off his chair. Bodien did fall off his. Basellecci uttered a sharp cry of alarm.

"We just *have* to!" Norman cried.

"What, what?" Gaylord asked, half standing, his eyes bulging.

Bodien clambered slowly to his feet, blinking.

Norman walked over to the toolbox, opened it, and examined what was there. "Ah," he said, picking up a short-handled pickax. "It's no sense waiting any more. Life is short. There's only the Trinity of . . . only love, dream . . ." He gestured graciously toward Basellecci, whose face filled with blood like a life-tinted corpse. "And . . ." He walked into the tiny chamber, raised the pickax, and drove it full force into the hideous bulge of the wall. "Courage!" he shouted. Then he began to chop away in a fury at the swollen thing. Plaster flew like a miniature snowstorm. Bodien picked up the toolbox in one hand, a wrench in the other. Gaylord stood with his hands out from his hips like a gunman ready to draw.

There came a rumbling, a choking, a gurgling. The wall exploded in a wet vomit of brown thick liquid. Norman was inundated. His eyes and mouth were clogged with a vile and odorous viscosity, his clothes soaked. The torrent went on for about eight seconds, then belched and fell off to a trickle. No one breathed or moved. The other three just stared at Norman in horror. He was a reeking, slimy figure gleaming in the harsh light over the toilet. The world waited for his outcry.

"*I'M BORN!*" he howled, with unimaginable ecstasy. "See, Basellecci, I'm born to you. See, see, smell me, see me. You'll be healed. Everything will be all right!"

"But I'll die?" Basellecci squealed in terrible excitement.

"Yes, yes, you'll die," Norman screamed, laughing.

"In terrible pain?"

"In terrible pain."

"Alone?"

"All alone."

Basellecci began to laugh and cry at the same time. "I'm drunk," he wailed. "I'm so drunk that I'm happy."

"The wall will be new and clean and worthy of you,"

Norman said, wiping his filthy face and shaking with laughter.

Basellecci drew himself up with great and reverent dignity. "Dreams then . . . yes, yes, I have had . . ."

Bodien, meanwhile, had pushed past Norman and was now groping with a screwed-up face for the meaning inside the rotten wall. Gaylord came in, crowding the tiny chamber, and began to do the same thing. Bodien began pulling ugly pieces of pipe and cloth-soft bits of wood out of the crater. They began to rip the whole wall apart.

Basellecci said, "Coffee, I will make more coffee."

Bodien ran downstairs. There came a crash as he fell a few steps, laughed, and continued down. Soon he came back, carrying a length of pipe and a pipe-cutter. There was a frenzy of labor, in which Norman was involved without knowing in the least what he was doing. Time passed without reckoning. Basellecci made an untold number of pots of coffee. Somewhere he found a full bottle of vermouth, which they had with coffee and then plain. The filth dried on Norman, and he was like a living creature cracking a fragile shell. They spoke constantly, yet none of them would remember afterward what they said. Heat and joy were generated; untold numbers of stories and reminiscences passed between them in an intimacy no normal men ever achieve. Norman's head rang with the tremendous noise of the experience, his heart filled to bursting, burst, and went on. Dimly he heard Basellecci enunciating Italian words with the fervor of a great lover. There was a clanging and a thudding loud enough to waken the entire city, and at various times screams of anger came in to them from below.

Perhaps, Norman thought, if we all reach our last day of life at the very same time, it will be something like this. He stole glances at the heathen faces of Bodien and Gaylord, the suffering, yet oddly consoled, eyes and mouth of Basellecci, noting the brave enthusiasm of men who had never dreamed of anything very definite, and it occurred to him through the reek of his person that there *was* only one hope for him, and for all people who had lost, through intelligence, the hope of immortality. "We must love and delight in each other and in ourselves!" he cried.

"You're drunker'n a . . ." Bodien could find no simile and just chuckled happily as he threaded the piece of pipe.

"That Norman's the craziest, insanest nut," Gaylord roared, acting as a vise for Bodien as he gripped the pipe with both hands from behind the plumber, so that it appeared he was embracing him. "That Norman Moonbloom got a idea he can *do* something to the world. He thinks he's a giant superman. He's so crazy he makes me crazy too, makes me think I'm building the pyramids in old Pharaoh country, or maybe the friggen Yewnited Nations. You hooked us, Norman, you got us mainlinin' the same fix you been taking. Hah, Basellecci, Bodien, ain't we all drunk on the same stuff he been drinking? You lousy rat, Moonbloom, this man here is dying, Bodien here is a disbarred plumber without no future who won't have another plumbing job after you go. And me, me, I'm just a poor shine with nothing to look forward to except sweeping up other people's shit till I'm too weak and old to do even that. So how come, how come I'm happy as a friggen lark? You got me drunk, Moonbloom; you got me so drunk I'll *never* sober up."

"No, no, what I'm saying is what Sugarman says. There's a Trinity—Love, Courage, and Delusion, I mean *Ill*usion . . . I *think* I mean *Ill*usion. I think I mean . . ." He raved as he carried cartons of filth down the stairs to the basement, raved to the angry faces of disturbed tenants who thrust their heads out of their doorways at him. "Of course I'm roaring drunk, and this is all probably delerious tremb . . . delerium treml

243

. . . But still and all, I'm born and I'm living and I worry and love. . . ." Once he fell, but by then he was so dirty that any further contact could only clean him.

He watched Bodien and Gaylord working and admired the cool dedication of their faces and bodies. He grew very tired and hardly spoke at all. A great serenity seemed to wrap them all as Gaylord stroked the surface of the plaster with a trowel, and there was such a silence that the silky rasp of metal on plaster was like a great toneless note. After a while Norman and Bodien and Basellecci sat down and watched the gliding trowel in Gaylord's dark hand, and they seemed to rock somewhere on the edge of sleep.

Basellecci made more coffee, moving in a dreamlike slant, and then, with their eyes narrowed to that one movement on the wall, they sipped and existed.

It was something as real and at the same time unreal as the hot coffee on his tongue, Norman thought. Or as real and unreal as sight, which takes in the huge depth of landscape with all its large movements and colors and planes and yet makes it all convincing in mysterious imprint on a dark whorl of tissue. Sentiment had to disintegrate under what his drunken mind knew now, and in its place come an immense capacity to consume. He felt carnivorous, as though he could devour all of them, himself included. Small, dusty man indeed! Why, he was huge, united with all of them! His eyes, his brain, his ears, all swallowed the universe. "Oh my," he belched.

Then, suddenly, a rosy glow suffused the new white plaster, and they were done and it was morning. Basellecci stood with a beatific expression on his wasted face, and the other three admired with him the straight gleaming wall.

"It is done," Basellecci said with a serene smile. "What more could I have asked?"

And the other three looked at him and at each other, smiled, and put things away. One by one they left the apartment, while Basellecci sat gazing at the transfigured wall, and his coffee boiled on the stove.

Outside was a wonder. The sun shone on the snow and made everything too brilliant to see. They parted, and Norman walked by himself, scabrous and weary. The air was warm, and already a dripping came from the roofs and drainpipes. There was a scent of earth.

In his office he sat happily, waiting for Irwin. As he waited, he noticed that the last letter of his name had now been totally scraped away. Somehow it freed the word, opened it up so that the o's bubbled out endlessly, carried the crooning sound of the name out to an infinite note of ache and joy. It thrilled him with his own endlessness, and, almost laughing, he followed its course.

Moonbloooo-ooo . . .

Books by Edward Lewis Wallant
available in paperback editions
from Harcourt Brace Jovanovich, Inc.

The Human Season
The Pawnbroker
The Tenants of Moonbloom